"Why do you care what a supposedly bad man is doing with me?"

Will shouldn't care. It was none of his business if she married Ben or not. And yet, he couldn't stand idly by.

"You lied to me about severing your connection with him."

Mary flinched at his words. "I did not. Ben's visit here tonight surprised me just as much as it did you."

Actually, Will had noticed that. He'd also noticed how Mary bristled at Ben's attention. But something wasn't right with the situation. "Then why did you announce your engagement?"

"*Ben* announced our engagement." Mary's eyes flashed as she emphasized Ben's name. Will had to admit, Mary had really pretty eyes. Green with flecks of gold, so deep a man could spend hours mining them and still— What was he doing mooning over her? Hadn't he learned his lesson?

"Why did you go along with it? Why not tell everyone that you'd broken things off with him?"

"Didn't you hear me try to explain that it was over?" Mary's voice was littered with the angst of unshed tears. "But I—" She shook her head. "It doesn't matter. I'll figure something out."

Will took a step closer. "I'll help you," he said softly. "Let me help you."

Danica Favorite loves the adventure of living a creative life. She loves to explore the depths of human nature and follow people on the journey to happily-ever-after. Though the journey is often bumpy, those bumps refine imperfect characters as they live the life God created them for. Oops, that just spoiled the ending of Danica's stories. Then again, getting there is all the fun. Find her at danicafavorite.com.

Books by Danica Favorite

Love Inspired Historical

Visit the Author Profile page at Harlequin.com for more titles

DANICA FAVORITE

The Lawman's Redemption

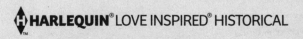
HARLEQUIN® LOVE INSPIRED® HISTORICAL

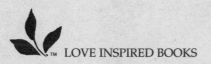

LOVE INSPIRED BOOKS

Recycling programs
for this product may
not exist in your area.

ISBN-13: 978-0-373-28320-0

The Lawman's Redemption

Copyright © 2015 by Danica Favorite

www.Harlequin.com

Printed in U.S.A.

Trust in the Lord with all your heart,
and do not lean on your own understanding.
In all your ways acknowledge Him,
and He will make straight your paths.
—*Proverbs* 3:5–6

When I married my husband, I found great riches in his family. Without their support, I could not do half of the things I do, especially when it comes to writing my books. Fred, you are always there for us, and give to us so abundantly, I can't even begin to express the depth of my gratitude, love and admiration for you. Pat, you didn't get to see any of this, but thank you. Gloria, you have been such a welcome addition to our family, and you mean the world to us. Ricky, not only do you help me blow stuff up, but you always make me smile. Debbie, thanks for all your support.

Bernard and Teri, you guys have invested so much in our family, and I'm so grateful for all you do. Most importantly, I'm thankful for the family traditions you've kept alive so my children will know about their Leadville relatives. And of course, I'm so grateful that you give us free access to the Leadville house whenever we want to go up. Without our time in Leadville, there would be no book.

To the Novaks—you bravely came to America and arrived in Leadville to create a future for your family at a time when life in Leadville couldn't have been easy. I hope my books honor your spirit.

And to Randy,
thank you for introducing me to all of them.

Chapter One

Leadville, Colorado, 1881

Someone was following her.

Each time Mary Stone looked around or tried checking behind her, she didn't spot anything unusual. But she was no fool. She'd learned to trust that feeling deep in her gut when she knew something wasn't quite right. If only she'd accepted her friend Polly's offer to accompany her on her errand to the mercantile. Selfishly, Mary had wanted just a few minutes to herself, away from her siblings' squabbles and the work of putting together their new household.

Selfishness never profited anyone. Maybe it wasn't an exact quote from the Bible, but it had to be in there somewhere. And now Mary was paying for that decision.

Teeming with saloons and miners celebrating the receipt of their wages, the busy street wasn't an easy place to find refuge. Two blocks ahead was the Rafferty Hotel, a respectable place where they'd stayed when they'd first come to Leadville. If Mary could get there, she could talk to Mrs. Rafferty and see if one of her hired men could escort her the rest of the way home. That was, if she didn't lose her pursuer first.

A wagon rolled by, kicking up dust and the loose slag that passed for a road. Mary coughed and pressed her nose into her handkerchief. Raucous laughter jolted her further as the doors to a saloon opened and several men lumbered out.

One of the men, having clearly imbibed too much of the drink, grabbed her. "Yer a pretty one, ain't ya? My ship's come in at the card table. Maybe you'd like to help me be respectable by marrying me."

His foul odor stung her nostrils, and as much as she wanted to get away, to loosen the man's grip on her arm, her legs were frozen to the spot.

Worse, she felt someone's eyes on her back. Her pursuer had caught up with her.

"Please. You're hurting me. Let me go." She tried jerking her arm away, but the man tightened his grip and pulled her toward his companions.

"Lookee here! I found me a wife."

The others, clearly miners who'd had just as much drink as their friend, laughed.

"She's sure a beaut," the one closest to her said as he tripped forward, extending his hand. "Name's Lucky. But Tom here's the lucky one if you're marrying him."

"I'm not marrying him." She gave her arm another tug, freeing herself from Tom's grasp and sending him sprawling to the ground in the process.

Freedom. But the only way out was through the man's friends, stepping into a dangerously busy street, or turning back to—

She spun, running directly into a sturdy chest.

"Is there a problem?"

The deep voice jolted her, almost as much as the feeling that she somehow knew this man.

"Y-y-yes," she managed to mutter. "These men, they—"

"Hey, now." Tom staggered to his feet. "No problem here. I just come into a bit of money. Was making this lady here the offer of her life."

A shudder coursed through her body. No way would she waste her life on a gambling drunk. She'd seen where that had gotten her poor mother.

"I don't think the lady's interested," the stranger answered for her.

Tom stepped forward, a determined look on his face. "Now, you see here. I promised my friends I'd turn my life around and marry the first respectable woman I saw, and that's what I aim to do."

Tom gave Mary a broad smile. "So, pretty lady, what's it going to be? You gonna marry me?"

"No," she said without hesitation. "But if you're serious about turning your life around, you can start by visiting Pastor Lassiter at the Leadville Community Church. He'll help you far more than marrying me would."

Pastor Lassiter, or Frank, as he'd asked them to call him when Mary's brother married his daughter, was always talking about how these men were lost and needed to be shown the Lord's love. Most of the time, though, when she encountered them on the streets, they always scared the words right out of her.

Until this moment, she hadn't even had the good sense to ask the Lord for his assistance. Well, that was something she could rectify. With a quick *help me,* along with a *forgive me*, she hoped her silent prayer would do for the intensity of the situation.

"Church?" Tom and his friends guffawed at the same time. The friends came around and slapped Tom on the back. "Boy, you just got lucky again, escaping that noose."

They continued down the street, Mary's safety again assured. She turned to the man who'd come to her aid. "Thank you for your assistance."

For the first time, Mary took a good look at her rescuer. Or rather, up at him. Though she wasn't nearly as petite as some of the dainty women at church, this man towered over her. Deep brown eyes stared back at her, not in the lustful way Tom and his friends had, but their intensity still left her feeling uncomfortable. This was a man who could see into a person.

If her sister Rose were here, she'd surely collapse into a fit of giggles about how romantic it was to be saved by such a handsome man. But Mary knew how deceptive looks could be, and a simple thank-you was as far as she'd take her gratitude.

"It's no trouble. I'm sorry you had to deal with those men to begin with. Had I approached earlier, I might have saved you the distress."

Mary swallowed the fear that started to rise in her throat and reminded herself that God had not given her a spirit of fear. If only that belief were easier to live out.

"Why would you approach me? Do we know each other?"

"No." He took off his hat and gave a friendly smile. "Will Lawson, at your service. I've been looking to speak with you on a matter of, uh…delicate nature."

Which was not at all comforting. He may not have

been as aggressive as the miners who'd accosted her, but he certainly didn't seem like the sort of man she should be speaking with. There was a reason she didn't talk to strangers. "I'm afraid it wouldn't be proper at all. While I appreciate your aid with those ruffians, I can't be of assistance. I've been too long on my errand. I'm sure I'll be missed. Good day."

Will studied her in a way that made her collar feel just a little bit too tight. Mary took a deep breath, ignoring the strange sensations in her stomach. Oh, they weren't unfamiliar, but she knew that just because a man made her feel slightly giddy didn't mean she could trust him. Even if he had a warm smile.

"I'd be happy to escort you home. We can talk then. A lady such as yourself shouldn't be walking the streets alone."

No, she shouldn't. A fact she was sure the older women in residence at the Lassiters' would remind her of as soon as she returned. She'd thought herself so clever, refusing Polly's offer of an escort and slipping out before Maddie, the housekeeper, or Gertie, Polly's mother, got wind of her plans.

"My family will be concerned if I arrive home with a stranger as an escort." She started toward Rafferty's, remembering her plan to find a suitable escort to ensure her safety.

"They should be more concerned that you're wandering around unescorted."

Clearly this man understood the dangers of the situation, but it didn't mean she had to put herself in more danger. There was something a little too… Mary shook her head. She didn't know what it was about him, but she wouldn't risk finding out.

"I'm going to Rafferty's hotel, just down the street. Mrs. Rafferty will have one of her boys escort me the rest of the way."

"Good." He stepped in with her. "That's where I'm staying, so I'll accompany you there, and we'll have a few moments to talk."

Mary stopped. "Fine. Say your piece."

Mr. Lawson handed a stack of envelopes to her. "I'd like to ask you some questions about Ben Perry."

The air whooshed out of her lungs at the mention of the name she'd hoped to forget. She didn't need to open the envelope to know its contents. Her own handwriting, bold and firm, told her everything she needed. The past she'd hoped to escape still followed her.

"Where did you get this?"

"Doesn't matter," he said, taking her by the elbow and maneuvering her through another group of drunken men. "I need your help in finding him."

Mary jerked out of his grasp and stopped, forcing him to turn and look at her. "If you read all the letters, then you know I have no interest in Ben Perry. I don't know where he is, nor do I care to. Now, if that is all, I will bid you good day, as I am perfectly capable of crossing the street to Rafferty's on my own."

She would have been better off with the drunken men who'd accosted her than to talk to anyone interested in Ben. Mary hastened forward.

Her words did not deter Mr. Lawson, who continued to walk in stride with her, even though she had picked up her pace considerably.

When her brother had found their late father's mine and moved the family from Ohio to Leadville, it was supposed to be a new start for the family. But how was

Mary supposed to start over when her past wouldn't leave her alone?

One more reason that selfishness led to disaster.

Her family could never know the part she'd played in the troubles that had befallen them.

Mr. Lawson reached in front of her to open the hotel door, only he didn't let her pass. "Please, Miss Stone. Just give me a few minutes of your time. Let me buy you a cup of tea, and we can sit in the open where everyone can see that my intentions are completely honorable."

Everyone seeing was precisely the problem.

"I'm sorry," she said in the tone she usually reserved for chastising her younger siblings. "There is nothing I can tell you that would be of any help."

"Let me be the judge of that." The earnestness in his face made her sympathetic to his cause. The man was clearly desperate to find Ben. But desperation meant one of two things. He was either just as wicked as Ben and looking to cash in on some evil scheme, or he was a lawman.

Either meant trouble for Mary.

Perhaps the right thing to do was to turn herself in, but with her brother Joseph and his wife, Annabelle, on their honeymoon, there was no one to look after her younger siblings. Particularly Nugget, the product of her father's liaison with a fallen woman. The last thing Nugget needed was more upheaval in her life.

Mary had to protect her family, and herself, from anyone knowing of her past involvement with Ben Perry—and his criminal history.

She stared long and hard at Mr. Lawson, ignoring the desperation in his eyes. Their sweetness reminded her of…

No. She simply would not have it. Sympathy for anyone wanting to know anything of Ben would only cause trouble.

"I haven't spoken with Ben in months, and as I'm sure you can tell from my letters, I severed our connection completely."

Oh, how she wished she'd not given in to the childish impulse to express her feelings in writing to Ben.

"Some of the contents of the envelopes were missing. But on top of the bundle of correspondence was a piece of paper that gave your direction in Leadville. If you severed your connection, as you and the last letter say, why would he have your new address?"

Was Mr. Lawson—this stranger—calling her a liar?

Mary had lied about plenty of things regarding Ben, but that was all in the past. Mr. Lawson couldn't possibly know anything about those things. All he had evidence of was a foolish young girl in love.

And that Ben had somehow figured out where to find her. Mary shoved the thought to the back of her mind. She'd figure out a way to deal with that later.

"Trust me, I have no reason to renew my acquaintance with Ben."

"He clearly wants to be reacquainted with you. I just need—"

"No." Mary grabbed the door handle he was holding and gave it a swift yank.

"If you could just hear me out, perhaps we can come to some kind of agreement."

"I can't." Mary gave him another hard stare while trying to keep her voice from shaking. "Please, leave me alone."

Her words apparently convinced Mr. Lawson, since

he let go of his hold on the door and let her pass. But as she entered the hotel and hurried to the front desk, she couldn't help but feel as if somehow, despite winning this battle, she'd lost.

As nice as this man seemed—whoever he might be—finding Ben would only spell trouble. Yes, that was it. She was saving this man from being cheated or hurt by Ben. And if he was the law, she was better off not saying anything that could possibly incriminate her.

When she'd threatened Ben with going to the sheriff, he'd laughed and told her that no one would believe her innocence. In fact, all the evidence pointed to the fact that she'd been a willing accomplice to his crimes. How could she have known that when she was inviting her suitor in to visit while she worked cleaning houses, she was inviting in a thief? The so-called family heirlooms she'd hidden in her home because Ben had asked her to keep them safe for him were actually stolen property. Worse were the gifts she'd accepted from him. While she'd tried making up for it by donating all she could of her newfound wealth to charitable causes, she still felt the stain of having possessed ill-gotten goods. She'd blindly believed in Ben and everything he'd told her. Too bad it had all been a lie.

Will Lawson admired Miss Stone's purposeful stride into the main lobby of the hotel. Pursuing her farther would only cause a scene, and with the looks they'd been getting at the door, he'd already pushed too far.

So close.

Mary Stone was the closest he'd been able to get to Ben Perry and his gang, and she refused to cooperate. Well, that wasn't exactly true. He'd gotten close once before, but he'd put his trust in the wrong person and ended up with a bullet in his gut, his badge taken away and any hope of respectability—gone.

Still, Miss Stone wasn't what he'd expected. While she was comely enough, with hair the color of pure coal and alabaster skin that hadn't yet been damaged by the mountains, she hardly looked the part of the sort of lady the notorious outlaw would be interested in. Reed-thin, not nearly as buxom as Perry typically preferred. And she seemed to possess a more genteel spirit than the bold women Perry cavorted with.

So, what was Perry's game?

Miss Stone spoke to the man at the counter, not looking in Will's direction or acknowledging him. Almost as though she didn't want anyone to know of their encounter. Which fit in with her reticence, but why?

What was Miss Mary Stone hiding?

When she finally left, Will headed for the hotel saloon, hoping he'd see a familiar face in the crowd. Ben Perry preferred the finer things in life, which in this town meant staying at the Rafferty Hotel.

Bold as the brassiest woman of the night, Perry sauntered right up to Will as soon as he stepped through the saloon door, as though he wasn't a wanted man in dozens of places.

Trouble was, Will didn't have the power to arrest him. Not anymore.

"I thought they'd taken your badge, Lawson." Perry gave a short, barking laugh. "Law*son*. Still gets me. You should change your name to Law-lost-his-badge."

Will balled his fists at his sides but forced himself to take the taunt. Yes, he'd messed up the Colorado Citizens Bank case, and, yes, he'd let Ben get away. But

Will *would* find a way to take down Ben Perry and his gang once and for all. Even if stopping Ben didn't get Will's badge back, at least there'd be one less evildoer on the street.

"Did you have something to say, other than to be childish?" Will glared at the other man, wishing there was something he could do besides follow Ben around and wait for him to strike.

Sure, Will could try to turn Ben in to the local authorities, but the price on Perry's head wasn't enough to make it worth anyone's while. At least not on the petty crimes they could prove.

Will's fault.

Will should have known that someone as pretty as Daisy Bostwick wouldn't have been interested in a man like him unless she wanted something. He just never figured that she'd be working for Ben Perry.

"Wondering what you're still doing this side of the Divide." The casual tone of Ben's voice was almost menacing. "I figured you'd hightail it out of these parts now that you've lost everything."

A nasty smile crossed Ben's lips. "Your poor mama. I can't imagine how lonesome she must be, taking in the waters at Glenwood all by herself."

Will tightened his fists at his sides. Not a man alive would blame him for laying Ben out flat. The rumors swirling around Will's involvement with the Colorado Citizens Bank robbery had caused Will's mother to take ill and retreat to Glenwood Springs.

Will was innocent. But the gun used to rob the bank and kill an innocent man was Will's distinctive weapon—the weapon used by one of the masked robbers. Because the robber's features had been hidden and the robber was the same height as Will, many had thought the robber had been Will.

Will's gun had gone missing from his rented rooms the day before the robbery. Will hadn't had a chance to report it yet. He'd left early that day because Daisy had sent him a note saying she'd finally found a way to run away from Ben and needed his help. And of course, Will would help her.

It was all a lie. A lie that had Will arriving back in town just in time to make it look as if he'd been helping Ben's gang.

Though he hadn't been charged in the crime due to insufficient evidence, everyone thought Will had been guilty. No one believed his gun had been stolen. No one believed that Will had been set up. But someday, Will would prove that Ben had been behind the robbery. Ben had pulled the trigger, and Ben would hang for it.

"My mother is perfectly well." Will's jaw barely allowed the words to escape.

"Glad to hear it." Then, as if to prove to Will exactly what kind of vermin he was, Ben turned and said, "I'll be sure to give your regards to Daisy."

With a wink, Ben headed out of the saloon, whistling.

Ben might believe he was untouchable. For now, Will would go on letting him presume that. Better for a man to think he had the upper hand and get cocky than to have him be on his guard.

When the marshals had raided Ben's previous boardinghouse, they hadn't had enough men to both give chase and search Ben's belongings. So Will had hunted for evidence. Ben was too good to leave much in the room, but Mary's current address written on a sheet of paper left with the letters had been enough to at least give Will an idea as to where Ben might be headed next.

Mary Stone might say she didn't know anything about Ben, but the fact that Ben had kept her letters told Will that the outlaw still had some interest in her. Ben didn't keep things for sentimental purposes.

The marshals hadn't done much to stop Ben anyhow, so it was up to Will to fix his mistake in letting Ben get away the first time. Ben had a scheme in mind, and Mary Stone was right at the center.

If only he had the missing pages from the letters. Then he might be able to see the full extent of Mary's involvement.

The shadows behind Mary's eyes had spoken of a deeper fear than just meeting a stranger. He'd seen the same shadows behind Daisy's eyes just before she'd shot him. Daisy, whom he'd thought so noble and pure. Not so.

Mary seemed like an innocent girl. But he'd been deceived once before. He wouldn't make the same mistake he had with Daisy. If Mary was involved, he'd have no problem helping the authorities put her away in a jail cell.

Chapter Two

Mary stirred the pot of beans before dishing out a serving to the miner who stood before her in the church-yard. "Here you go. Polly's got some cookies over there if you'd like one."

A smile peeked out from his bushy mustache. "Thank ye kindly."

The next miner approached, and Mary barely glanced up as she dished out another serving. "Enjoy. If you want some cookies—"

"I don't want cookies. I want to talk to you."

Him. Mary glanced around to be sure the rest of her family was busy with their tasks before looking at Will Lawson. "I already told you, I have nothing to say. Now, please go, before someone notices."

"I hear you made these beans," Will said with a twinkle in his eyes. "And I aim to enjoy them, then when folks clear out, I *will* talk to you."

Not if she could help it. Mary looked down the line to see a number of others waiting to be served. At least it would give her time to figure a way out of this confrontation.

"Fine. Have your fill." Mary plopped more beans on his plate.

"You know I want more than beans from you." He touched her hand, sending a small jolt through her body.

Oh, she knew what that jolt was. Mary looked hard into Mr. Lawson's eyes, letting him see that she was not affected by his charm. Not one whit.

The one good thing about her time with Ben was that she'd learned a lot about the way men thought they could get a woman to do their bidding with a pleasing look and flirtatious smile. And she wasn't falling for it. Not now. Not ever again.

Only, the steely expression Mr. Lawson gave her in return was far from flirtatious. In fact, he looked deadlier than an unexpected blizzard in winter—and just as cold.

"I can't help you," Mary said slowly, quietly, trying not to draw attention to the conversation. "Please, go."

Mr. Lawson's gaze remained firm. "I'll be waiting when the meal's over. Talk to me, or I'll be speaking with Pastor Lassiter about finding assistance."

Mr. Lawson didn't seem the type to make idle threats. And while Mary knew that Frank Lassiter preached forgiveness, she wasn't sure she deserved it.

She'd done so many bad things in the name of love. No, she hadn't known the various baubles she'd sold on Ben's behalf were stolen, but she knew the law wouldn't see it that way. And if there was one thing she knew for certain about Frank, it was that he believed in owning up to one's mistakes and facing the consequences. If he knew the truth, he'd make Mary turn herself in.

How could Mary risk going to jail when her only crime was believing Ben's lies?

When her brother Joseph had discovered the silver mine, making her family wealthy, she'd tracked down every family Ben had stolen from and anonymously made restitution. They didn't know it was Mary, of course, but surely it was enough. Everything had been returned to the victims, as best as Mary knew how.

But for people to actually know what she had done?

Her family needed her. More important, now that her family was linked to the pastor's through Joseph's marriage to Annabelle Lassiter, they needed Mary's reputation to be untarnished. Who would welcome Mary into their homes, knowing what she'd done? And how much damage would it do to Frank's ministry?

Jail and pariah-hood. That was what Mary faced if the truth came out. Yet here stood Will Lawson, thinking he could just stare his way into ruining lives.

"So, what's it going to be?" he asked, not breaking his stare.

"Meet me after. I'll slip out, and we can talk over by the fence."

She'd become good at slipping away and meeting with people undetected. Well, *a* person. Ben. She'd vowed to be different now that she knew the truth. But here she was, sneaking around again.

Would she ever be free of her past?

"You're holding up the line!" Ernie, one of their regulars, shouted from the back.

Mary didn't bother hiding her relief as Mr. Lawson moved on. She continued serving the men in line, giving Ernie an extra portion for his patience. He rewarded her with a toothless grin.

"I'll be naming my next big strike after you, Miss Mary."

"I'm honored," she told him, ignoring the sick feeling in the pit of her stomach. She already had a mine named after her—by her father, who had done unspeakable things in pursuit of those riches.

At least Ernie didn't have a family back home relying on him. Like her father, he put every dime he had into prospecting. If it wasn't for the church feeding him on a regular basis, Mary had no idea how the poor man would survive.

She watched as Ernie took a seat among some of the other men, grimacing as she realized he'd sat right next to Mr. Lawson. Mr. Lawson caught her eye, and she turned away.

"Well, if it isn't Miss Mary Stone." The familiar drawl jerked her attention to the man standing before her.

Ben Perry. The reason her life was in such disarray.

"What are you doing here?" she said, looking around again to be sure none of her family noticed that two of tonight's visitors, both of questionable character, knew Mary.

"Now, that's not the way to treat a man you promised to marry."

His voice slid down her spine, making the hairs on her arms stand on end.

"I sent you a letter ending things." Mary looked around. A letter, she realized, that Will Lawson now had in his possession.

Fortunately, Frank was engaged with a group of men, eating and talking. Her siblings all seemed to be occupied with their respective tasks. Even Polly, her friend and possibly the only confidant she'd consider telling, was busy.

"Please, leave," she told him in the harshest voice

she could muster without drawing too much attention to herself.

Gone was the charming smile he'd used to lure her in. Something evil glittered in his eyes as he said, "I don't think so."

Then, in a voice so loud it would have been impossible for anyone not to hear, he said, "My darling Mary, I've finally found you."

Ben looked as though he was about to try to embrace her, so Mary did the only thing a woman in her situation could do. She dumped the plate of beans square down the front of his shirt.

"You will regret that." His voice remained low and menacing, all while he was putting on an act of the charming, debonair man she'd once fallen for.

"Dear, sweet Mary. You're so overcome with joy that your clumsiness has come upon you again."

People began surrounding them. Polly was first at her side. "Mary! I can't believe it. A secret beau!"

Somehow she found herself brought around the table and next to Ben with his arm around her.

"My Mary made me promise to wait until she'd heard news from her brother. I left only briefly to find a job to support us, but when I returned, Mary was gone, and it's taken me all this time to find her."

Mary's eyes narrowed at the vile man pretending to be the loving suitor. What was he up to? When she'd refused to participate in his foul plans, he'd cast all sorts of insults at her.

"Imagine my surprise at finding her here, her brother building the family a fine home down the block, the pillars of Leadville society caring for the poor."

Of course. Ben knew they had money. What he'd stolen back in Ohio hadn't been enough to keep him long. So now he was here, trying to get himself a rich bride.

Mary removed herself from Ben's grasp, noticing that Mr. Lawson had wound his way to the front of the crowd that had gathered. At least now he wouldn't be confronting her. He'd said he'd wanted to find Ben. Well, here he was.

"That was a long time ago, Ben. So much has happened since we last saw each other." She gave him a long, hard look. "I'm afraid it wouldn't be right to take up where we left off."

"So, that's how it is." Ben gave a long, exaggerated sigh. "Now that she's a wealthy heiress, she doesn't want anything to do with a lowly workingman, taking what odd jobs he can to support himself."

With a long look of sadness that she couldn't believe the others didn't see through as being completely fake, he continued, "Back in Ohio, Mary said that love was all we needed. But now that she's had a taste of the good life, she can't bear the thought of a simple rented room."

Oh, the nerve of the man... Mary shook her head, wishing she could ask God for a way out, but knowing that since her sin was what had gotten her here in the first place, God wasn't likely to offer his assistance.

Of course!

Mary gave him what she hoped was a look of deep regret, then turned her attention to the crowd. "While it's true that at one point I may have had feelings for Ben, I've had time to grow and reflect upon my relationship with the Lord. Given that Ben doesn't have a relationship with Christ, it isn't right for us to be together."

Of all the things Ben most despised, it was anything to do with the church. In her foolishness, she'd thought that by loving Ben, she could get him to love the Lord, but in the end, it had only rent a hole in her own faith that she wasn't sure could ever be repaired. At least that was one mistake she'd not repeat.

Ben stepped in front of her and clasped her hands with such fervor she thought they'd break. "Oh, Mary darling, then all your prayers have been answered, because I've been going to church."

More lies, she was sure, but with the oohs and aahs from the gathered crowd, she wasn't going to let him get away with it.

"Which one?" The words came out more peevish than she would have liked, but she simply couldn't allow anyone, least of all Ben, to think they had any future.

His grip on her hands tightened, making her wince with pain. "Lots. I've been moving around, searching for you. But now that I've found you, and I see what a wonderful job this church is doing for the poor, I believe I'll be staying."

She knew she'd been beaten. The only way out was the truth, and by the way everyone had all fallen under Ben's spell, Mary knew that not one of them would believe it. An accomplished thief and scoundrel, Ben knew all the tricks of worming his way into people's hearts. .

"Please," she whispered, "don't do this. Just go, and I promise, we'll talk later."

But Ben didn't release her hands. "I could never bear to leave my beloved's side."

He bent, and as he kissed her hand, he whispered, "I still have your aunt's brooch. If you don't cooperate, I'll be sure it's found in your possession."

Every hope of getting out of this situation undamaged shattered. To Ben, it was just a brooch he'd stolen.

From what she'd seen in the satchel that night, one of many. But to Mary, it was one more reminder of how she'd failed her family and wreaked so much havoc on their lives.

How much more would she have to suffer for the foolishness of believing herself in love? For thinking that a man could love her? No one would believe she hadn't stolen the brooch. Just like they wouldn't have believed her the night she'd discovered the extent of Ben's deception. He'd planned things too well and set her up to look too guilty.

Mary pulled her hands from his grasp, shaking them to rid herself of the lingering kiss he'd placed there and to bring the blood back to the fingers he'd crushed.

"Then I hope you know how to do dishes." She gestured to the pot that lay nearly forgotten on the ground. "Because now that supper's over, we'll have plenty to wash."

Never mind the fact that she hated washing dishes. Ben hated doing them even more. Actually, the man hated any kind of work, so if there was any blessing to be found in the situation, this was it. Surely he couldn't keep up this act with dishes to be faced.

"Now, darling." He grabbed her hand again and brought it to his lips. "You know that I would love to help, but I've only just got to town, and I still need to secure lodgings. I'll return first thing in the morning, and we can talk about our wedding then."

She fought the urge to slap the face so close to her hand. Instead, she turned away, trying to ignore the whispers of how romantic it was.

"Tomorrow, my love, tomorrow." With a look that could only be described as a threat, Ben was gone.

She should have felt relief as she watched him leave. Even more relief at noticing that Mr. Lawson had also disappeared. She gathered the dishes and brought them next door to the parsonage. But when she entered the kitchen, the murderous glance her sister Rose shot her only brought more discomfort.

"You evil, evil sister," Rose hissed, standing in Mary's way. "Oh, I recognized him right away. All those trips to the mercantile and errands to town. To think you almost had me fooled."

Rose knew. She'd known all along. What should have brought relief to Mary's torment only made it worse.

"Rose, I—"

Her sister gave her another look of sheer hate. "Don't bother. Nothing you say can make it better. When I think of all the times I had to stay at Aunt Ina's to look after the little ones so you could go to town on an important errand."

With a shake of her head, Rose continued, "All that time, you were going to see him, weren't you?"

Mary couldn't deny it. Couldn't pretend that she hadn't done her best to find every excuse in the world to see Ben, leaving Rose to mind their younger siblings. Rose hadn't been as good as she had been at protecting them from Aunt Ina's wrath. But Mary hadn't known that at the time.

Or maybe she'd been too head over heels to notice.

Either way, it didn't matter. Because Mary had been wrong, terribly wrong.

"I'm sorry," she said simply, wishing there were other words she could say to make her sister feel better. To take away the harm she'd caused.

But Rose wasn't looking to feel better. She wanted

blood. "You're sorry? Sorry isn't going to get Silas back. While you were off wooing your beau, mine got tired of waiting and married Annie Garrett. Annie Garrett! I could have been Mrs. Silas Jones, but you were too busy lying to me and catering to some dandy so you could be first."

Silas? Rose was mad about losing Silas to Annie? Was it wrong to be relieved that her sister wasn't accusing her of greater sins, of which Mary was indeed guilty?

"Rose..." She softened the look she gave her sister. "That had nothing to do with Silas marrying Annie. She was the only child of the family who owned an adjacent farm. Their fathers wanted to combine the farms and expand the holding. Silas was always going to marry Annie."

"It was me he loved," Rose wailed. "He told me so by the cottonwood behind the church. Silas carved our initials in it to seal the promise of our unending love. He didn't bring Annie there, he brought me, and he kissed me, and he said he'd love me forever."

Tears rolled down Rose's face. "I was supposed to meet Silas so we could run away together. But you were late getting home from taking the eggs to town. You said you were delayed helping Mrs. Burdoch's lame horse. Now I know it was a lie. You were meeting him. And since I missed my meeting with Silas, he married Annie instead."

Nothing Mary said would convince Rose of the truth. She *had* been helping Mrs. Burdoch. Ironically, it had prevented her from meeting Ben—the first time they'd planned on running away together. Unlike Silas, Ben had been more patient. Who would have thought that one lame horse could wreak so much havoc?

If Mary could kiss that horse, she would. It had saved her from making the biggest mistake of her life even worse.

"Rose, you were there when Mrs. Burdoch brought over the pie to thank me for helping her. It's true that I did lie to meet Ben on a number of occasions, but that wasn't one of them. I'm sure Silas was meeting you to tell you that the wedding had been arranged, not to run away with you."

The sting of her sister's hand against her cheek was wholly unexpected. It should have hurt more, but as the side of her face throbbed, it felt almost good to finally receive some of the punishment Mary deserved.

"You know nothing of my relationship with Silas. Just as I knew nothing about your beau. And now you sit here telling me that Silas never loved me because you're so smug about having a man track you down. I hope you remember at every happy moment of your life with him that it came at the expense of mine."

Rose turned and ran out of the house. Mary took a step toward her, but Polly reached out a hand to stop her.

"Let her go. She needs time."

Mary turned to face her friend. "How much of that did you hear?"

"Most of it." Polly shrugged. "If she'd done more than slap you, I'd have stepped in. But she needed to get it out. She's been nothing but angry and bitter since she got here. Now I know why."

And here Mary had thought it was about having to accept an illegitimate sister. Maybe Nugget was the least of their problems. As much as Mary thought she'd been listening to her siblings, perhaps she'd been making a lot of assumptions.

"I had no idea." Sure, she'd seen the flirtatious glances in church, but with everyone knowing that Silas and Annie had been promised for just about forever, Mary had assumed it to be meaningless. If only her sister had been more forthcoming, perhaps her heartbreak could have been prevented.

Of course, Mary herself hadn't been all that forthcoming, either. She'd never been as close to Rose as she had been to their brother Joseph. When Joseph had left to search for their father, she'd kept her own counsel about things she'd usually have talked with him about.

"You and Rose will work things out." Polly gestured to the pile of dishes they had yet to wash. "How about we get to work, and you can tell me all about this beau of yours?"

Her friend gave a wicked grin, then splashed her with some water. "All this time you've had a secret engagement and didn't even tell me!"

If Mary thought that facing her angry sister was hard, this was going to be an even tougher conversation. Rose was right to hate her for her deception over Ben's courtship. Though her sister was wrong about Mary's part in her failed romance, she was all too correct about the damage Mary's absences had done.

How could she tell Polly the truth? It was something that would make Polly turn from her in disgust.

So much to atone for. An entire lifetime wouldn't be enough to earn absolution for her sin. Mary had already made up her mind to take on most of the burden of raising her younger siblings so that Joseph and his new wife, Annabelle, had the chance to raise their own family without the burden of their siblings. They deserved a chance at happiness. Especially Joseph, who'd worked so hard to keep the family together. Hopefully, Mary would find a way to extricate herself from whatever mischief Ben was cooking up without causing even more damage to her family.

But just as she put her hands in the dishwater, Mr. Lawson passed by the kitchen window, sending her a meaningful glance. He hadn't forgotten their meeting. She watched as he strode purposefully toward Frank.

Frank could not be told the truth, particularly now that Mary knew Ben still had Aunt Ina's brooch. Of all he had taken, the brooch had cost Mary the most. Aunt Ina had been merciless in her accusations of Mary, Rose and their other siblings. She'd even snatched the spectacles off poor little Bess's face, demanding to know if her brooch had been sold to pay for them. It hadn't been Mary's doing at all. Their Sunday school teacher, Miss Beverley, had noticed Bess's reading troubles. When Mary confessed it was due to Bess needing spectacles they couldn't afford, Miss Beverley had purchased them and told Mary she wished to remain anonymous. So, Mary had said she'd taken on extra work to purchase them. At the time, Mary had thought herself so smart, because saying she'd taken on extra work had given her more excuses to go meet Ben.

If she could take it back, she wouldn't have lied about those spectacles.

But wishing didn't solve the problem of having to meet Mr. Lawson. Mary glanced over at Polly, who was hard at work doing her share of cleanup. She'd never lied to Polly and didn't want to start now. When Ben had left town, Mary had promised herself to never lie again.

How was she supposed to keep her promise and keep her secrets?

"You've barely touched the dishes." Polly caught her gaze, then looked down meaningfully at the pile. "You're worse than useless now that your beau is back in town. Combine that with your disagreement with Rose, and I'd just as soon do all the work myself for all the help you're being."

Mary swallowed. "I'm sorry."

This was the point at which she should have confessed, but her throat tightened.

"Don't be. We all have our days. Go get some air and I'll finish up in here. You've done my share of the chores a time or two."

The weight should have fallen off Mary's shoulders, but it only seemed heavier. Polly was being a true friend. And Mary had nothing to offer her in return. At least not while the troubles with Ben hung over her.

Chapter Three

Mary joined Mr. Lawson and Frank in the yard. Ordinarily, Mary would never dream of interrupting one of Frank's conversations, but this was no ordinary discussion.

"Mary!" Frank smiled warmly at her. The gesture only made her feel worse.

"Good evening." Mary tried to think of a reason for having interrupted the men, but her mind went blank. It was as though all of her excuses had been worn out with Ben.

"Mr. Lawson was just telling me how welcome you made him feel at tonight's dinner."

She glanced over at Mr. Lawson, who smiled innocently. Oh, he wasn't innocent at all. He was a conniving, manipulative snake who—

Was making her miss the rest of what Frank said about their conversation.

"I'm glad he told me, Mary. You know how I feel about you girls wandering the streets of Leadville alone. There are too many unsavory elements, and I'm extremely grateful Mr. Lawson came to your assistance.

Had someone of less exemplary character been present, you might not have fared so well."

Mary closed her eyes and took a deep breath before opening them again and looking at Frank. "Trust me, I learned my lesson, and I am very grateful for Mr. Lawson."

Mr. Lawson gave a small smile. "Please. It's Will. I was more than happy to render assistance."

Unfortunately, Frank smiled back. "Of course. We don't stand much on ceremony in these parts, do we, Mary?"

Her only option was to give a polite nod. Referring to Will as Mr. Lawson had been the means of keeping him at a distance. Now even that was being taken from her.

Why was everything in her newly safe world being turned upside down?

Frank twisted his head toward some men entering via the back gate, giving Mary enough time to catch Will's smirk. Could a human being be any more insufferable?

"If you'll excuse me—" Frank turned his attention back to them "—I need to take care of this."

He didn't wait for a response but immediately went over to the men at the gate. Though Mary was used to the pastor's business, she turned to Will to give an apology for the abruptness.

Will seemed to sense what she was about to say and held up a hand. "I understand perfectly. He's a good man, your pastor."

Some of the tension fell off Mary's shoulders. "He is. He's done a lot for our family."

"Once he finds out the kind of man Ben is, he'll never consent to your marriage."

Mary swallowed. On one hand, she was counting on

it. On the other hand, she had no idea how to let Frank know without letting her own secrets be known.

"You seem like a nice girl. You have a good family. A pastor who is loving and kind. I'm sure whatever you are mixed up in with Ben, if you come clean now, they will support you through it."

Easy for him to say. He had no idea what she'd done. Moreover, if he knew the kind of man Ben was, he would know that whatever she had done wasn't anything a person admitted to. So, that left the question of who Will Lawson was and why he was so interested in Ben Perry.

"What's it to you? You said you came here looking for Ben. Well, you found him. So, go about whatever business it is that you have with him, and leave me out of it."

Will looked at her with an intensity that made her want to hide like the little ones did when some of the rougher miners came to call on the pastor.

"Ben Perry is a bad man."

She wished Will could have told her that a year ago. Of course she probably wouldn't have listened. Ben had preyed on her every vanity. Her every desire to be admired by a handsome gentleman.

"Why do you care what a supposedly bad man is doing with me?"

Will shouldn't care. In one respect, Mary was right. It was none of his business if she married Ben or not. And yet, he couldn't stand idly by as Ben ruined another life.

"You lied to me about severing your connection with him."

Mary flinched at his words. "I did not. Ben's visit here tonight surprised me just as much as it did you."

Actually, Will had noticed that. He'd also noticed how Mary bristled at Ben's attention and how she'd tried to remove herself from his grasp. But something wasn't right with the situation. With Mary's reticence.

"Then why did you announce your engagement?"

"*Ben* announced our engagement." Mary's eyes flashed as she emphasized Ben's name. Will had to admit, Mary had really pretty eyes. Green with flecks of gold, so deep a man could spend hours mining them and still— What was he doing mooning over her? Hadn't he learned his lesson?

"Why did you go along with it? Why not tell everyone that you'd broken things off with him?"

"Didn't you hear me try to explain that it was over?" Mary's voice was littered with the angst of unshed tears. "But I—" She shook her head. "It doesn't matter. I'll figure something out."

Will took a step closer. "I'll help you," he said softly. "Let me help you."

"If he is such a bad man, why would you involve yourself? Are you the law, with the power to do something about him being a bad man?"

"No." Will's gut churned. It was still hard to face the fact that he had no legal authority. But if he could gather enough evidence, he could take it to the authorities, and they could finally put Ben where he belonged.

"Then why?"

"Because it's the right thing to do." In so many ways, but most of them were things he couldn't make Mary understand. Ways he wasn't sure he understood himself. Ultimately, his gun had been the cause of an innocent man's death. Whether Will pulled the trigger or not, he bore some responsibility.

It was easier remembering that layer of guilt, and how he needed to bring closure to Eldon Wormer's family, than it was to look into the eyes of a woman as sweet and innocent as Mary.

Surely she was innocent.

But how was he ever to trust his instincts where women were concerned when he'd been so easily conned by Daisy? Her eyes had appeared innocent as well, and look where that had gotten him. Gut-shot and badgeless.

"In my case," Mary said, giving him a tiny smile, "the right thing to do is walk away. I didn't ask for your help. I don't want your help. And I don't know anything about Ben that can be helpful to you."

Her head turned, and Will realized that the pastor was making his way back to them. They wouldn't be able to talk freely soon.

"You didn't ask for my help earlier today, either, but I probably saved your life."

As she turned to speak to the pastor, Will thought he might have heard her say "Perhaps you shouldn't have bothered," but he couldn't be certain.

The one thing he was certain of, however, was that, based on the information he had about Ben's activities in the area, no matter what level of involvement Mary had with them, she was in for a world of trouble.

How else could he get her to talk? And would it be the truth? He wasn't sure he was capable of telling the truth from a lie any longer, especially when it came to a pretty woman.

Will returned to the Rafferty Hotel, noting that Ben

wasn't in the saloon or in any of the public areas. He attempted to make discreet inquiries about the man, but no one seemed willing to talk.

When Will finally retired to his room, it was with a heavy heart. Locating Ben had been the easy part. Finding evidence against him—well, that might be as difficult as counting all the silver in this fine country.

Will hadn't been sleeping long when a scuffle outside the window roused him. He climbed out of bed and peered out the curtains. A group of men were arguing. Will sighed. Last night's sleep had been interrupted by the same.

But just as he started to let the curtain drop, one of the men turned, his face briefly illuminated by the coming dawn.

Ben.

As quickly as he could, Will dressed and headed out, hoping to catch up with the other man and ascertain his activities. When he exited the hotel, the other men had scattered, but Will caught a glimpse of Ben scurrying down Harrison Avenue.

He quickened his pace as Ben turned down State Street. The most notorious red-light district in the state, if not the country, and Will was going in without a gun or a badge. Fortunately, Ben entered the closest saloon, The Pink Petticoat.

Approaching cautiously, Will looked around to make sure he wasn't walking into a trap. It was probably safe, given how brazen Ben had been in the other saloon. Ben knew that even if Will wanted to, he couldn't do anything to stop him. But someday…things would be different.

No one seemed to notice as Will entered the saloon.

With dawn upon them, most of the men were too far into their cups or sleeping it off to pay attention. Ben had already found a table and was in deep conversation with the men seated there. Will moved in for a closer look.

"See something that strikes your fancy?" A kitten-soft voice spoke into his ear as a woman wrapped her arms around him.

At first he didn't recognize the painted features. But something about her seemed familiar. "Daisy?"

The woman jumped at the name, then shook her head. "No, but for the right price, you can call me anything you want."

Her voice was husky, as if she'd spent too much time in the smoke-filled room. She put her arm around him, turning him toward the stairs.

Will's face heated, and he pulled away. "Sorry. I think you got the wrong idea. You reminded me of my old friend Daisy. I can see I was mistaken."

Something flashed across the woman's face as her woman-of-the-night expression softened.

"It's not safe to talk here," the woman whispered harshly. She took his hand, then led him out a side door linking the saloon to another building.

"I think you've got me wrong. I just want—"

She turned and pressed her fingers to his lips. "I want the same thing. But if you don't come with me, we're both going to be in trouble."

Clearly this woman knew something about the situation. Was this another one of Ben's games, designed to keep him from spying on whatever conversation was happening?

At this point, he wasn't sure who to trust. It was on the tip of his tongue to ask God, but that had never done him much good, either. For all the prayers he'd prayed, his father was dead, his mother was still suffering from consumption, Ben Perry was still on the loose, and Will had lost his badge. No, it was up to Will to make sure things turned out right.

Before he could make up his mind about what to do, the woman had led him into a room and closed the door behind them.

"What's your name?" he asked. "And what's this got to do with Daisy?"

Though the lamplight wasn't as dim as it had been in the saloon, it still wasn't bright enough to make out more of her features, especially with the curtains drawn tightly closed. Only enough to confirm that while she looked like Daisy, it was only a faint resemblance.

She reached into a drawer and pulled out a handgun, aiming it directly at him.

"I'll be asking the questions here. Starting with the ones you asked me. Who are you, and what do you know about my sister?"

Sister? At least it explained the resemblance. He took a step toward her. "Lady…"

With practiced movement, she cocked the gun. "Don't come any closer. Answer my questions, or I'll shoot."

Will didn't move. She held the gun as if she knew what she was doing. Even though he couldn't see the look in her eyes, he was pretty sure she meant business. "With everyone around? They'd hear the gunshot. You'll hang for sure."

"No one's going to hang a woman for defending herself against a robbery." She gestured toward a chair in the corner of the room. "Sit. I can put a bullet in your skull faster than you can take a step to disarm me, so don't even try."

Cunning, he'd give her that.

"My name is Will Lawson. I knew Daisy back in Century City. We were working together to bring down Ben Perry and his gang, but she betrayed me. The last I saw her, she was riding on the back of Ben's horse headed out of town."

"Liar!" The woman took a step closer, making a point of getting him in her sight. "Daisy would have never willingly gone with Ben Perry."

He could hear the doubt in her voice. "Then what are you doing here? It can't be an accident that you're in the same saloon."

The woman loosened her grip on the gun. Not enough for him to feel safe in disarming her, but enough that he knew he could eventually talk her down. Especially if she hated Ben as much as he did.

"I knew Ben and his men back in Denver. Daisy disappeared from the convent school about the same time Ben was forced to leave town due to some unpleasant business. I'm a favorite of one of Ben's men, and he sometimes tells me things. Just nothing about Daisy. But I know they had to have taken her. They're working on a big score here in Leadville that'll keep them here for a while. This may be my only chance to find her."

Information that matched what Will knew about Ben's activities shortly before arriving in Century City, including how Daisy had come to be with Ben in the first place.

But it still didn't answer the question about why Daisy had betrayed him.

While he couldn't offer the woman any comfort

about Daisy's last known whereabouts, at least he could offer himself as an ally.

And maybe gain an ally for himself. Did the big score she spoke of have anything to do with Mary? Could this be the break he needed to take Ben down once and for all?

"We're on the same side," Will told her. "I used to be a deputy in Century City. Daisy had told me that she wanted to get away from Ben. She sent me a note, saying she wanted me to meet her. While I was off trying to save Daisy, Ben and his gang robbed a bank. They fired me when Ben got away. I'm pretty sure the sheriff was on Ben's payroll, but I can't prove it."

"So, what do you want with Daisy?"

Will shook his head. "Nothing. I was here trailing Ben, hoping to see if I could find out anything about his plans. I saw you and thought for a moment you might be Daisy, that's all."

"When did you last see her?" Her posture had softened enough that he didn't think he was in danger of being shot anymore, but as long as she held the gun, he wasn't taking any chances.

"Why don't you put the gun down and then we can talk?"

"Fine." She sat in a chair across from him and set the gun in her lap. "But don't think I won't shoot you. You wouldn't be my first."

Hard. In all the places where Daisy was soft. Where Mary... Will pushed the thought of the other woman aside. She had no business sneaking into his brain now. Not when he was face-to-face with the reminder of why he wouldn't even consider getting involved with anyone connected to Ben Perry.

Will cleared his throat. "Now that we've got that out of the way, are you going to tell me your name?"

From this angle, the light hit her face in such a way that he could see the detail of her features better. In daylight, he'd have never mistaken her for Daisy.

"Melissa. But I'm known as Mad Mel." She picked up the gun again and studied it. "Came by the name honestly, if you know what I mean."

Mel looked up at him. "I believe you were telling me about when you last saw my sister."

Will took a deep breath. If she truly was mad, then she wouldn't like his side of the story. Especially since she'd already made clear that Daisy would have never gotten involved with Ben.

"Last I saw her, she was getting on the back of a horse with Ben and riding out of Century City."

A dark look crossed Mel's face. "He must've been forcing her. Why didn't you stop them?"

"Because I'd just been shot and lay bleeding in the middle of the street." He declined to add the fact that Daisy was the one who'd shot him—on Ben's order. Out of habit, he rubbed the still-healing spot that had laid him up for weeks. Sometimes he could feel the bullet still burning a hole in his belly, even though the doc said he'd gotten it all.

"He pulled a gun on her, then?" The tone in Mel's voice was so hopeful that Will couldn't let her keep believing a lie. Maybe Daisy had been that person at one point in time, but that wasn't who she was anymore.

"No. She went willingly. Kissed him passionately before he helped her onto the horse."

Oddly, that fact didn't sting the way he'd thought it would. He'd replayed the scene over and over in his mind while recuperating, thinking that she'd have been kinder to him had she just killed him outright. But she hadn't. She'd shot him and left him in a pool of his own blood, then kissed the man she'd once promised to help him bring down.

"Why would she do that?" Pain slashed across Mel's face, and Will almost felt bad for telling her the truth.

"I don't know," he simply said. "I honestly don't."

Mel must've believed him, because she stood, then put the gun back in the drawer she'd taken it from. "Daisy always said she hated him."

"She'd told me the same thing." And if he hadn't been shot, then seen her kissing Ben, he'd have still believed it.

Silence filled the room, and he looked around. The room was just as nice as what he'd been given at Rafferty's hotel, only made a little more like home with some personal items strewn about. Mel was clearly not some throwaway woman of the night.

Will walked to the bureau and picked up a framed portrait of two young girls. "This the two of you when you were younger?"

Mel stood and joined him, taking the frame out of his hands. "Before our father died, yes."

It was easy enough to piece together the rest of the story on his own. Without anyone to care for them, Mel had adopted the world's oldest profession to provide for her younger sister. He looked at her, wishing he could do something about the tears in her eyes or the way she gripped the frame tightly.

"I did everything to give her a good life." Mel returned his look with a mournful expression that made his gut wound ache even more. "Why would she take up with Ben Perry?"

Will would like to ask that question himself. *Why would she take up with Ben Perry?* Not just of Daisy, but of Mary, a sweet woman who spent her time working with a preacher and feeding down-and-out miners. How could such goodness be attracted to such evil?

"I wish I knew," he said softly. "I'm sorry I couldn't give you better news of your sister. If I hear anything, I'll let you know."

Then he turned toward Mel. "I still plan on taking down Ben Perry. I'd be obliged if you'd keep an ear out for me."

"We'll see." The hard expression had returned to her face. Mel wasn't likely to do anything that would jeopardize her chances of finding her sister. For Mel's sake, Will hoped Daisy wanted to be found.

He gave her a nod, then turned toward the door.

"Not that way," Mel said, pointing to another door. "We're not supposed to bring men into the boardinghouse, so I need to take you back through the saloon. Alma will be furious if she finds out I had you in here."

"Alma?"

"She owns the place. Thinks that if she gives us women of the night a good home we'll eventually see the light and repent of our sins. Alma means well, even if it'll never get her anywhere."

Mel's frank assessment made Will sadder for Alma than he would have thought. The realities of the lives of women like Mel were not that they changed.

Yet he couldn't forget the wistful look in Mel's eyes as she talked about wanting a better life for Daisy. He had wanted a better life for Daisy. Stupidly, Will had thought he'd be able to provide it for her.

Perhaps he and Mel weren't so different after all.

A lightness he hadn't known since the shooting filled his heart. Yes, he'd loved Daisy, but for the first time it hit him that maybe it wasn't the romantic kind of love he wanted in a wife. Maybe it was the sister kind of love. Sure, he'd kissed Daisy, but most of them had been on the forehead. The couple of times he'd tried to kiss her on the lips, she'd turned her head, and he'd gotten her cheek instead. He'd already known that he was over her, but now maybe he could accept that he'd never truly loved her at all.

A knock sounded at the door. "Mel?" The whispered voice was urgent.

"It's okay, you can come in," Mel called back. She glanced at Will. "Get behind the changing screen."

He moved quickly, positioning himself to be out of view but able to see what was happening through a crack in the side. The woman who entered looked even younger than Daisy and was sporting a bleeding lip and what would probably be a bruised cheek in the morning.

"What happened?" Mel rushed to the woman and escorted her to one of the chairs.

"Ben said I sassed him, so he had Big Jim hit me." Tears filled the girl's eyes. "I didn't mean to sass him, I promise. Ben said that I'd be all his last night, but he just got here, and the sun's almost up. When I asked him about it, he told Big Jim to take care of me."

The girl's words brought a new fire to the hole in Will's gut. What kind of man asked another man to do his dirty work like that? Bad enough that he'd wanted to strike a woman, worse that he'd made someone else do it.

The woman's sobs strengthened Will's resolve. Someone had to take down Ben Perry. Not only were the banks not safe, but countless women were in danger, as well. It was as if Ben made them impervious to his misdeeds. To what a foul person he was.

Once again, his thoughts drifted to Mary Stone. Everything about her spoke of a kind and decent woman. But somehow, Ben had managed to trick her into thinking that...

That what? Was it really his job to save Mary from Ben? He'd tried with Daisy. If he'd just done his job and followed the evidence and arrested Ben, he'd have never been shot. Never let Ben get away. But no, he'd thought Daisy had needed rescuing.

He glanced back over at the woman Mel consoled. She was putting some kind of poultice on the woman's injuries.

"Thank you, Mel. I just hope it doesn't show too badly so Ben doesn't send me away. I'm sure if I tell him I'm sorry, things will be fine."

Will looked away, but not before catching the warning look on Mel's face.

No, he wouldn't be saving anyone. At least not here. But if someone didn't do something about Ben Perry, and get him in jail where he belonged, there'd be more women like Daisy, like this woman before him and, God help him, like Mary Stone, who'd fall victim.

He'd just have to find a way to do it and not let himself get entangled with Mary. No matter how often her image popped into his thoughts.

Chapter Four

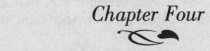

This time, when Mary went on her errands, she brought Polly with her. Rose still wasn't speaking to her, but perhaps that was for the best. Mary wasn't sure she had any energy left to defend her position while keeping her secrets.

"Can we finally talk about Ben?" Polly's eyes glimmered in the early-morning sunlight, perfectly matching the blue sprigged muslin dress she wore.

Mary let out a long sigh, wishing she felt half the energy her friend appeared to have as she swung the basket of goods Maddie had given them to deliver.

"Ben was a youthful—" well, there was only way to put it "—indiscretion." Trite as it sounded, it was the only fair way to describe things without revealing the whole truth.

"I thought I loved him, but once I found out his true character, I knew he wasn't the man for me." Mary looked at her friend, hoping to convey the full depth of her lack of feelings for Ben. "But he doesn't seem to understand that."

They passed by a pawnshop, and Mary couldn't help

but notice a brooch displayed in the window. Not her aunt's, but enough to remind her of Ben's threats. How was she going to fully extricate herself without being implicated in Ben's evildoings?

"Could you have played a role in the change of Ben's character?" Polly gave her a long look. "He said he's going to church now. Maybe he realized the failings you pointed out and decided to improve upon them. He sounded quite earnest."

Mary stopped. Stared at her friend for a moment. "Have you gone mad?"

"What?" Polly's eye held the twinkle Mary knew and loved. "He is rather fine-looking. And unlike most of the men in this town, he's got nice manners. He seems to be everything a man ought to be."

That was precisely the problem…he *seemed* to be a lot of things. The trouble was, he was none of them.

"And to think just yesterday, you were telling me how all men were less useful than the sludge that comes from the smelters."

Polly sighed. "True. I'm sure your Ben is just as useless despite being so handsome to behold. Still, a girl can always dream that there's happiness to be found for someone, at least."

"A man's looks can be deceiving, surely you know that."

The darkness Mary had come to recognize being part of Polly returned to her face, and Mary regretted teasing Polly about hating men. The man who'd recently broken Polly's heart had supposedly been very handsome. Mary hadn't meant to rub salt in Polly's wounds.

"I'm sorry, I didn't mean—"

"Leave it. You don't want to talk about Ben, I don't want to talk about the past."

Polly adjusted the basket she'd been carrying. "Let's hurry and deliver these baked goods to Miss Betty's, then meet up with the other girls from church for the picnic. It'll be good for you to get to know them, and it'd be a far sight better than sitting around the house with Rose still sore at you."

Mary's own basket was starting to get heavy, and she'd appreciate finishing the task, as well. Even though she understood Frank's mission was about helping the less fortunate in Leadville, Mary still didn't always understand why it had to be *those* women. It didn't matter how many times Frank told the story of the sinful woman and how no one cast a stone at her, she still didn't feel comfortable entering dens of sin.

Were it not for Miss Betty's kindness, though, who knew what would have happened to Nugget, Mary's youngest sister. Most notorious women would not have cared for the child of one of their deceased workers, but Miss Betty had taken care of Nugget until their brother Joseph came to town. Surely she could muster some grace for the sinner who saved her sister.

She and Polly bustled down the street, picking up their pace as they entered State Street. Most decent folks avoided this part of town. Ruffians could attack at any time, and no one would come to their aid. Usually one of Polly's brothers came with them, but they'd been too busy up at the mine, now that it was finally in production.

As they passed the saloon a few doors down from Miss Betty's, a man stumbled out, disheveled.

"But I can still win it back," he slurred.

Mary lifted her skirts slightly and attempted to move past when another man followed.

"I don't think so, Hank. You're in to me for far more than you can ever pay." The man gave a barking laugh, so distinctive that Mary was forced to look at him.

Ben. His shirt was unbuttoned, and a scantily clad woman had her arm possessively around his.

Mary glanced over at Polly, who gave a shrug.

But Mary wasn't going to accept that. Not when it could possibly give her a way out.

"So this is where you've been keeping yourself," she told him, giving her best glare. "Despite your words last night, I think it's clear that we no longer have a future together."

He stepped toward her, stuffing his shirttails into his pants. "A little meaningless fun, that's all."

"Not in my book." Mary tucked her free arm into Polly's and took another step down the street. "Let's go."

Another man rounded the corner, blocking their path. She didn't need to look up to know it was Will. Something about his presence…

Whatever it was, it couldn't be a good feeling, the way her windpipe felt as if it was closing up. Mary cleared her throat. "I see you've found each other. Now you both can leave me alone. I want nothing more to do with the lot of you."

She tugged at Polly's arm to go around them, catching Polly mouth the question *Two beaus?* at her. No, she didn't have two beaus. She'd only ever had the one, but…

Will's eyes were firmly upon her. Deep, probing eyes that made her feel more undressed than the woman standing next to Ben.

Ben said something, but she didn't hear. Didn't want to, for that matter. Determined not to be caught up in further conversation with either man, she practically sprinted to Miss Betty's, pulling a breathless Polly behind her.

Only once they were seated in Miss Betty's kitchen, cups of tea in front of them, the serving girl dispatched to fetch Miss Betty, did Mary speak.

"So now you understand why I can't marry Ben." Polly gave a nonchalant look. "They all do it. Might as well accept that fact. You'll marry eventually, then look aside when he seeks his entertainment."

Mary's face burned. Not just with the casual treatment of marriage, but with the reminders of what her family had suffered due to her father's indiscretion.

"Frank isn't like that," Mary retorted. Some men could be trustworthy.

After casually setting her teacup down, Polly gave half a smile. "But he's a rare one. Most men think nothing of visiting State Street."

"Polly MacDonald!" Mary glared at her friend. "Your mother would tan your hide if she heard you being so vulgar. Like one of—" she looked around, hoping none were listening, and lowered her voice "—those women."

Polly picked up one of the cookies the kitchen maid had set before them. "Those women happen to be onto the truth about men. I've talked to some of them on our visits, and I think they're quite nice."

Then, as though she was sitting in her own mother's kitchen, Polly took a large bite of cookie.

Quite nice. Mary squeezed her eyes shut and forced herself to count to ten. One of those quite nice women had trapped her father and foisted a child on him, a child that her brother was forcing them all to accept as their sister. Oh, it wasn't little Nugget's fault. In truth, Nugget completed their family in a way she never thought possible.

But it didn't make her father's actions right.

She knew she should be able to forgive and move on, especially as Frank's sermons were full of lessons about everyone falling short of the glory of God, but somehow, these women and their sins bothered her the most. What was the benefit of finding riches when your soul would burn from your evil deeds?

She'd thought that after two months of helping Frank's mission to these women, it would be easier. That reminding herself of the good Miss Betty had done for her family would lessen the pain of witnessing so many mired in sin.

But it hadn't. Maybe her inability to come to terms with her father's deception was more about her own. If only Mary hadn't been so enamored with the idea of having a beau that she'd been blinded to the truth. She'd lived in the fantasy that she and Ben would get married and get her and her siblings out of Aunt Ina's home. She'd thought that temporarily deceiving everyone about Ben would be worth it in the end because they'd finally be free. But Ben had lied, and Mary's lies had all been for naught.

Was that what her father had done?

No, she couldn't dwell on such things.

Mary opened her eyes to see the mirth in Polly's. "It still bothers you, doesn't it?"

"Wouldn't it bother *you*?"

Polly's casual shrug was meant to catch her off guard,

but Mary saw the pain in her eyes. "It's what men do. The sooner you accept it, the better off you'll be."

Now she knew Polly wasn't talking about Mary's father, but about the man who'd courted Polly—as a lie. It was probably hard for Polly to accept that there were still some honorable men out there.

Lies. Responsible for hurting so many people.

The maid returned to the kitchen and offered a small curtsy. "Miss Betty's not up to receiving today, but she says to tell the pastor that she appreciates his kindness in remembering her."

Mary smiled as politely as she could, hoping that her harsh words hadn't been overheard by Miss Betty. It wasn't Miss Betty's fault that Mary's life had been upended by another woman in her profession. But if her father hadn't met that other woman, then perhaps he would have come home in time to save their farm. Maybe then her mother would still be alive. And maybe she might have never met Ben at all. Then her life and family wouldn't be the horrible mess it was now.

Will caught up with the ladies as they exited the brothel. What were they thinking, visiting a house of ill repute? Two single ladies, alone? Thankfully, he'd decided to return to the saloon to see if he could learn more about Ben in the daylight.

"Allow me to escort you home," he said, stepping in stride with them. "It's not safe for you to be here."

Mary's glare was sharper than any of the glaciers that had carved out these beautiful mountains. "We come here every week to bring food to Miss Betty. We're perfectly safe."

He might not have known her well, but Will could

still hear the fear in her voice. But what was she afraid of? Him? Or State Street?

"But we'd be delighted to have your escort," her friend added, giving him a dazzling smile. "I don't believe I've made your acquaintance, though you're clearly familiar with Mary."

The scowl on Mary's face gave him an impish pleasure, almost like when he used to pull Nancy Shaw's braids back in school. Oh, how she'd hated it when he did that. But there was something about giving those braids a tug that always made him grin. At ten years old, he'd been sure he'd marry Nancy Shaw. But she'd moved away and left him with no one else to tease.

So it was with a giddy feeling in his stomach that he tipped his hat to Mary's friend and said, "Will Lawson, at your service."

"Polly MacDonald." She gave a mock curtsy and wink that told him she was enjoying tormenting Mary just as much. "And don't mind Mary. She's just—"

Mary's elbow to her friend's side was not at all discreet. "Enough. We're due home, so let's not dally. I'm sure your mother could use our help with the little ones."

"Help?" Polly's indignant sputter forced Will to hold in his laughter. "I thought we were going on the picnic with the other girls from church."

Watching Mary's face turn as purple as her dress almost brought him the same satisfaction as he'd had as a kid, only now…there was a strange sensation in the pit of his stomach. As if maybe there was something more to be desired.

Insanity.

He could tell by the way her face contorted as she tried to come up with an answer that she didn't want to let her friend down, but she also wanted out of his presence as soon as possible. Something he wished he could oblige her on, but first, he needed to know what she knew.

After spending time in a place his mother would be ashamed to know he'd ever entered, Will had to do something more to stop Ben. He'd hurt too many people, and it would be Will's fault if Ben hurt any more.

Will looked past Mary to Polly, who seemed more peacefully inclined toward him. "If you'd like to go to the picnic, I'd be happy to escort you. Mrs. Rafferty said I could use her wagon anytime. It'd be a shame for you to miss out because Mary's got work to do."

His words had the desired effect. While Polly beamed, Mary's face turned a dark crimson. "No need for you to borrow a wagon. We're meeting at the church and going as a group."

He wasn't going to let Miss Mary Stone off the hook so easily. Sure, she was mad, but what had he ever done to her? If it took making her explode in the middle of Harrison Avenue, then fine. But he was going to get to the bottom of the situation and figure out just what she had to do with Ben.

Will gave her an easy smile, then turned his attention back to Polly. "Still, if Mary is unable to go, I'm happy to take her place. I would like to get to know some of the community better."

That did the trick. Mary stepped in front of him, then stopped to turn to face him. "You are not needed to take Polly to the picnic. I said I'd go with her, and I'll go with her. Now that we've safely arrived to the respectable part of Harrison Avenue, you can be about your business."

Was she so mule-headed that she didn't understand that she was his business? With the way her eyes sparked, he didn't think so. Mary knew exactly what he wanted— to talk about Ben. Though he'd be lying if he said he wasn't interested in the raven-haired beauty who could give as good as she got.

However, this time, as much as he'd like to further a more personal acquaintance with Mary, he would keep it all business. His heart was not going to get in the way of apprehending Ben.

"Like I told Polly, I would like to get more involved with the church community. It'll be my pleasure to escort you both. Surely there's room for one more."

Mary's shoulder's sagged. She looked defeated—for now. But Mary wasn't one to give up easily, and that was something he liked about her.

"If you insist." The words sounded so forced, he almost felt bad for her. And if her feelings were the only thing on the line, he'd have relented.

"Oh, Mary, have a little fun for a change." Polly took her friend by the arm and gave Will a smile. "Don't mind her. She's always too busy thinking about her responsibilities to remember that she's young and supposed to enjoy life."

Will regarded Mary carefully. Again, he was struck by the way her personality seemed to be in contrast with the sort of woman Ben carried on with. Ben Perry only concerned himself with the party and would have never wanted to be tied down by responsibilities.

He'd like to be able to accept what she said at face value, except something in the sensitive part of his gut, the part where he'd been shot, still said that Mary was hiding something. Only it didn't keep him from wanting to bring a smile to her face.

They crossed over toward the church, and Polly deftly slipped her arm out of Mary's and moved to the other side of him, leaving him between the two ladies. Despite Polly's cheerful chatter, he could still feel Mary seething. Perhaps at the picnic, he could explain to Mary that he didn't mean any harm. As long as he obeyed his aching gut and kept his mission close to his chest.

When they arrived at the church, a large wagon was already parked in front, and several young people milled about, laughing. A young woman spied their approach and waved.

"I'm so glad you came! You'll never guess who's here. Jasper Jackson!"

Will's ears perked up at the name. He'd done some security work for Jasper's father when they had a bank in Denver. When the Jacksons moved to Leadville, Will had opted to take a deputy position in Century City to be close to his parents. Though they'd parted on good terms, Will had to wonder if the reunion would be positive after Will's disgrace. Surely word of his failure had gotten back to the Jacksons.

His musings had put him behind in the conversation, drawing him out at the mention of his name.

"And this is Will Lawson. He's a…friend…of Mary's." Polly's emphasis on *friend*, along with her wink, told Will exactly what Polly thought of his association with her.

He tipped his hat to the woman and murmured the most polite "How do you do?" he could muster.

"Quite well," the woman said, then turned to Polly. "Can you help me with the food?"

As Polly and the young woman walked away, giggling, Will was painfully aware of being alone with Mary.

Despite the tightness in his throat, he looked over at her. "I'm sorry if I said or did anything to have given her the wrong impression. I didn't mean to embarrass you."

Her cheeks tinged pink, and the tightness in her jaw softened. His apology was enough to loosen the tension between them. Maybe the rough start they'd gotten off to could be redeemed.

"You can make it up to me by not coming to the picnic." Her tone was all sweetness, but just like he knew her earlier acceptance of his presence was forced, there was nothing sweet about Mary's demand.

Good thing he wasn't very sweet, either.

"Then I guess we're sworn to be enemies." He took her hand, gave it a well-placed kiss, then turned to join the others.

Chapter Five

Everyone had seen The Kiss. Mary's ears still rang
from Polly's squeal about Will's being her secret beau.
Worse, she found herself seated next to him on the
wagon, where he chatted amiably with everyone around
them. And worst of all, Mary's hand still tingled from
the press of Will's lips against her hand.

Mary finally caught his eye, but when she tried giving him her best "you're in trouble" glare, he merely
winked back.

How could any human being be so positively insufferable?

Will settled back against the seat and gave her what
she imagined to be his best lady-killer smile. But Mary
knew better than to fall for that ruse.

"What are you most looking forward to at the picnic?" Were not there so many eyes upon her, wondering about the secret romance that had been whispered
about, she might have been tempted to give him yet another dismissal. But he wasn't one for accepting them,
and in present company, she was in no mood to argue
with him.

Mary hesitated. She had been looking forward to visiting with some of the others. Other than Polly, she didn't have friends her age, with being so busy caring for her siblings. How was she to make friends with others if Will monopolized her time?

Perhaps, if there was any compassion in the man, he would understand. "I was most looking forward to getting to know the other ladies. We haven't been here long, and as much as I adore Polly, it would be nice to establish myself in the community."

His warm smile almost made her think he could be among those she counted as friends. "Then we are of the same purpose. Perhaps we can conquer them together."

Oh, to be able to trust that easy look. But his connection to Ben made it impossible. What had Ben told him of her? Was he of the same character as Ben?

"You are just as much a stranger to me as they are." She cast a glance over at Polly, who was chatting with the young lady to her left. "I fear too close an association will only fuel the tale that you are a beau."

The expression on his face finally seemed to register his understanding of her predicament. "I suppose I should apologize for kissing your hand. I sometimes go too far in my teasing."

Though he looked chastised enough and possibly even regretful, she didn't fully believe it. Perhaps it was because she kept too many secrets of her own to trust in the veracity of others. But mostly, it was because his eye still held the same twinkle it did when his lips burned a hole in her hand.

"I'll believe that when I see it," she told him with the same kind of severity she usually reserved for the children.

"And here you thought me a stranger." His wide grin seemed to fill the entire wagon. "You seem to have me already sorted out."

Being so familiar with this man was dangerous, to be sure, but Mary couldn't resist teasing him right back. "As I've said, I have a great deal of experience with children."

Her zinger broadened his smile, and before he could send another comment back, Polly interrupted.

"I will not have you ruining our perfectly nice time by speaking any more of the children, Mary Stone. You and I have barely had a break taking care of your siblings and mine, and I intend to enjoy every last moment of it."

Her indignant glare reminded Mary that this was indeed a rare break from their responsibilities. And while it felt good to get away, even for a moment, part of Mary felt guilty for neglecting her family. It had been neglecting her responsibilities that got her into trouble with Ben in the first place. Oh, had she only not allowed herself to get caught up in the fancy of believing herself to be in love.

Unfortunately, giving her friend a smile was not enough reassurance about their time away.

"Promise me, Mary. No more talk of our responsibilities. We're here to enjoy ourselves."

It would have been a simple enough promise to give if only Will's eyes were not upon her. Why did he care? He seemed to hang on every one of her words.

But maybe that was his intent. To throw her off guard so that she was willing to talk more about Ben. Fine, then.

"Of course I promise," she told Polly. "What more can I do to show you my desire to have fun?"

Polly grinned. "Just stick with me, my friend." She turned and indicated the girl sitting on the other side of her.

"This is Beth Williams."

The freckle-faced girl held out a gloved hand. "So pleased to make your acquaintance. I know your sister-in-law quite well. Annabelle is a dear, and we were all so happy to see her settled with such a fine man as your brother."

Mary would have been flattered by the compliment to her family except for Polly's barking laugh and quick retort.

"You mean you were glad that you no longer had to worry about her competing with you for Jasper's attention."

Fanning herself furiously, Beth hid behind her fan. "I'm sure I have no idea what you're talking about. Are we almost there? Suddenly it's grown quite warm out."

Some of the girls around them giggled. A perky blonde whose name Mary thought might have been Rachel leaned forward.

"There's nothing to be embarrassed about. Everyone's been infatuated with Jasper at one point or another. Who wouldn't? His father runs with the high rollers and has even sat in Mr. Tabor's box at the opera house. Plus, he's the most handsome man I've ever seen."

At those words, all the girls sighed and glanced in the general direction of one of the dandies sitting with the driver of the wagon. The glorious Jasper, she presumed.

In Mary's eyes, he wasn't so terribly much to behold. Certainly he had a thick glossy head of dark hair, but not so shiny as to give it the heroic description some of the girls were talking about. And his eyes…why, she'd seen much nicer eyes on—

Will.

She stole a glance at him, only to find him staring right at her with an amused look on his face.

"Do you find Jasper as wonderful as the others are saying?"

His eyes held the same twinkle they'd had the entire time, and Mary was forced to admit, at least to herself, that they held a kindness to them that she rarely saw in others. Ben's eyes always had a coldness that never left. Will, even when tormenting her, had a warmth that made her want to trust him.

But where would that get her? Perhaps Will had no idea of the extent of Ben's criminal enterprise. Maybe he saw Ben as so many in Ohio had—as a perfectly amiable man who was all kindness and civility. After all, Ben had very quickly and easily taken in those at the church last night, convincing them, despite her protests, that he was a loving fiancé.

How could she expose the truth of Ben Perry to everyone without exposing herself?

If anyone from her family saw her aunt's brooch, she'd be in trouble for sure. They would all believe she'd had a role in its theft, as well as the other thefts that had taken place. Several families had jewelry and other valuables stolen—and all of them were connected to Mary and her work. The sheriff had even questioned her about the losses. It wasn't until the mercantile and bank had been robbed that they'd cleared Mary of suspicion. She'd honestly never thought that Ben, who'd patiently waited for her while she worked, was actually robbing the place behind her back.

Why had she been so desperate for romance as to keep Ben a secret, even from the sheriff?

Ben was right. With all her deceit, who would believe her completely ignorant of his actions?

Will nudged her in the side. "I can introduce you, if you like. I know Jasper from my work in Denver. Pleasant fellow."

Mortified that her woolgathering over Ben had led to the belief that she was interested in Jasper, Mary shook her head. "That won't be necessary, thank you. I have no romantic illusions at this point in my life."

"Say it's not so." Will gave her a look that would have melted the heart of any woman who hadn't had hers irrevocably broken. "A beautiful woman, of marriageable age?"

Before answering, Mary stole a glance at Polly, who had returned to her animated conversation with the other girls. "I won't marry until after I'm certain I've fulfilled my responsibility in raising my siblings."

On this point, she was determined. She'd failed those responsibilities already in believing herself ready for romance and marriage. From here on out, she wouldn't fail. Couldn't fail.

"Why is that mutually exclusive? Plenty of people marry and take on another's children."

The conversation was clearly headed in a direction she didn't need to go. Didn't need to consider.

"Not when there are six of them," she said. Mindful of Polly's gaze turning in her direction, Mary changed course. "What work did you do in Denver with Jasper?"

Will coughed slightly. "I…uh…I did some security for his father's bank."

* * *

Will had supposed that at some point or another, his previous line of work would come up. At least it had been about the security he'd done for the Jacksons as opposed to his fall from grace in the sheriff's office in Century City. Though it was only a matter of time before the gossip got back to people, he'd like that piece of information to remain confidential for as long as possible.

Who wanted to associate with a disgraced lawman? It had been his fault Perry's gang had gotten away with robbing Colorado Citizens Bank. He'd been so wrapped up in his romance with Daisy, so intent on saving her from Ben's nefarious schemes, that he hadn't realized that she was spying on him for Ben. He'd been a fool. And in so doing, everyone believed that he'd willingly given them information, willingly let them go.

Plus, despite Mary's denials about Ben, he still had to wonder what she knew. What her involvement with the gang might be. Could he get her to trust him enough to tell him the truth? And given his past poor judgment when it came to women working with Ben, could he trust that whatever she told him was the truth?

No, letting Mary know his story was not a safe option at this point. Much as he'd like to, there was too much at stake.

"Is that what you're doing in Leadville? Working for Jasper's father?"

He didn't like the way her eyes narrowed at the question.

"No," he told her honestly. "I'm here in pursuit of Ben."

She gave him a look similar to what she'd given

him every other time the other man's name came up. "Why?"

If she was in on Ben's schemes, the truth would only serve to make things harder for him. But surely nothing could make Mary more hostile than she'd already been.

"He robbed a bank in Century City, and I aim to bring him to justice."

Easy enough to share the gist of what was going on. Harder to read the expression that crossed her face, which darkened, but just as quickly turned back into the stone mask that matched her name.

"So you're a lawman?"

Not anymore. But that was a shame he couldn't face. "No."

She looked doubtful, chewing on her lip ever so slightly, almost imperceptibly, except that he'd somehow gotten to know the very fullness of her lips. What kind of cad was he, thinking of her in this way?

"How much is the bounty on his head?"

"None." Because he'd botched the job too badly to get the evidence on Ben.

"Then why do you care?" she snapped, turning away and leaning in toward the other girls.

Yes, Mary's reactions to his investigation of Ben definitely held an air of suspicion. He tapped her on the shoulder.

Mary turned, and the other girls giggled. Definitely not helping diminish the mistaken impression that he was Mary's beau. But he couldn't afford to fight fair. Not with all the money to be stolen in Leadville. Not with his reputation on the line. Not with the women Ben kept abusing. He'd make it up to Mary. Somehow.

"What Ben's done is wrong. All I want is to find out

what you know about him because there might be something in that knowledge, no matter how insignificant you believe it is, that can help put him in jail."

Her face softened for a moment but then hardened again. "There's nothing I can tell you. I knew him in Ohio, before he came to Colorado. He left Ohio before I did, and we hadn't spoken from then until he showed up last night at the church."

Will stared at her and examined her expression for any sign of prevarication. "He claimed you were engaged. Last night, you looked every bit the happy couple."

That part might have been an exaggeration. Through the cheers and Ben's loud proclamations, Mary looked like a rabbit caught in a snare. Will had replayed the scene in his mind over and over, trying to figure it out. She'd looked just as miserable with Ben as she had when Will questioned her about him. Which would almost have convinced him that Mary would be an ally—except that Daisy had told Will over and over that she wanted nothing more than to escape Ben's clutches.

The wagon hit a bump, jostling everyone and sending Mary nearly into his lap.

"Easy there." He tried to steady her, but Mary jumped again.

"I'm fine." She glared at his hands, then smoothed her skirts. "As for my supposed engagement to Ben, it's a misunderstanding that will soon be cleared up."

Her voice shook as she explained her status with Ben. Will didn't need his aching bullet wound to tell him something was definitely not right with Mary. But how could he get her to trust him? And how would he know to believe her?

The wind picked up, blowing tendrils across her face and stirring something inside Will. Was he stepping into a trap by thinking that somehow Mary was different? That his feelings for her were different?

"I can help you with that," he told her quietly. "Help me, Mary. And I'll help you."

The words echoed dangerously in his brain as he recalled saying that exact phrase to Daisy. Of course, he'd been trying to help Daisy escape her work as a barmaid, where she'd claimed to fear that Ben was pushing to get her to work above stairs, as well. Surely this was different.

But Mary remained stiff, straightening beyond her already perfect posture. "I don't need your help. I don't know anything about Ben robbing a bank. So, please, leave me alone. It's going to be hard enough to maintain my reputation as it is. Don't make it worse for me."

Her clipped tone made him realize how different the situation was. Daisy had never been a lady. But Mary… not only was she a lady, but by all accounts, she was a lady with standing. Building on their father's first discovery, Mary's brother was mining one of the richest veins of silver found in Leadville to date. Mary was an heiress of significant worth. Even though the fortune would be enough to tempt any man, the women of the community still refused to accept any woman who failed to follow proper standards of behavior.

Will's brain started to spin. What if Mary had been honest with him? What if things really had been over between her and Ben? Could Ben only be chasing her because he wanted access to her fortune? Marrying a fortune would surely be easier than stealing one.

The wagon rumbled over a number of rocks, making it too noisy to carry on a normal conversation. Will leaned closer to Mary. "If Ben's after your fortune, he'll go to no end to get it. Even if it means ruining you in the process."

Mary's face blanched, and he knew he'd hit his mark.

"I hadn't considered..." She uttered the words so softly that he almost didn't catch them. A lone tear trickled down her face.

Though he wished he could dry it himself for being the one to suggest the painful truth, Will merely pulled a handkerchief out of his pocket and handed it to her.

"If you don't help me, you may have no other choice but to marry him."

You couldn't fake the level of horror on Mary's face.

"Will Lawson!" Polly's shrill voice interrupted any chance he had of gaining Mary's cooperation. "Whatever have you said to make my friend so upset?"

Mary glared at him with such malice, he knew he was right back at square one. She'd made it clear that she wanted as little attention drawn to her and the situation as possible, and here he'd created the kind of scene she'd probably wanted to avoid.

"I, uh..." Will looked at Mary, who shook her head.

Mary dabbed at her eye, then handed the handkerchief back to Will. "I'm not upset. Something caught in the breeze and got in my eye, that's all."

Polly didn't look convinced. Moreover, the other ladies had turned their attention to the scene.

"Truly, I'm fine," Mary said with more calm than he'd thought her capable of with the way her hand shook. "But Will here was just telling me how he knew Jasper in Denver."

All the girls giggled, and Mary smiled at the pretty

redhead next to Polly. "You should ask him about their time together. I'm sure he has all sorts of tales that would interest you."

The girl's face turned the shade of her hair, and Ben knew that the only way to salvage his chance with Mary would be to play along and regale the women with tales of Jasper Jackson. Only he didn't know anything that would excite a woman beyond the fact that he was a nice enough guy who played a good game of billiards.

Still, if that was what it took to put Mary back at ease, then that was what he had to do.

"Jasper," he called to the gentleman at the front of the wagon. "These ladies here would like to hear about our times in Denver. Any particular tale you'd like me to tell?"

His old friend glanced his way, and recognition dawned on him. "Will? How are you? Why didn't you tell me you'd come to town?"

Jasper quickly picked his way through the wagon to join him. The other man clapped Will on the shoulder and addressed the women. "Ladies, you won't meet a finer man than my friend Will Lawson. I was just telling someone about him the other day and how he'd saved my father from being robbed."

Will's stomach sank as Jasper launched into a tale of Will's heroism. It had been happenstance that day, him riding down the street at the same time Mr. Jackson was being held up. Will had been fast on the draw and managed to get a shot off that had wounded the bandit and given Mr. Jackson the space needed to get away. Of course, in Jasper's version...

"Hey! I didn't kill anyone. And there was one man,

not ten." Will gave his hearty denial of the exaggerated story.

"You still saved my father," Jasper admitted jovially.

With Jasper's hearty endorsement, it was clear to Will that he hadn't yet heard of Will's disgrace. Which should have been reassuring; only, it served to make Will feel more like a fraud. What would his friend think of him once he knew how far Will had fallen?

That would be resolved easily enough—as soon as he brought Ben to justice. He stole a glance at Mary, whose expression lacked the mistrust he'd come to expect from her. Could Jasper's endorsement be the ticket he needed to get Mary to open up?

Chapter Six

The party arrived at the picnic location near Soda Springs, and Mary couldn't help but notice how the other young ladies had gathered around Will and Jasper. Once Jasper had filled their heads with tales of Will's heroism, he'd gained estimation in their eyes.

Mary sighed and helped Rachel spread one of the blankets they'd brought for the excursion.

"Have you ever had the water here? It's like drinking a real soda." Rachel pointed to the spring a few yards away.

"Let's go before the others crowd in."

Nodding her assent, Mary followed the other girl down a well-worn path toward the soda spring. When they reached the water, Rachel handed her a cup and together they dipped them into the water.

As Mary drank, the bubbles tickled her nose. The water had a tangy flavor she found quite refreshing.

"It's good, isn't it?" Rachel grinned as she refilled her cup. "The others can gawk at Jasper and Will all they want, but they're wasting their time."

"Because we're drinking all the water," Mary said, taking another sip.

Rachel shook her head. "There's plenty of water for everyone. What I meant was that Jasper has never shown an inkling of interest in any one of us, and as for Will…" She looked around slowly, then back at Mary. "Will only has eyes for you. I see him looking over here, watching you."

Almost as if Rachel could predict the future, Will chose that moment to break free from the crowd and head in their direction.

"See?" Rachel looked mighty puffed up over her proclamation. "It's a good thing I already have my heart set on someone else. Otherwise, I might not forgive you for stealing the heart of one of the few worthwhile eligible bachelors in town."

Mary frowned. "But I'm not—"

"Oh, no. Don't try to argue. We all noticed how he monopolized you on the ride over."

So much for trying not to draw too much attention to herself. More specifically, to her and Will.

Rachel continued, "What I don't understand, though, is last night, when mother came home from helping serve the meal to the miners, she said your fiancé arrived. It was quite the to-do, from how she tells it. Such a dashing man, and yet here you are, having secured the interest of another."

Wasn't it Sir Walter Scott who said, "What a tangled web we weave, when first we practice to deceive?" So much of her world was mixed up all because of a secret romance gone awry.

"It's a long story," Mary told her. "The truth is that

I broke off my engagement some time ago. And Will is not my beau. He's—"

One more thing she couldn't explain. Apparently, he wanted to bring her former fiancé to justice. But at what cost? Would her aid in proving Ben's guilt also put her behind bars? Will looked so determined in his desire to see Ben punished. What would he do if he knew her involvement?

"Well, I don't know what he is," Mary finally said. "I met him on the street yesterday when he saved me from being accosted by a group of drunken miners. Since then, our paths keep crossing, and I—"

She what? Was growing to like him more at every moment? And with that like, growing to fear his reaction when he knew the truth? Mary tried not to sigh, but she simply couldn't help it.

Fortunately, her sigh was all Rachel needed. "It sounds so romantic."

Only if one thought a hangman's noose was romantic. Did they hang accomplices to thieves? Or was Will a thief himself?

Will was almost upon them. "I see you two have already been drinking the water. Is it as good as everyone claims?"

"Here you go." Rachel thrust her cup into Will's hands. "You two enjoy. I need to finish getting the rest of the picnic things ready."

Before Mary could argue, Rachel was off, leaving her alone with Will.

"I'm sorry about that," she said.

"I'm not." Will bent down and filled his cup. "It gives us a few moments alone to finish our conversation from the wagon."

Precisely what she didn't want. Will had a point in his observation about Ben being enticed by her fortune. He was probably even right that he'd stop at nothing to marry her. If he was willing to rob good people of their money, ruining someone like her wouldn't be beneath him.

If she wasn't already ruined.

"You don't understand the position I'm in," she said by way of explanation.

"Then help me understand."

His face was filled with such kindness that she was reminded of Frank and how he cared for those around him. Though she knew the pastor cared for the worst of the population and encouraged them to minister to the fallen women in their community, she wasn't so sure that he'd be able to forgive her actions. If the pastor couldn't forgive her, how could a man as ordinary as Will?

"With my brother on his honeymoon, I'm responsible for caring for my siblings. They need me. I can't get caught up in some scheme to take down a man who's as wily as they come. If something happened to me…"

Mary shook her head, then drained her cup. "I know you think it's the way out, but I'll find another. Even if it means ruining my reputation so that no one else will marry me. The important thing is to make sure my brother and sisters are cared for."

Perhaps that was the price she'd pay for her vanity—remaining a spinster her whole life. None of the men had ever paid her a bit of attention, before Ben. That should have been her warning that Ben wasn't on the up-and-up. Amazing what a little flattery could get. And how disastrous the results could be.

Mary started back to where they'd spread the picnic blankets, cognizant of the voices headed their way. She'd go back to the group and follow her original plan of getting to know her contemporaries.

"Don't go," Will said, catching up to her. "The others are almost here. I know you wanted to spend time with them, and here I am, monopolizing you with things you don't want to talk about."

Pausing to look toward the group heading for the spring, then back at Will, Mary knew there was no easy escape. Could Will's olive branch be genuine?

A dark lock of hair had fallen over his forehead, giving him an innocence that made her want to trust him.

"Come on, Mary. We'll call it a truce for now, and I promise, I won't speak of Ben for the rest of the outing." He held his hand out to her as though he were making a solemn business deal. She'd learned that such promises mattered none to Ben, but with Will, well, he was different.

She accepted his handshake, noting the firm grip of his fingers around hers. He treated her as an equal, and in his eyes shone trust and respect. It hit her again how stupid she must've been to trust in Ben. He'd been a selfish fop, something evident in his too-eager smiles, lazy posture and glib tongue. Will, on the other hand, was everything a man should be.

When he released her hand, it tingled from the absence of his strong presence.

"It's settled, then," he said. "Friends."

The warmth of the word made her insides churn as though she'd drunk a whole gallon of the soda water.

"Hello, lovebirds!" Jasper's booming voice jolted her. "Sneaking away for a little private time?"

Mary's collar suddenly felt tight around her neck, preventing her from any speech. Her face warmed, and she tried desperately to think of ice and snow and cold, anything to keep herself from betraying the disquiet inside her.

"Not at all. We just wanted to get some of this famous natural soda water before my gluttonous friend took it all." Will gave a fake punch at Jasper, who dodged.

"I see we'll have to go to one of the boxing matches at the Tabor Opera House one of these days. Sparring with you has always been a challenge, but wait until you see what the real pros can do."

The other girls filed around them, giggling, she supposed, at the manly demonstration between Jasper and Will.

"Goodness," Polly said, linking her arm with Mary's. "You and Will seem awfully cozy for someone who denies that he's her beau."

Mary blew out a breath, wishing that she hadn't made such a muck of her life that she could confide in her friend. Of all people, Polly might be the one who would possibly understand what it was like to fall for a man who was nothing but trouble. Polly's former beau had turned out to be one of the thugs who'd kidnapped Mary's sister and sister-in-law.

"For someone sworn to never give her heart away again, you sure have a lot of interest in my love life."

They found their way to a grassy spot near the edge of the spring. "So, how about you let it drop, and let's enjoy the water."

Polly ignored the cup Mary held out to her. "I'm not very fond of the water. It has a strange aftertaste I've never gotten used to."

The intense look Polly gave her indicated that she had no intention of letting the subject drop. Would that it were as simple as telling Polly that Ben was a bad man and Will determined to bring him to justice, the questions would cease. Polly would understand. But Polly would ask questions and want Mary to talk to the authorities. Authorities who would more likely than not arrest her.

"It just seems strange," Polly said finally, "that you have so many men interested in you, yet you claim complete indifference. I may have sworn off having a beau for myself, but I admit to being completely fascinated by your having so many."

It was on the tip of Mary's tongue to offer one of her unwanted beaus to Polly, but she wouldn't wish Ben on anyone. Will, on the other hand…

She turned to glance at him just as he threw back his head and laughed. A warm laugh that invited everyone with him to join him, not the kind that was at anyone's expense. The automatic comparison to Ben started to pop into her mind, but she willed it away. There was no reason for her to compare him to Ben at all. Absolutely none. Except that traitorous voice deep inside her reminded her that she might be uncomfortable in offering him up to Polly for very different reasons.

Will had not enjoyed himself more thoroughly in a long time. He'd forgotten what great company Jasper had been. Work had kept him too busy to notice Jasper's absence when the Jackson family had moved to Leadville.

The girls giggled at something Jasper said, and Jasper gave him a look that seemed to say *What can you do?* Silly girls, that was what the whole lot of them were. While he'd been amused by Jasper's antics and stories, he was about sick to death of the constant prattling about dances and fashions and hats coming from the women. Mary was a much more sensible girl, and while most of their conversation had been about his case, he appreciated that she wasn't afraid to spar with him. She took him on directly and didn't hide behind giggles and frantic playing with her fan.

Just then, he caught a glimpse of her looking at him. Those bright eyes were hot enough to melt a man's soul.

"What's the story with you and Miss Stone?" Jasper gave him a playful nudge, then walked away from the crowd, indicating he should follow him.

Now, that was a complication he wasn't sure he could answer fully. "I wish I could tell you. She's…"

He'd liked to have said that she was just a case, but that would have made him a liar. Why couldn't Mary have a hooked nose, bad teeth and an equally sour disposition?

"Is it part of a case you're working on?"

At least in that he could be frank with his old friend. "Yes, but it's becoming more complicated than that."

Looming above them was a hillside littered with the remains of trees that had been taken for the mines and town. "Come on. You're going to love the view."

They climbed for a while, and Will appreciated the silence amid the scrape of their boots against rock, the occasional heavy breath blown out at the exertion and the twittering of the ladies below.

Will paused to rest. "You realize that we're putting on an exhibition for them, don't you?"

Jasper's only response was a wide grin. He climbed

a bit higher, until he'd reached the crest of the hill. It took several more minutes for Will to catch up before they were both seated at the top.

"Amazing, isn't it?" Jasper gestured at the expanse of the valley before them.

At this spot, they could see the sprawl of the town. Some said that nearly thirty thousand people lived there, rivaling the size of Denver. From this vantage point, Will would have to agree. Though the smokestacks from the smelters nearest them billowed thick, dark clouds, Leadville was indeed an impressive sight.

To the south lay some lakes, barely visible from this spot, but Will had seen it from other places along the way. The mountainside east of them was bare save for the skeletal images of mine shaft after mine shaft, the source of the town's riches.

The contrast of beauty with the booming town and mines reminded Will of Mary. How could someone as wonderful as she get mixed up with someone like Ben?

He looked to the base of the hill, chuckling at the irony of calling something at such a high elevation a hill, and noted that while many of the girls waited at the bottom, not one had ventured up. He scanned the crowd for Mary, but didn't see her among Jasper's admirers.

"Don't worry. They won't follow. They're too intent on keeping their dresses fresh." Jasper's trademark grin lit up his face. "A man's got to escape his admirers every once and a while."

Will couldn't help his belly laugh. Good old Jasper.

Jasper walked over to a rock and sat on it. "Those women make me crazy. Sure, it's nice to be so flattered, and my family has more dinner invitations than we know what to do with, but it'd be even nicer to have a real conversation with a person that didn't involve money."

The conspiratorial look Jasper gave him was all too familiar.

"And your plan is?"

A hummingbird whizzed by them. The sound of its wings against the air echoed the imaginary whirling of Jasper's mind.

"Tell me about the case. Let me help."

Will had been the one to teach Jasper how to fire a gun. To defend himself against others in a fight. Jasper had thrived on the energy of it all. Had he not been his father's only child and counted on to carry on the family business, Jasper would have followed him into law enforcement, Will was sure.

"Your father would kill me."

"He doesn't have to know."

The smooth tone to Jasper's voice made Will shake his head. "How many ladies have you kissed with that line?"

Jasper grinned. "Enough to know it works."

Unfortunately for Jasper, Will was no lady. "Father or no, I can't have you a part of this."

"Why?" Jasper jumped down from the rock. "Because you lost your badge? I don't have a badge, either. That's what makes this perfect."

The air whooshed from Will's lungs. "You knew? But you've been so…"

Jasper picked up a rock and chucked it down the hillside as if he was skipping it across a lake. "You had to have been set up. I figure, whatever you're up to here in Leadville, it's about clearing your name. And I aim to do what it takes to help you."

He hadn't expected such ease of acceptance, not when everyone in Century City treated him like a criminal himself. The breeze picked up, and Will turned to see dark clouds moving in behind them.

"They still want to charge me. Still might, if George Bishop has anything to say about it. The robbers got away with several thousand dollars. He's out for blood, and if mine's all he can get, then he'll take it."

His friend fell in beside him, his voice taking on a more serious tone. "All the more reason to help you. I know you, Will. There's not a dishonest bone in your body. You did all you could, and more."

He wished it were that simple. "You weren't there. The truth is, I made a mistake. I trusted the wrong person, and because of it, a bank was robbed, I was shot, and the culprits got away."

At least his words would serve to kill the hero worship that shone in Jasper's voice when he spoke of Will. He wasn't deserving of such high praise, so maybe now, all of Jasper's exaggerated stories would cease.

Only Jasper didn't see it that way. "You're not perfect. Doesn't mean that you deserve to be punished for what happened. In fact, it makes me even more determined to help clear your name."

The earnestness in Jasper's voice eased the ache in Will's gut that had plagued him for so long.

Since pursuing Mary had been nothing but a dead end, maybe Jasper would be able to give him a new perspective that would finally break the case open.

Will took a deep breath, then spilled the details of the case to his friend. From meeting Daisy and believing her to be in danger from Ben's abuse and trying to help her, to that fateful day when he acted on the information she fed him about wanting to meet him outside town to escape Ben—only to be shot by her as she fled the scene of the bank robbery.

He left no detail out, even the humiliating part about believing himself in love with the girl. The hardest part, though, was telling him about Mary and the letters he'd found in Ben's things. Maybe Jasper, whose heart wasn't getting entangled, would be able to sift through the information to be able to tell him whether Mary was lying or not.

As soon as he finished relaying his tale, the distant rumble of thunder and a few stray raindrops prevented him from gaining the benefit of Jasper's opinion.

"We need to make haste," Jasper said, scurrying toward the base of the hill. "The ladies aren't going to like getting caught in the storm."

As wordlessly as they had made their way to the top of the hill, they made it back down, and in half the time. Below, the women were carrying on and dithering about the rain.

Except Mary.

Even before his feet touched the bottom of the mountainside, he could see her standing about, giving directions to the others for gathering their belongings and loading the wagons. By the time Will and Jasper arrived back at the wagons, almost everything was loaded and ready to go, save for a crate that Mary and a couple of the other girls were struggling with.

"Let me help," he said, grabbing one of the ends of the crate. Together, they lifted the heavy wood into the wagon.

The rest of the party filed into their respective wagons, just as the sky opened up completely, sending a deluge of water over them all. Will glanced at Mary, her chest heaving from the exertion, water pouring down her ruined bonnet and dress.

Was it wrong of him to think her the absolute most beautiful creature he'd ever laid eyes upon?

As he helped her into the wagon, Jasper passed by and tossed a blanket at them.

"You're a goner," he whispered.

If it weren't for the rain and the now-shivering woman beside him, Will would have thrown the blanket right back at his friend. So much for getting sage advice.

Chapter Seven

The finale of the picnic was, without question, an unmitigated disaster. Mary huddled in the blanket Will had wrapped around her as the wagon lumbered back toward town. Though the trip to the spring had taken less than an hour, as the rain poured down, they made significantly slower progress toward home.

Despite the men working to get canvas to cover the wagon, rain poured in from all sides. They'd likely not be dry again until they reached home.

Polly squeezed in next to her, and Mary released a corner of her blanket to let her friend in.

"Some outing, huh?" Polly snuggled in with Mary. "At least you got to know some of the others better."

"Yes. Rachel and Beth are as nice as you said they were, and it was good to get to know everyone else. Sarah Crowley has one of those lace-making machines, and she promised to teach me how to use it. Nugget's dresses could use some lace at the edges."

It seemed odd to be talking so casually of such things while some of the other ladies wailed around them.

Emma Jane Logan, one of the girls she hadn't gotten to know well, was sobbing over the condition of her hat.

Such a silly thing to be trifling over when there was nothing to be done about it.

Polly sighed. "Back to responsibilities, are we? Well, have at it, then. I suppose I should accept it, since you at least looked like you were enjoying yourself today."

"Oh, I did enjoy myself." Mary gave her friend a smile. "I actually liked the water, and I'm so glad to have made the acquaintance of so many nice girls."

Polly appeared to be relieved by the statement. A gust of wind broke loose a corner of the canvas, sending a flood of water at them.

"Ack! Are we ever going to be out of this misery?" Polly jumped up and vainly tried brushing the water off her. "I don't think a one of us will be able to salvage anything we've got on."

As they turned a corner in the road, the horses stopped suddenly. Everyone murmured around them, wondering what was going on. Will rejoined them.

"The road's washed out. Flash flood. We're going to have to wait out the storm."

The cries of the girls around them were so loud, Mary thought she might have to cover her ears. Will looked at her. "No tears for you?"

"What good will that do, other than make me wetter than I already am? Since we can't go forward, what other options are there?"

Rivulets of rain ran down Will's face. "I think we passed a turnoff for a ranch a ways back. I'll talk to Jasper and see if we can unhitch one of the horses so I can ride for help."

She shouldn't have been surprised by Will's gallant

offer. It seemed such a sharp contrast to the man who'd accosted her in the street and kept pressuring her to reveal things about Ben that she'd prefer to be left alone.

As Will plucked his way back to the front of the wagon, she couldn't help but notice his confident, manly form. Even in the midst of the storm, he'd kept his wits about him. Could she have been wrong about him?

She'd been so intent on fighting this battle alone, but Will's words about her reputation washed over her, harder than the deluge from the clouds. Was she a fool to think that she could do this on her own?

Watching closely as Will consulted with the other men, she noticed how they all seemed to respect him, nodding at his words. Could he possibly be trustworthy in her situation? Would he believe in Mary's innocence? Questions best left alone for now. Emma Jane's sobs were beginning to subside, and instead, she made loud hiccuping noises, as if the rain had won the competition with her tears. For the first time, Mary noticed that the woman's fine gown, which Emma Jane had been overly proud of, was soaked nearly through, and Emma Jane was shivering.

"I'm going to offer Emma Jane the blanket," Mary told Polly.

Polly's brow crinkled. "Why? She's such a sourpuss. Why should we make ourselves cold for her sake?"

"Because it's the right thing to do."

Mary got up and carried the blanket to Emma Jane. "Here. Take this and come sit with us. It's drier on our side of the wagon, and the blanket hasn't gotten too wet."

Emma Jane's head remained down, and she wouldn't look at Mary. "No, thank you. I'll be fine."

The other girl's hair lay in flat clumps; the curls which she'd probably so painstakingly made were now a mess of knots. Beside her lay a parasol, practically shredded from the weight of the rain. No, she hadn't chosen her accessories for the weather, but Mary supposed none of them had given thought to the fact that in September, afternoons typically had showers. Monsoons, on the other hand, were a rarity.

"Let me at least help you with your hair," Mary said. "I could quickly get it out of your face, and it will be so much more comfortable."

Emma Jane jerked away. "No! I said I would be fine. Now go with all of your friends and leave me in peace."

She ought to do exactly what Emma Jane asked. After all, she'd done her Christian duty by reaching out to the other girl and attempting to share her blanket. Emma Jane had said no, and that should be that.

But something in the wounded tone of the other girl's voice made her feel sorry for her.

"If you change your mind, there's plenty of room with Polly and me. We'd be delighted to have you join us. You could tell us more about your hat, and we could put our heads together to figure out how to fix it when the rain stops."

Emma Jane's head snapped up, revealing a face that was more than just tear-stained. Clearly, Emma Jane had been wearing some form of paint, and the water had washed it partially away, revealing deep pits and a smattering of color in all the wrong places.

"There's no fixing it. My hat is ruined. And there's nothing you or anyone else can do about it."

"Maybe not, but we won't know until things dry out." Mary pulled out a handkerchief. "At least take my handkerchief and you can use it to wipe your face. You'll feel better if your face is clean."

The gasp that come out of Emma Jane made Mary feel even worse. "Don't look at me!"

She huddled down and once again hid her face. So that was it. Emma Jane was ashamed of how her face looked in the rain. Until now, Mary hadn't realized that the other girl wore so much paint.

Another gust of wind blew through the wagon, and Mary shivered. She couldn't help but notice that Emma Jane's shivers had grown worse. Mary knelt beside her and put the blanket around the other girl's shoulders. If they didn't get out of the rain and cold soon, they were all at risk of taking ill. Pneumonia was a particularly bad threat here, and many died from the dreaded illness.

"You'll catch your death for all your pride," Mary told her. "Everyone looks terrible right now, so who are you to think that you're any more hideous than the rest of us?"

Fortunately, Emma Jane wasn't a stupid woman, and she took hold of the end of the blanket, wrapping it around her. "Everyone." Emma Jane sniffed. "They've been saying it all day. You can't pretend you haven't noticed the way everyone has been mocking me."

The pain in the other girl's voice made Mary's stomach turn. She had noticed the other girls whispering and giggling about Emma Jane. Mary had thought that not participating in the conversation was enough, but as tears streamed down Emma Jane's face, she wished she'd done more to reach out to the other girl.

"I'm sorry," Mary said, tucking a flap of the blanket that had gotten loose around Emma Jane.

Emma Jane looked up with watery eyes. "It's not

your fault. They're right. I am ridiculous. I should have never come today or agreed to my mother's silly plan."

Mary thought back to all the times in Ohio when the girls mocked her for her outmoded dress, or how her family faced ridicule for their poverty. It was one of the reasons she'd fallen so easily under Ben's spell. After being tormented for so many external trivialities, she couldn't believe she could find someone who'd seen past it all.

She'd been wrong.

But that didn't mean that her newfound wealth had to turn Mary into that same kind of girl. She might have been wrong to trust in Ben, but looking past the surface of a person was always the right thing to do.

Mary gave Emma Jane an encouraging smile. "Your dress might not be the latest fashion, but you are far from ridiculous. The other girls have no right to be unkind to you. I'm glad you came on the picnic, because I'm very pleased to make your acquaintance."

Tears rolled down Emma Jane's cheeks. "Don't be. I'm a nobody, which will be all too clear once news of my family's downfall becomes public. Mother thought coming to the picnic would change things, but I fear it's only made everything worse."

"How so? What could possibly be so important about a picnic to change your life?"

Emma Jane finally looked up. "You wouldn't understand."

"You keep saying that, but how do you know I wouldn't understand when you haven't given me the opportunity to?" The words that were supposed to comfort Emma Jane grated on Mary's conscience. How many times had she used that as a justification in her situation with Ben?

Surely Mary's situation was different.

"You probably already know that my father has lost everything to the gambling hall." Her words were so strained with the humiliation Mary had been used to with her own father.

"I'm so sorry," Mary said quietly. "I do understand. Before my father made his strike, he had gambled away our family's money, as well. We were living on the charity of an aunt whose cruelty was almost too much to bear. But I don't understand what that has to do with this picnic."

Mary handed the sniffling girl a handkerchief. "Here. I must insist this time."

Emma Jane's nose had puffed up, and it had to be uncomfortable. She clearly knew Mary's intent and took it, blowing with a force that startled the girls around them. Fortunately, they were all too focused on their own misery to pay more mind.

"My mother is going to be so upset with me. Not only did I fail in getting Jasper to marry me, but now I've ruined her hat and dress. She'll never forgive me."

Another loud wail erupted from the girl, nearly piercing Mary's ears. Did Emma Jane really think that her only hope of salvation came from marrying a man who clearly did not know she existed? How could she have assumed that after all this time of not being noticed, that a hat, a dress and some paint would do the trick?

"I'll help you," Mary said, putting her arm around the girl. "I know Pastor Lassiter will help your family. As a member of our church, you should know how willing he is to help."

Emma Jane recoiled. "My father refuses to take charity. Mother says that the only solution is to marry well. You have no idea what I've had to endure. I'd hoped—" Another stream of tears interrupted more of Emma Jane's arguments.

So many thoughts ran through Mary's head in that moment, but not one of them came together coherently enough for her to speak. Though she understood the pressure Emma Jane faced to care for her family, how could she think that making a spectacle of herself would achieve that end?

Then again, who was Mary to judge? She'd made her own attempted matrimonial mistakes. In that, Emma Jane was the better person. Willing to risk it all, even marrying a man she didn't...

"Do you even like Jasper?" The question burst out of Mary's mouth before she could control it.

"Everyone likes Jasper," Emma Jane said a little too quickly. As if she'd been feeding herself the same story over and over just to convince herself of what she was doing.

Mary took a deep breath and looked at the other girl. "I don't care what everyone says. How do you feel about him? Does your pulse race when you see him? Do you light up at the thought of being near him?"

True, they were all the sensations she'd felt with Ben, but Mary wasn't completely ignorant in the ways of men and women. Especially because those were the things she felt when...

No. Mary closed her eyes for a moment to remind herself of what this was about. She was not going to consider her feelings for Will.

Emma Jane sighed. "Honestly, I'm just nervous.

Afraid of doing or saying the wrong thing and he will end up not liking me."

Clearly not true love. Despite everything Mary had gone through, she had to believe that it still existed and that nothing less was proper inducement for marriage. The problem, though, lay in the difficulty of deciphering the difference between the real and the fake. Ben had taught her all about counterfeit emotions.

But real love? She hadn't seen it with her parents, nor with Aunt Ina. She knew of it through Christ, and she'd recently witnessed the deep abiding love between her brother Joseph and his new bride, Annabelle. Surely others, like Emma Jane, could experience it for themselves.

Before she could share any of these thoughts with the other girl, some horses rode up. Even through the blowing rain, Mary recognized Will.

"Will's back." Mary stood, letting the rest of the blanket fall around Emma Jane. "Hopefully, he has news of a rescue."

"Is Jasper with him?" Emma Jane's voice was strained, probably half hopeful, half nervous.

Though Mary couldn't tell, it didn't hurt to appease the other girl's fears. "I'm not sure. But let's get you cleaned up so that when he does see you, he'll see as pleasing of a creature as we can provide."

"It's no use. I'm hideous." Emma Jane started sobbing again, and Mary almost regretted her words. But the truth was, without all the paint, Emma Jane was prettier.

Mary pulled out another handkerchief, glad for Maddie's warning that she should take some extra. "You are not hideous. I've never liked paint on anyone, and if we clean off your face, and I put a braid in your hair, you'll be as pretty as anyone in this rain. If Jasper has any sense in him at all, he'll admire you for doing what you can in this horrible weather."

Emma Jane continued sniffling, more tears running down her face.

"And you absolutely must stop your crying. It's doing far worse for your complexion than all the rain and paint combined. Turn, and let me fix your hair."

That did the trick. Emma Jane took the handkerchief and began using it to wipe her face. The handkerchief came back filthy, but at least it revealed a clean girl. Surely that added to her beauty more than anything else.

With nimble fingers that had gotten far too much practice braiding several little girls' hair before church, Mary unpinned Emma Jane's hair and, though tangled, was able to put it into some semblance of a neat braid. She'd have to get the knots out later, but at least it looked better than the mass of washed-out curls and snarls.

Though Mary wanted to go see what news Will brought, her work with Emma Jane kept the other girl calm. Polly caught her eye and smiled. They'd know soon enough what was going on. Until then, Mary could bring comfort to a girl who was certain her life was over.

Will dismounted, grateful that the nearby ranch had provided them with fresh horses. They'd also provided another wagon, already covered, and would keep everyone dry for the return to the ranch. With the road washed out, continuing home was out of the question. But at least they'd have a warm place to spend the night.

He joined Jasper and listened as Jasper explained

what would be happening. Another rider had been sent into town with word of their whereabouts, and they'd spend the night at the ranch. In the morning, after things had dried, there was a back road they could take back to town.

As Jasper spoke, Mary and another girl joined them. He was glad to see that Mary looked to be in good spirits, but then he hadn't expected anything less of her. Such a cool head in the midst of a crisis. How on earth had she found herself mixed up with Ben?

He watched Mary interact with the girl, recognizing her as one of the ones who'd gone into hysterics at being caught in the storm. Now, as she stood near Jasper, taking in what was happening, a serene smile replaced the lines of worry. He saw how Mary patted her hand. Clearly, the change in the girl's demeanor came from Mary's influence. Mary could be such an asset to him in bringing Ben to justice. If only he could convince her.

Shortly after Jasper explained the situation, the ranch wagon arrived. From the steam rising from the horses' bodies and nostrils, they'd been ridden hard to get here as quickly as possible.

Will helped load the ladies onto the new wagon, pausing slightly at Mary. "Save me a seat next to you. I want to know how things went."

The girl next to her giggled, and Will wished for a moment he hadn't been so bold. Mary was so concerned about people thinking they were a couple, and it seemed that every move he made, even those he intended as mere kindness, were continually misinterpreted.

Still, her warm smile almost made him change that wish.

"Certainly," she said. "Have you met my new friend Emma Jane?"

He glanced briefly at Emma Jane. "It's a pleasure."

"Is everyone ready?" Jasper came up behind him, and Will turned his attention to the other man.

"I think so. I'm getting Mary and her friend…Emma Jane? Settled."

Movement between the two girls momentarily distracted him. "Sorry, it is Emma Jane, right?"

Jasper made a noise, then turned away. From the pained expression on the girls' faces, Emma Jane must have been one of Jasper's many admirers.

"We need to get moving," he said instead. And to his relief was rewarded with a small smile from Mary.

Her smiles shouldn't matter as much. And he shouldn't notice things such as her kindness to others like Emma Jane. Daisy had never struck him as particularly kind. One more thing to remind him that what he'd felt for Daisy wasn't real, wasn't lasting. The trouble with his growing admiration of Mary was how much he wanted to like her. How much he wanted to help her. Whatever her relationship with Ben Perry had been, surely he could save her from—

What was he thinking?

That was exactly the kind of disastrous thinking that had gotten him shot in the first place.

"Thank you," Mary said quietly, making his insides quiver.

If she could be avoided, he would run as far away as possible. Mary was not the kind of distraction he needed. And yet, she might possibly have the information he needed to finally apprehend Ben Perry.

Chapter Eight

The smell of hay and dust hung thickly in the air, tickling Mary's nostrils.

The rancher who came to their aid had a small spread, with a small cabin, not big enough for all of them. So they were dispatched to the barn. When it came time to retire, the men would be able to bunk with the rancher's hired hands, and the women would have the barn to themselves. From what Will had said, the women were getting a much more comfortable place to stay than the men. Though she heard some of the girls complaining, it wasn't nearly as bad as what she'd lived through in the past. And after being in the rain for so long, it felt so good to finally be dry that she didn't care.

The rain had finally slowed to a gentle drizzle, and most of their party was huddled around a small fire the men had built to take the chill off.

"Why aren't you with the others?" Will asked, appearing beside her.

She glanced at him, noting how his hair had started to curl slightly at the base of his neck as it dried. It seemed as though he grew more handsome every time she saw him. Certainly he'd grown in her regard with the evenhanded way he'd handled their detour.

And the way he looked at her… Warmth shone in his eyes, as if he actually cared. For a brief moment, it reminded her of the way her brother Joseph looked at her, only it was somehow…warmer.

"I'm not cold." Mary watched as one of the girls fumbled with the blanket she'd been given. There hadn't been enough for everyone, but Mary was grateful for even this small shelter.

Polly and Rachel glanced her way, then giggled before turning away. Mary tried not to groan, but enough creaked out that Will caught it.

"I'm sorry. I keep trying to be nice to you, but again, it seems like I've stirred up more talk."

How had she not noticed that he had a decent side to him? If not for his connection to Ben, she could almost imagine herself feeling something for him. They might even be able to be friends.

Will left her side and went to join the others. She watched as he shook his head at whatever Polly said to him. Polly glanced her way again. Mary probably ought to rejoin her friend, but she couldn't bear the thought of having to endure any more teasing about Will. She offered a smile, then looked around at the others. Emma Jane stood alone at the edge of the fire.

Instead of joining Polly and the others, Mary walked over to Emma Jane. "Are you getting dry?"

"Enough." Emma Jane shrugged and looked in the direction of Jasper. "He'll never marry me, will he?"

Given his earlier reaction to Emma Jane, probably not. "Maybe if you got to know him and he got to know you—as people, not as a woman hunting a husband…"

Mary didn't want to elaborate, lest she give the poor girl false hope.

"I don't have the luxury of getting to know him. Everyone likes Jasper, so I'm sure I will, too." A dark look crossed Emma Jane's face. "Not that it matters. He hates me."

The group by the fire laughed, a joyful sound that drew Mary's attention, just in time to see Jasper tug on someone's deflated curl.

"Why can't I be pretty like Flora?" The words came out like a half sob.

Mary hadn't yet gotten to know Flora, so she couldn't speak to the other girl's character. "Surely there should be more to a person than their looks. Or, in Jasper's case, their money. Don't you want a husband who has qualities you respect and admire? Someone who loves you and you love back?"

Oh, what a mistake she would have made in marrying Ben. Yes, he was handsome and charming, but she couldn't pinpoint a time when he'd done something she respected and admired. As for love, perhaps she'd been too hasty in claiming such affection for the man.

"That's easy for you to say," Emma Jane grumbled. "I heard the other girls talking about how you have a fiancé already, and here you are making eyes at Will. You have options. With your brother's wealth, you don't need to marry for money."

How many times would she have to deny her relationship with Ben before people accepted it? And if they did, would he carry out his threat of blaming her for the theft of her aunt's brooch?

Oh, to be able to shout out the truth so everyone here would leave her alone. She was not going to marry

Ben. She was not involved with Will. Honestly! Though she'd always feared dying a spinster, it would almost be worth it if it came with the blessed silence from gossip.

"Things aren't always what they seem," Mary finally told her. "I would gladly trade places with you, only I would never wish my circumstances on anyone. Be grateful for Jasper's lack of interest and your poverty."

The irony of her situation wasn't lost on Mary. If she'd remained poor, Ben wouldn't be pursuing her so strongly.

"You don't understand what it's like to have nothing." Emma Jane's face contorted in pain. "My family—"

"I do understand. We've only been wealthy for a few months. Before that, we lived with an aunt who forced us to work on her farm in place of hired hands. We were barely fed, barely clothed, and in addition to doing chores for our aunt, I cleaned houses and did laundry for many of the ladies in our town. I worked from sunup to sundown, and for several hours after everyone went to bed for good measure. If my aunt was displeased in any way, she'd beat either me or my siblings."

Emma Jane looked at her solemnly. "I'm sorry, I didn't know."

"Before my brother discovered the mine, no one was interested in me. Do you think Ben likes me for my charming personality or my desire to help my brother raise my siblings? No. He wants my money."

Emma Jane's flinch told Mary she was finally on the right track. "Don't do this to Jasper. He deserves a woman who loves him and cares for him. Just as you deserve the same. Don't do it to yourself."

"It doesn't matter. Jasper won't have me anyway."

The sadness in Emma Jane's voice told Mary that her words wouldn't have convinced the girl otherwise.

"Someone will." She should add in one of Frank's platitudes about the Lord providing for their needs, but it wasn't advice Mary would have accepted while in Aunt Ina's home. Moreover, Mary wasn't even sure it was true in her current circumstance.

Instead, she offered Emma Jane a smile. "I know your father won't accept charity. But my brother needs people to help with the mine. He's on his honeymoon right now, but Collin MacDonald is running things in the meantime. I'll put in a good word for your father if he'd like a job."

At least it was something practical she could do for Emma Jane's family. And maybe give Emma Jane the hope of a future outside of marrying a man who despised her.

"Collin won't hire him. My father once fired him for being too drunk." Emma Jane sniffled as though she was about to start sobbing again. "You see? My life is hopeless."

"Don't you dare start crying again." Mary gave her the same stern look she gave the children. "I heard my brother and Collin talking about your father once. Collin said that your father is one of the most brilliant men at following a vein. So don't lose hope. There is always hope."

Emma Jane's eyes watered. "I don't know...."

"Let's at least try. If it doesn't work, we'll find another solution for your family. I refuse to give up, and neither should you."

Will approached them. "Mrs. Haggerty brought us

some food. It's not much, but along with the leftovers from the picnic, it'll tide us over until morning."

"I am hungry." Emma Jane said. "I haven't been able to eat all day, on account of being so nervous."

Will's smile made it almost impossible for Mary to breathe. "Then go eat. If it's not enough, let me know. We're each to have one piece of chicken, and I'm happy to give you mine."

Didn't Will know that men needed more food than women? Mary stared at him, and he winked. "I'll be fine. She looks like she'd have blown away in that storm had it not been for all the people in the wagon."

Mary turned to reassure Emma Jane, but Emma Jane had already gone. Once again leaving her alone with Will. It wasn't so much that she worried about what people would say anymore. From the conversation she'd had with Emma Jane, they'd already said plenty.

The worry now was that the more she saw this kind side to Will Lawson, the more she wondered how she was ever going to resist him.

Will hated interrupting the girls, particularly as he listened to Mary encourage Emma Jane. It again made him wonder how Mary could have played any part in Ben's actions. Maybe he could contact the sheriff in their old town to see what the connection was. Had Mary simply turned over a new leaf since coming here?

No. As he'd heard Mary tell Emma Jane not to lose hope, he couldn't believe that. Such conviction was borne of many years of believing in God's provision. She might not have mentioned Him, but Will could tell by the way she said it, she believed. If only Will could believe for himself in God's ability. He'd like to believe

God was there, but when He allowed such evil as Ben Perry to continue to walk the earth, Will had to wonder if God was active or merely present.

In his line of work, as much as Will hated to admit it, he'd arrested many a churchgoing man. Mary's faith meant nothing in relation to her culpability for crime. Still, Mary didn't seem the type. If only she'd talk to him.

But he'd promised to leave it alone—for now.

They watched as Emma Jane joined the others, and when the other girl was out of earshot, Mary turned to him. "You can have some of my chicken if you like. I hate the thought of you going without."

How could a woman like Mary have associated with Ben Perry? It didn't add up, and yet he knew he couldn't push her for the answers he needed.

"I'll be fine. When we came for help, Mrs. Haggerty wouldn't let us leave without having a bowl of stew. She's a good woman. Reminds me a lot of you."

He shouldn't have offered such a bold compliment, nor should he have enjoyed her blush so much.

"You shouldn't say things like that. You don't even know me."

"Whose fault is that? Mary, I want to know you. You have been so kind to Emma Jane, a girl everyone else shuns, and when we were in crisis, you stepped up and did what you needed to do. So, give me a chance."

For a moment, Mary almost looked as if she wanted to say something different. She shook her head slowly. "I want to, but I can't. There are so many things you don't know about me, things that would ruin everything."

She turned to go toward the food line, but Will stopped

her. "Weren't you just telling Emma Jane to have a little faith? Where's yours?"

Mary's jaw tensed. "That's different. Emma Jane hasn't… That is, she didn't…" Then Mary sighed. "Well, it's just different, that's all."

Will's heart sunk at her words, or lack thereof. Her guilty conscience set off all kinds of alarm bells in his head, his heart and, more importantly, in that tender place in his gut.

Mary knew something.

As much as his heart didn't want to accept it, he even had to wonder if maybe she had been involved. He'd been loath to do it, but it was time to stop thinking only like a man and remember that he was a lawman. He may not have his badge, but he'd taken an oath, and he was going to see to his duty of keeping the world safe. Especially from men like Ben.

When they got back to town, he'd send a telegram to the sheriff in their old town to see what he could find out.

In the meantime, if he could only convince Mary to tell the truth, surely a judge would give her a lighter sentence if she'd be willing to help put Ben behind bars.

He looked at Mary, trying to be as comforting as possible. "Whatever it is, it can't be that bad. I'll do whatever I can to help."

"I'm sorry." Mary truly looked regretful. "I can't. Perhaps when Joseph and Annabelle are back from their honeymoon…"

He should have been pleased at the victory, only he didn't have the luxury of time. "And in the meantime, who knows what Ben will do. Mary, this is more serious than your pride or your reputation."

But his words seemed to have no impact on Mary. She gave him a wan smile before brushing off her skirts. "I suppose I should get my share of the meal. You may not be hungry, but I'm starving."

Will would have liked to have stopped her, but when he turned in the direction of the others, he saw Polly's watchful eye on them. She seemed determined to pair him with Mary. And every time someone's tongue got flapping about him being Mary's beau, Mary shut herself off to him even more.

He clenched and unclenched his fists. There had to be a way to get more information about Ben from her. Maybe he shouldn't be so reliant on information from an attractive woman. How could he trust in Mary after being burned by Daisy?

Something was different about Mary, a small voice told him. But he brushed it aside. He had to remain unattached. Let the whole story come out, and then decide.

Jasper stepped in next to him. "You sure you're not interested in Miss Mary Stone? She's a looker, that's for sure."

Will shook his head. "Maybe if you looked past outward appearances, you might find a woman worth pursuing. I've already learned my lesson in that regard."

He wanted to add that there was so much more to Mary than her looks. But that would only serve to fuel the fire. She'd joined the others and was laughing and eating as though she didn't have a care in the world. He didn't miss the fact that she'd joined Emma Jane and had brought out more smiles from the seemingly troubled girl.

Will had never known such kindness in Daisy.

Jasper clapped him on the shoulder. "I've given up

on that line of thinking. The women around here are only interested in my money, and if that weren't inducement enough, they twitter about my fine looks. I suppose at some point, my father is going to insist I marry one of those silly misses, and I'll abide by his decision."

His old friend's words were tinged with enough bitterness that Will wondered what had happened to him. But it wasn't his place to ask. At least not if he wanted to leave the Daisy stone unturned. The only trouble was, another Stone was rearing its head in Will's life, and he wasn't sure he'd escape that one so easily.

If only she weren't completely entwined with a case that had Will's entire life held hostage.

Jasper cleared his throat. "I think I'm going to check out our accommodations for the night. Want to join me?"

Will looked in the direction of the women, who'd clearly finished eating. Now that they were reasonably dried out and their bellies full, they'd returned to casting longing glares at Jasper. Since the roof was still pinging with raindrops, outside was the only place Jasper would find some peace.

Foolish as it was, Will couldn't help but glance in the direction of Mary. She and Emma Jane were engaged in a seemingly intense discussion. Whatever Mary was trying to say, Emma Jane was having nothing to do with it. Emma Jane turned and stomped off to a set of hay bales lying to the side. He returned his gaze to Mary.

Though he shouldn't care so much about her, the disappointment streaking her face drew him.

Surely someone as compassionate as Mary, who cared about the feelings of a prickly girl she barely knew, could hardly have willingly gone in league with Ben Perry.

Mad Mel's words returned to Will. She'd claimed there was no way Daisy had willingly come under the influence of Ben. Though Will had never seen any evidence of coercion, could he have been pulling her strings behind the scenes?

Again, he thought of Mary, and her desperate words about Ben. She'd claimed to want nothing to do with the man, but when Ben had announced their engagement at the church supper, she'd worn a smile.

A tight and unenthusiastic smile. Unlike the genuine expressions he'd seen from her today.

Something was not right with the situation.

But what did Ben have on her?

And could Will overcome whatever it was enough to give him the information he needed?

Chapter Nine

Most of the girls were bedding down for the night when Mary realized she hadn't seen Emma Jane for a while. Polly patted a pile of hay near her.

"I saved you a spot. Surely you're not going to abandon Rachel and me for Emma Jane? I mean, it's wonderful that you're being so nice to her and all, but your real friends still want the details on your many beaus."

Mary groaned. There was no way she was going to escape the questions. But maybe something in her story would help Emma Jane understand that chasing after Jasper Jackson wouldn't solve any of her problems.

And, maybe if she shared some of the details, avoiding the ones implicating her in Ben's crimes, the other girls would finally understand that she was absolutely not interested in either Ben or Will.

Mary looked around one more time for Emma Jane. "Perhaps if we all share our stories of love gone wrong, it'll be an encouragement not to chase after the wrong sort of man."

"Not that again," Polly huffed. "I've already done

told you that all men are all alike. You just have to find the one that's most tolerable and learn to look the other way when they get into their scrapes. It's what my ma did, and what yours did, as well."

If Mary weren't still looking for Emma Jane, she would have glared at her friend. Just because it was what her ma did didn't make it right. And it certainly wasn't how Mary was going to live her life. If she couldn't have an honorable man, then she wanted no man at all.

"Have you seen Emma Jane?" Mary finally stood on one of the hay bales to see if she could catch a glimpse of the other girl.

"She's probably out using the necessary. I saw her go out a while ago."

Mary had seen her leave as well, but she'd assumed the other girl had returned. "That was hours ago. She hasn't come back in?"

Polly patted the straw next to her. "How would I know? I'm here to take a break from always watching everyone else and making sure they're out of trouble. You should be, too. Come tomorrow, we'll be back at the Lassiters' making sure all the little ones stay out of trouble. Knowing Maddie's frustration with Daniel's escapades, I'm certain that she'll have taken to her room by then."

Polly was probably right. Mary sighed. Part of her younger brother Daniel's problem, she was sure, was all her fault. Why hadn't she brought her courtship with Ben out into the open so that Daniel could have a male's influence with their pa and Joseph gone?

Because Ben had insisted, that was why.

One more thing that had, in hindsight, rankled about their relationship. There had been so many signs that everything wasn't on the up-and-up. But she'd ignored them.

Just as well that she hadn't allowed Ben to influence her younger brother. The poor child would have been corrupted—maybe on his way to living a life of crime.

Something she had to be mindful of as Will approached. He'd been so kind, so compassionate and, were she to be honest, so many of the good things that had been lacking in Ben.

But even Will's kindness would not extend to accepting the truth about her role in Ben's misdeeds.

"Are you ladies settled for the night? It's time for the men to head to where we'll be sleeping, so I want to be sure you have everything you need first." Though he spoke in the plural, Will's eyes remained focused on her.

Mary shook her head. "I'd like to be, but I haven't seen Emma Jane anywhere. I'm sure I won't sleep a wink until I know she's got a comfortable place to sleep."

"I'll take a look," he said, already glancing around the barn. "I'll even get Jasper to help. I'm sure that'll bring a smile to her face."

Mary wished he wouldn't tease about Emma Jane's fixation on Jasper. But if she took him to task, it would only fuel Polly's belief that there was something between Mary and Will. And from the weight of Polly's eyes on her, the other girl's mind was already turning.

Plus, she was getting mighty tired of everyone speculating on other people's relationships. Emma Jane was pursuing Jasper. Half of the ladies in the barn were. It didn't make it right to make remarks. Just as it wasn't right for everyone to be remarking on her and Ben—or her and Will, for that matter.

But as Mary glanced at the expectant gazes of Polly and Rachel, she knew it wouldn't be that easy.

As much as she'd like to go with Will to search for the other girl, it would only serve to create further talk Mary was loath to have to explain away.

"Thank you, Will. I'm sure Emma Jane will appreciate the effort on her behalf."

Then, without looking at him, a fact of which Mary was quite proud, she sat on the spot Polly had indicated.

"All right, girls, what would you like to know?"

Polly and Rachel giggled and glanced in the direction of Will's retreating back. Mary forced herself to not groan. She'd almost rather face Will's questioning than talk to these two.

"You're truly not engaged to that other fellow?" Rachel looked intently at Mary, as if she could somehow whittle out a truth Mary had not yet revealed.

"Absolutely not. We broke things off in Ohio, then he left town in search of his fortune. Him showing up here in Leadville is the first I've spoken to him since. I'm sure he's only here because of the family's silver mine."

At least that was a truth she could reveal. As for his character and all the reasons why she could never marry a scoundrel like Ben, well, those were things she had to keep private.

Rachel gasped. "He's a fortune hunter, then?"

Finally Polly seemed to get the idea as she nodded sagely. "Of course. I should have known. Now that you're wealthy, he sees himself a bride who can give him a life in style."

Her friend sobered, and a sad look crossed her face. "I suppose…" Then she looked away.

Was Polly thinking of the man who'd used her so harshly?

Mary touched her friend's arm. "I'm sorry if I made you think of the past. But surely you can see why marrying a man like Ben would be intolerable."

"What other option is there?" Polly said, her voice thick and murky. "We all say we dream of honorable men, but it doesn't seem they exist."

"I shan't marry." Mary straightened and looked at both girls with utter seriousness. "If a man isn't honorable, then I want no part of being his wife."

She looked down at the straw around her. Her brother was an honorable man. So, too, was Frank. But, out of every man in her acquaintance, how could she only know of two?

"Easy for you to say," Polly grumbled. "Rachel and I don't have the benefit of owning our own stock in a mine. At some point, we'll need to find a man to support us. I've been a burden on my family for too long."

Mary understood. She'd thought that very thing until she'd met Ben. Of course, Mary had always tempered it with the thought that her family needed her to take care of them. Still did.

Polly, at least, had both parents living.

"And we're not getting any younger," Rachel added. "Every week, some new, pretty young thing moves into town and takes up one of the few remaining decent men in town."

Polly nodded sagely. "You'd do well to snatch Will up."

Mary stared at her. "Did you not forget that we saw him on State Street only this morning?"

"Men have needs." Polly's well-used answer tore at Mary's heart. Such men were not husband material.

"Then you can have him. I won't tolerate a husband who visits such places."

But something twisted in Mary's stomach as she thought of Polly and Will together.

"Will's not for me," Polly said. "He doesn't look at me the way he looks at you."

Rachel sighed, as if she, too, had noticed the way Will looked at her and found it hopelessly romantic.

Only there was nothing romantic about the way Will looked at her. He wasn't after her for romance. No, he wanted to know about Ben. His eyes fixed on her not because he harbored desire for her, but because he was hoping to ferret out her secrets.

"Well, I don't want him," Mary stated firmly. "The other girls can help themselves. Will Lawson isn't the man for me."

Will hesitated rejoining the girls as he overheard their discussion of his relationship with Mary. He shouldn't be surprised, except that as Mary hotly denied anything between them, the back of his neck burned in a most painfully peculiar way.

He was not going to get attached to Miss Mary Stone. It should have been a relief to know that she had no attachment for him. Besides, he had bigger problems. His hunt for Jasper had turned up neither Jasper nor Emma Jane.

"Will!" Polly greeted him with an overeager smile. Given the bit of conversation he'd just overheard, he could only imagine what Polly thought of him. Something he should correct with the girls, but how could he let them know the truth of his visit to The Pink Petticoat without telling the whole story? For now, it was best to let them think what they wanted to think. After all, it wasn't as though he cared what Mary thought of him.

He gave Polly a slight nod and turned to Mary. "Not only is Emma Jane missing, but I can't find Jasper."

Mary's brow crinkled, but before she could answer, one of the girls who'd been hovering gasped. "That horrid little tart!"

Mary turned toward the girl. "You don't even know what happened to Emma Jane. She could be out there injured, or worse, and you're afraid that she's gone and stolen Jasper out from under you."

"He doesn't even like her," another girl chimed. "He told me that he thought I was the fairest flower of them all." She preened slightly. "I can't help but be named Flora, you know."

The first girl gasped. "That's what he told me! You obviously were spying on us when he stole a kiss earlier tonight."

"I always knew you were loose, Sarah Crowley." Flora gave a final humph and stomped off, a couple girls trailing after her.

Sarah started to say something, but Mary finally spoke. "Enough. We don't know that Emma Jane and Jasper are together. Last I saw Emma Jane, she was going to use the necessary, and that's been quite some time ago."

She looked toward Will. "When did you last see Jasper?"

"Near suppertime, I think." Will tried to think if he'd seen Jasper since, but he'd been too focused on Mary to even think about his friend. Besides, Jasper needed time alone. And with all the kisses it seemed his friend had managed to steal, he'd probably needed plenty of room.

What was Jasper thinking? He hadn't been so thoughtless in regard to a woman's reputation in the past. As far as the accusation that he was off with Emma Jane, Will didn't believe it for a moment. Not only was he clearly not interested, but Jasper wasn't so mule-headed as to steal away with a woman so blatantly desirous of trapping him into marriage. Jasper was smarter than that.

The weight of Mary's eyes on Will made him realize that he, too, had made a number of mistakes he was too smart to make. Like being so focused on Mary that he'd not paid attention to his friend or the fact that one of the women had gone missing.

"Did you look outside?" Mary's voice sounded strained.

"Yes. I searched around as far as I could, and I called both of their names."

"I wonder if Emma Jane was simply too embarrassed to answer, if she's in distress of a personal nature. I should go check."

The firm set to Mary's jaw told him that it would do no good to argue, even though he'd found the outhouse empty. Plus, such a thing wasn't mentionable in the presence of so many ladies.

"I'll walk outside with you."

"I think it's best if I go alone. Her pride..." Mary didn't need to finish her sentence.

"I'll leave room for you to have some privacy. Besides, I still need to find Jasper."

They walked out the door, and Will did his best to

ignore the giggles of Polly and Mary's other friend. Such silly girls. He'd had no time for pursuing ladies in the past because he couldn't get past their giggles and the fact that they all seemed to be more vapid than he had patience for.

And then he'd met Daisy, and for a brief moment, he'd thought that things could be different. But he was wrong. Just because she wasn't as vapid as the rest of the girls didn't make her any better. In fact, it made her capable of a heinous crime.

So where did that leave Mary?

He watched as she strode earnestly to the empty outhouse. She made great show of walking around it, calling Emma Jane's name.

All for nothing, of course.

The furrow in her brow had deepened as she returned to his side. "I can't imagine where she might have gotten. Perhaps we should put together a search party."

Will lifted his lantern. "Not only do we not have enough for all of us, but I don't want to needlessly put anyone else in danger. With the rain, the paths are slippery, the land unstable. It's best to wait until morning."

"We can't leave Emma Jane out here alone all night."

"She'll be fine." Words meant to convince Mary, but even Will knew they probably weren't true. The woman had gone into hysterics at getting wet. Mary was strong enough to tolerate being out alone all night, but she also wouldn't have been so foolish as to get lost in the first place.

Who was he kidding? If it were Mary out there, he'd go after her.

Mary wasn't supposed to be special.

"Go inside with the others. I'll see if I can get Josiah Haggerty or his sons to help me look."

"I'm not going to abandon her."

"You're not abandoning her. I'm going in your place."

"But Emma Jane doesn't trust you. Plus, her reputation will be ruined if she is alone with you."

He raised a brow. "And your reputation won't?"

"I don't care about my reputation. Perhaps if you're the one to ruin it, then Ben won't have any reason to continue his pursuit of me."

"You want me to ruin you?" His words were meant to shock her into reason. The look on her face told him he'd succeeded.

"I can't just sit around dithering while Emma Jane is missing."

She barely knew the girl, and yet, Mary was staking her honor on making sure Emma Jane was safe. Unquestioning loyalty. Was that what kept her from revealing the truth about Ben? Would that Ben were so loyal. His loyalty was only in advancing himself, without care to who he ruined in the process.

He needed to be careful. Gaining her trust was one thing. Getting attached was another.

"You won't be dithering. You'll be sleeping with the others, getting rest so that you can be of use to us in the morning."

Mary appeared to consider his words. After all, they were of the kind of logic she was sure to appreciate. Her desire to be useful was something he admired about her. Surely he could find qualities to admire without sinking in too deep.

"I won't be able to sleep a wink. I'll be too worried about Emma Jane."

Compassion. One more good quality that defined Mary. Had he ever noticed that in Daisy? He could hardly remember for the betrayal he'd suffered. He caught himself before he was steeped in memory. Perhaps he needed to not focus on Mary's finer qualities, but on the qualities he found not so attractive. Like her connection to Ben Perry.

"You're not equipped for a search in the dark. Sleep or not, you need to go back inside with the others."

Mary squared her shoulders. "I don't think you understand me clearly. I categorically refuse to go back inside until Emma Jane is found."

Stubbornness. Now, that was a quality he could find to be lacking in her character. Only it didn't bring him closer to solving the problem at hand.

"I can't put you in danger."

"If you go without me, I'll go on my own once you leave."

Not just stubborn, but downright mule-headed. Worse than mule-headed. Mary Stone was completely daft in her refusal to see sense in this matter.

The look on Mary's face said that she'd brook no refusal. And maybe letting her search with him was an opportunity to talk to her and get her to open up to him about Ben without giving her the excuses to run off. But he needed to be mindful of her reputation—especially given the biddies in the barn who were already stirring up way too much talk for his comfort.

"If we can get Mrs. Haggerty or another lady to come with us, then fine. But I'm not risking your safety or your reputation to rescue a woman who didn't have the sense to stay close in the first place."

His answer appeared to mollify her, and his only hope in succeeding lay in procuring someone to chaperone them and save Mary's reputation—and his heart.

Chapter Ten

Mary ate the breakfast Mrs. Haggerty provided as quickly as she could, trying to ignore Will's smug eyes on her. Not only had Mrs. Haggerty refused to chaperone her in the search for Emma Jane last night, but Mr. Haggerty had joined in the discussion and insisted they wait until morning for the search. While they were wasting time eating breakfast, Emma Jane could already be dead—or dying.

None of the other girls seemed to care that Emma Jane was missing. Most of them seemed more put out that Jasper was also gone, and in the minds of a bunch of busybodies who didn't have any facts, they were all certain Emma Jane had somehow absconded with the catch of the century.

Mary forced herself to take another bite, making exaggerated motions to show that she'd slowed down her pace. "I don't care what the others say. I'm certain something terrible must have happened to Emma Jane."

Will's face darkened into an unreadable expression. "Saying it more often isn't going to make a difference.

We'll find her. But we've got to do it right, or else we risk others being harmed in the process."

Mary nodded slowly, his words clunking together in her brain. When had she become a ninny, wringing her hands and dithering about when it did no good? She'd done everything she could to get the rescue party moving, yet none of her efforts had done any good.

"I'm sorry. I feel so helpless right now, and Emma Jane must be cold and afraid. I can't imagine how horrible it must have been, spending the night alone. If she survived..."

She was doing it again. "I should help Mrs. Haggerty clean up." The first sensible thing Mary had managed to put together since they'd first discovered Emma Jane missing.

Mary walked past Flora and one of the other girls who'd been particularly nasty about Emma Jane's disappearance.

"I'm sure Emma Jane kidnapped Jasper. Everyone knows she's desperate to restore her family fortunes. A man like Jasper would never be interested in her."

Mary's skin prickled on the back of her neck. Flora had been nothing but nasty, and what did she know of Emma Jane? Certainly nothing to indicate a level of kindness or compassion. Merely mean-spirited gossip.

She turned toward the other two women, screwing a pleasant smile on her face. "We don't know what happened to either of them. Perhaps if you joined in our efforts to find them, rather than engaging in idle gossip, we'd find them sooner."

Flora tossed her head. "As if any of us give a whit for Emma Jane Logan. What's she to us?"

Mary opened her mouth to defend the other girl, but Mrs. Haggerty took Mary by the arm.

"Will said you were on your way to help me. You're so thoughtful." Mrs. Haggerty smiled, then looked at the other girls. "I'm sure if you were lost in the mountains, you'd want your church sisters to be praying for your safe return. Perhaps that would be a better use of your time than idle speculation about what might have happened to Emma Jane and Jasper."

Though Mrs. Haggerty's words were meant to shame the other two girls, guilt nibbled at the corner of Mary's heart. In all of her fury at not being able to search for Emma Jane during the night and her fretting over what might have happened, not once had it occurred to Mary that the most useful thing she could be doing was to be praying.

"We could do so now," Mary suggested, but Mrs. Haggerty shook her head. "Josiah is loading up the wagon. Those going back to town need to gather their things and join him."

The barn erupted with activity as the others scurried toward the doors. Only Mary and Mrs. Haggerty remained.

"None of them want to help?" Mary didn't need to ask the question, not really. Her words fell on the empty air.

Polly reentered the barn. "You're not coming?"

"I can't leave Emma Jane out there alone. She's so sensitive that I think having a familiar face will ease her discomfort, having endured such difficult circumstances."

Polly scowled. "What's it to you? Emma Jane is an odd woman at best, and she spurned the friendship you offered. You've done your Christian duty by her, so shake the dust off your feet, and let's go home to our family."

If only Polly hadn't reminded her of her Christian duty. The truth was, Mary *hadn't* done her Christian duty by the other girl. And maybe if Mary could help find Emma Jane and spend time with her, it would somehow help her.

"Weren't you the one who argued that we needed time away from them when we first left for the picnic?"

But Polly seemed ill-inclined to show kindness toward Emma Jane. "I'm sure Daniel is wearing on Maddie's nerves, and even my mother hasn't got the patience to mind him for long."

"I know. But something deep inside me says that helping Emma Jane is the right thing to do."

"What of your reputation?" Polly's eyes narrowed.

"What of it? Mrs. Haggerty will be with us, so no one can accuse me of impropriety."

Her words didn't erase Polly's frown. "Impropriety with Will is the least of your worries. The other girls are spitting mad that you'd take up for Emma Jane when she is clearly—"

"And you would put their good opinion over doing what's right?"

That, at least, had an effect as Polly winced. "They can make life in town difficult."

Before Polly's father had been put in charge of Joseph's mine, many of the prominent women in town had mocked Polly and her family's lower circumstances. Mary would think that, of all people, Polly would understand what it was like to be in Emma Jane's position. Perhaps, though, it was such a relief to no longer be in Emma Jane's shoes, she wasn't willing to risk it.

Mary, too, understood that feeling. "When we lived in Ohio with Aunt Ina, the other girls mocked us for being poor. For our scandalous family and no-account father. I could barely hold my head up high walking through town. I had no friends."

Perhaps that was why she'd so easily fallen into Ben's trap. He knew that she wouldn't have anyone to talk to, to find out that he was not the man he claimed to be. He'd made her feel special when no one else acknowledged she existed.

She stared hard at Polly. "The reason I could hold my head up high, though, was that I had done nothing wrong. If I go home without trying to find Emma Jane, the ladies in town will think more of me, but will I be blameless? I let a defenseless woman suffer."

"You almost make me want to stay." Polly's face softened. "But it doesn't change the fact that someone needs to manage Daniel. I can admit to not nearly being as good a Christian woman as you."

Arguing that she was hardly the picture of a good Christian woman would mean that Mary would have to own her other flaws. The things Ben still held over her head.

Perhaps someday she'd be able to be so open about her flaws. However, she couldn't forget that Ben held evidence that could put her in jail. Maybe even… Did they still hang thieves?

"Last call to leave for town." Will's voice broke through any decision Mary might have made to be open with her friend.

"You should go," Mary said.

Polly gave her a quick hug. "I still think you're crazy, but I respect what you're doing. I'm sure we'll get on fine without you."

As Polly walked away, Mary's conscience nagged. Surely she was doing the right thing in searching for Emma Jane. Her family could do without her for another day.

Will still didn't like it. He watched the wagon head back to town.

"Can we go now?"

He shouldn't have minded her forceful tone. He'd already seen that Mary was a doer. But it was starting to feel as if Mary didn't trust him to do the right thing. He'd already fouled up an important job. If there was anything she could count on, it was the fact that he wouldn't rest until both Jasper and Emma Jane were found.

But his reasoning? Well, that was something he couldn't share with her. The good Lord wasn't going to lend a hand, that he knew already. If something was to be done, it was up to him to do it.

Josiah and two of his sons approached. Mrs. Haggerty had pulled Mary aside, and they were talking quietly. Hopefully, the older woman would find a way to talk some sense into Mary. Even with a chaperone, it wasn't a good idea for Mary to be wandering the wilderness. Ladies such as she weren't familiar with the survival skills needed. Even if she was, Will's heart wasn't safe around her.

Maybe that was the most dangerous part of the proposition.

Hopefully, this detour in finding Jasper and Emma

Jane wouldn't be a setback in his quest for justice against Ben. At least, since Mary was with Will, Ben wouldn't have the opportunity to entangle her in any more of his schemes.

"We've got the horses loaded with supplies. Britta is helping Mary into some of her clothes. They're more suitable for the search, and she's got an extra pair of boots besides."

At least someone besides Will had a lick of sense.

They began their search on foot. Although Will had poked around the area immediately surrounding the barn and outhouse as soon as it was light, more sets of eyes wouldn't hurt. He couldn't imagine Emma Jane going very far. Surely she had to be nearby. If only it hadn't started raining again during the night. Any hope of finding usable tracks had washed away.

"There's some broken branches over here," Josiah called.

As Will headed in that direction, he noticed Mary had eagerly gone ahead to attend the find. He couldn't fault her in her dedication to her new friend. As much as it pained him to admit, the comparisons he'd been making between Mary and Daisy were not fair. The only thing the two women had in common was their attachment to Ben Perry.

So why would Mary have let herself get involved with a vermin like Perry?

Mary seemed almost terrified of the man. He'd tried convincing her that he could help her, if only she told him the truth. Will had thought all of these things before, but nothing in that thinking had gotten him to a place of figuring out how to get through to her.

"She's been through here!" Mary held up a scrap of lace.

Will closed the short distance between him and Mary, then took the lace from her hand. "Where was this?"

"Stuck on the tree, there." Mary pointed to where Josiah was examining the dirt. Will looked around. Less than a furlong from the barn, but in the opposite direction of the outhouse.

What had possessed the girl to come this way?

He shook his head. Probably she'd been so addle-pated that she hadn't even realized she was going the wrong way. But the signs on the ground as well as the torn lace in the tree had indicated she'd been afraid of something.

"Any sign of blood?" He asked the question quietly, addressing Josiah.

Fortunately for the ladies present, Josiah shook his head. Maybe having the ladies on this mission had been a bad idea. Actually, it was most likely the worst idea in the history of bad ideas, but convincing Mary of that fact was almost as impossible as—

"There's a ribbon here," one of Josiah's sons shouted.

Will looked farther up the hill. No wonder they hadn't found Emma Jane. She'd been going away from the ranch, away from civilization, the entire time.

They clambered up the slope. Rocks and loose soil gave way under their feet. Mary lost her balance, falling into Will.

He caught her in his arms. "Are you all right?"

"Fine." Mary struggled in his embrace, making him slip farther down the hill.

"Calm yourself, or we'll both go tumbling down. I mean no harm."

Mary stilled, allowing him to get his bearings, then he let her go.

"The ground is unstable through here. Perhaps you should wait where we found the lace."

"I'm fine." She stepped away and began climbing back up the muddy slope.

Though she'd only been in his arms for a few moments, he missed her warmth almost immediately as she departed. She'd spent the night in a barn, yet all Will could think of was how sweet Mary smelled.

Maybe he was the addlepated one.

They reached the crest of the hill. Despite the rain washing away most of the evidence of human activity in the area, slide marks were clearly imprinted against the ground. Emma Jane had most likely slid down the other side of the hill. But what of Jasper? So far, there had been no sign of his friend.

Hopefully, they wouldn't find a mangled body at the bottom. But as Will's eyes followed the path, he couldn't see finding anyone alive as being a likely outcome. Not with the jutting rocks and brush scattered about.

Mary seemed to follow his gaze. Seemed to understand his thoughts. "It doesn't look good, does it?"

Her voice cracked a little, and Will wished he could spare her this pain.

"I can take it from here, if you wish."

Mary shook her head. "No. She's been alone for so long, I can't bear for her to endure this alone, as well."

Who was Mary Stone that she could love a near stranger so deeply? Will couldn't help himself. He took her hand in his and squeezed hard. "I'll take good care of her."

"I know. But I still need to do this." Mary squeezed back and didn't let go.

Could this mean Mary was finally starting to trust him?

The crunch of gravel behind them reminded Will that they weren't alone. Such familiarity with Mary would be seen as improper, even though he had no ill intent. He let go of Mary's hand and turned in the direction of the sound.

"We think someone fell down the slope here." Will pointed at the disturbance in the soil.

"I should get the horses." Josiah's solemn tone said what none of them could say. The horses would be needed to transport the body.

Will swallowed the lump forming in his throat. He'd seen dozens of dead bodies before. Had delivered the bad news more times than he'd care to remember. But he'd never had to be with a lady as she saw the body in its natural state.

He started to pray, to spare Mary the pain of what they would find. But then stopped himself. If God hadn't helped him save innocents from a bank robbery, why would the Almighty lift His hand in the case of their missing friends? No, it was up to Will to make this right.

"We'll follow the trail," Will said, looking at Mary. He wouldn't try talking her out of it, not when it hadn't done any good before. But he'd do what he could to protect her.

Will and Mary followed the trail down the hill while the Haggertys went for the horses.

As they got farther down the mountain, Will could hear a faint cry for help.

"Did you hear that?"

Mary nodded and picked up her pace.

"We're coming," Will called back. "Keep talking, so we can find you."

"Help!" A man's voice.

"Jasper?" Will picked up his pace.

"Yes. We fell down an old mine shaft. Watch your step." The voice, an echo, but clear.

Will held out his hand. "Mary, the ground is likely unstable near here. Walk slowly toward me and take my hand."

She did as she was bidden, understanding the danger without having it spelled out for her. One more thing to admire about her. Will knew few women of that level of sense.

"Is Emma Jane with you?" Mary's plea made him remember the object of their search. Finding both Emma Jane and Jasper would be a boon they desperately needed. At this rate, he could have both ladies safely delivered to town by nightfall.

"Yes, but she's hurt."

Hurt, not dead. The heaviness in Will's heart lifted. At least that was one pain he could spare Mary.

"Emma Jane!" Mary's yell echoed against the forest.

Will looked at the terrain around them, spotting a disturbance in the dirt a few yards ahead. He guided Mary in that direction, testing each step to be sure of the ground's stability.

Several yards ahead, he spotted a hole in the terrain, a rough, jagged spot that looked as though the edges would cave in at any point.

"I think I see where you fell. Let me see what I can find to get you out."

Mary started in the direction of the hole, but Will stopped her. "See the cracks in the ground there? It's too unstable. If we get too close, we're liable to make the cave-in even bigger and end up right with them."

"Emma Jane!" Mary called again, but Emma Jane didn't answer.

"She's unconscious," Jasper called back. "Still breathing, so I think she'll be all right."

Jasper had no medical training, but now was not the time for Will to let Mary know.

"I'm going to find some felled trees to put across the opening as support." Will spoke loudly so Jasper could hear, but looked at Mary.

"What shall I do?" Mary's voice was quiet, almost as though she finally understood the seriousness of the situation. But, because she was Mary, she wouldn't be satisfied to simply sit and do nothing. How could he not admire her?

"Put our water together in one canteen, and whatever food we have left. Toss it down to them, but warn Jasper before you do so."

He wanted to add a caution about not getting too near the edge, but as he watched Mary in motion, he could see that she'd already figured that out for herself. Smart, capable and honorable. What was not to like about Mary?

The sound of riders approaching in the distance brought Will back to attention. He started in that direction to warn them, grateful for the extra hands that would be available for the rescue.

Finding Emma Jane and Jasper had been much simpler than Will had imagined. And with happier results than he could have anticipated, even with Emma Jane hurt. He hadn't needed the Lord's aid in finding Jasper and Emma Jane; perhaps that was where he'd gone wrong the first time in his quest to bring Ben to justice. Too much time praying and not enough doing what his own hands could do.

Chapter Eleven

The Haggertys had decided that it was closer to bring Emma Jane and Jasper to the Spruce Lakes Resort rather than back to their ranch. This time of year, they had a doctor in residence at Spruce Lakes to cater to the wealthy families who frequented the vacation spot. The time saved in going directly to the nearest doctor would be well worth the expense of such an extravagance. At least that was Mary's line of thinking. She'd already determined to cover the cost, no matter what it took. The last thing Emma Jane needed was another financial worry on top of her family's ruin.

Will interrupted Mary's pacing along the front porch of the hotel. "I sent word to town to let folks know Jasper and Emma Jane are safe."

Mary nodded slowly as she watched the light breeze ruffle the water of the lake. "*Safe* is relative, I suppose. I would feel better if Emma Jane would awaken."

"The doctor says she was hit pretty soundly on the head. Give her time."

Time was a luxury she didn't have. Even though her family knew she was safe, and Mary was confident in

Polly's ability to keep the peace in Mary's absence, it didn't make her any less nervous.

But how could she leave Emma Jane now?

"I should go sit with her." Mary turned to enter the hotel, but Will stopped her.

"The doctor and Mrs. Haggerty are with her now. I heard Mrs. Lewis offer you use of a bathhouse and some clean clothes. You should take advantage while you can."

Mary didn't look at him. If he were Joseph, she'd make a joke about him telling her she smelled bad, but as much as she tried convincing herself to only have the sisterly sort of feelings toward Will, she couldn't muster the ease of being a sister to the man.

The trouble was, Will was all man. The more time she spent with him, the more she saw him performing such noble deeds as rescuing a poor woman like Emma Jane, the more she couldn't see him as anything but a man.

She should go. Do exactly what he mentioned. Yet, a part of her couldn't bear to leave him.

"It's nice out here. After all that rain, I can't bear to not be in the sun." It suddenly felt warmer on the porch but not because the clouds had moved. Will's gaze seemed fixed on her, despite her resistance to looking at him.

"Why Ben Perry?"

The words came from Will quietly, but the force of their meaning was not lost on her.

"I told you. We're no longer engaged. It's a misunderstanding, that's all." Perhaps, if she stayed away long enough, Ben would set his sights on some other heiress. No, she wouldn't wish that on anyone. But was it too much to hope that his misdeeds would catch up with him, and he'd be run out of town?

"You were once. Why?"

Though gently spoken, Will couldn't have asked a harsher question. Oh, she knew what he was about. Trying to persuade her in all kindness and goodness to share things that she could not. Would not.

"My life was different then." Mary smoothed her skirt, noting the mud caking the bottom. "I should go bathe."

Will stepped in front of her, gentility lacking in his movement. "Why do you keep avoiding my questions?"

"For the same reason you keep asking them." Mary met his gaze, refusing to flinch. "You say you can help me, but you have no idea what kind of man he is. What he's willing to stoop to. There's too much at stake."

His eyes set firmly on her. "Don't you think I know that? It's the reason I aim to bring him down. But I need your help."

"Who are you to go after a man like Ben Perry? If the law hasn't caught up with him by now, surely an ordinary man such as yourself can do no better."

Not that Mary wanted him to be anything other than an ordinary man.

He looked at her with the same intensity as the sheriff in Ohio who'd questioned her. Oh, why couldn't she have just admitted to the truth then?

So many things she would have done differently.

Will's expression had become more solemn and contemplative. Perhaps he, too, was realizing the foolishness of trying to do something best left to the authorities.

She turned to go back into the hotel. "I think I will

take Mrs. Lewis's generous offer now. I'm sure they'll be needing me soon to help with Emma Jane's care."

"How can you be so mule-headed?" Will's words tore into Mary's retreating back.

Mary stopped. "I told you, there's nothing I can do in the matter." She brought her attention back to Will. "Leave the things of the law to the law. They're equipped to handle the likes of Ben Perry. Not me."

This time, she continued her trek to the cabin. She could feel the heaviness of Will's gaze. But she wasn't going to let him get to her. Not now, not ever.

Even if she could get someone to believe her side of the story, what good would it do? Speaking up was fruitless. In fact, with Rose's rage at her secret engagement, it would only further strain family relations. Rose already didn't believe the facts Mary had shared. There was no way her sister would believe that she'd had nothing to do with the thefts.

"Mary," Will called.

She stopped but didn't turn around.

"Despite the fact that Emma Jane was nothing to you, you risked your life and reputation to care for her. Why would you have compassion on a woman with such a prickly personality, but allow a man like Ben Perry to roam free?"

Mary took a deep breath. Saving Emma Jane, mostly from herself, was a penance that gave her soul some comfort for all the torment it suffered because of her actions with Ben. The wind whipped up around her, chilling her through the thin cotton dress Mrs. Haggerty had lent her.

Allowing Ben to roam free? Surely there was nothing she could do, save pray that the next time he crossed the line, the law would catch up to him.

As Will watched Mary leave, it was tempting to call her back. To finally confess the entire story. But he suspected that might only make things worse. Besides, he wasn't a lawman. Not anymore. A disgraced lawman held little attraction to anyone looking for safety.

Footsteps crunched behind him, and Will turned. Jasper approached, leaning on a makeshift crutch.

"Should you be up and about?"

Jasper shrugged. "Better than having Mrs. Haggerty and Mrs. Lewis fussing about me. I appreciate Mrs. Lewis's kindness, but if I have to hear another word about the eligible women here at the resort, not to mention her own daughters, I think I'll go mad."

"You'll have to marry eventually."

"I know." Jasper kicked at a rock with his bum foot. "But is it so much to ask for a man to be allowed to have a little adventure first? My father wants me to learn the ins and outs of the business. My mother is so busy trying to keep me safe that I could suffocate from her efforts. Maybe if I help you bring down Perry, I'll finally feel like I can settle down."

Or it would give his friend enough of a taste of the life he craved that he couldn't give it up. But Will would be stupid to not accept Jasper's help.

"Could be," Will said slowly. "You know I can always use an extra man. So long as the doctor says your leg is up to it."

"Nothing a few days' rest won't fix. He's leaving now. You can go ask him."

Will turned and watched as the doctor left the house. "I hope Emma Jane is going to be all right."

The air stilled around them. "I don't know what I'll do if she's not. I owe Emma Jane my life," Jasper said quietly. "I mean, sure, she was the one who got herself trapped in an old mine going out in the dark by herself. She was fortunate I happened to be outside and heard her cry out. But I didn't do any better, falling in while trying to save her. Still, when the mine caved in, she risked herself to push me out of the way. If she hadn't…"

Jasper's voice trailed off, and he turned toward the lake. Will recognized the speech of a man who'd faced death and was looking for redemption. A far better calling than having to apprehend an outlaw.

Then Jasper looked back at Will, his face contorted with pain.

"Emma Jane's not as bad as everyone thinks she is. She even apologized for throwing herself at me. Said talking to Mary made her realize that she'd pursued me for the wrong reasons. I think Mary needs to have that same talk with all the ladies in town."

With that last sentence, Jasper's voice lost its solemnity and returned to the old Jasper Will had known. The accompanying wink told Will Jasper was going to be all right.

That Mary had played such a role didn't surprise Will. In fact, it served to grow his admiration for her. If only she would trust him enough to be an ally against Ben. Surely Mary had more sense than what he'd witnessed Daisy possessing. Despite his vows not to compare the women, he was beginning to wonder if perhaps he should. Mary wasn't the same woman as Daisy. She was a stronger, much more rational woman. If only

Will understood her connection to Ben. That was the only area in which he could accuse Mary of being completely clueless.

"Speaking of Mary…" Jasper's voice almost matched that of the silly girls he'd so recently put down. "You two seem awfully close for her only to be part of a case you're working on."

Trust Jasper to know the leaning of his thoughts. He'd make a good investigator, and if he weren't the sole heir to a large banking fortune, Will could see Jasper having a promising career in law enforcement.

"We're—" Could he venture so far as to call Mary his friend? In other company, he'd do no such thing. He wouldn't dare risk a stain on her reputation. But this was Jasper.

"I don't know," Will said instead. Probably the closest to the truth if he knew what that truth was. "I need her help, but she won't talk to me about Ben Perry. I find that the more time I spend with her…"

He glanced in the direction of the hotel. If he had to be honest, he'd say that he enjoyed her company, and not just because he hoped to get information from her. Mary Stone was a good woman. He admired her. He respected her.

"You're falling in love with her, aren't you?"

Will's head whipped around at Jasper's question. "I can't afford to fall in love with anyone."

He knew he was wrong to keep bouncing back and forth in his opinion about comparing the two women. But he'd tried love once, and all it had done was leave him gut-shot and badgeless.

"Didn't you just tell me that I was going to have to marry sometime?"

Before Will could answer, Jasper nodded slowly. "You're like my father, then. You don't think love and marriage have anything to do with one another." He let out a long sigh. "Perhaps it's just as well. My mother's old school friend has a daughter of marriageable age coming to visit next week. She's been hoping for a match between the two of us. I suppose it's time I resigned myself to my fate."

Jasper turned and started toward the house. Will wanted to call out to him and tell him that Jasper had misinterpreted his words. True, he did not believe in the power of love, but neither was Will willing to accept a marriage based on someone else's wishes. Which was why Will had determined never to marry.

These thoughts, however, seemed more appropriate for the giggling young women Will and Jasper so disdained. Love and marriage. Subjects they were ill-suited to manage. Jasper had the family business to carry on, and of course he'd need sons. But Will had no legacy to pass on, other than that of a disgraced lawman.

Yes, it was best for Will to never marry. To not examine any positive feelings toward Mary. He'd do what he could to foster a cooperative relationship with her so that he could put this case with Ben Perry to bed, and then he'd move on.

Chapter Twelve

From the moment Mary left the bathhouse to return to the main hotel, she knew that she wasn't going home soon. It wasn't just the tiny snowflakes that had seemed to appear out of nowhere, but also the way the wind had suddenly picked up and begun whipping down the mountain. Colorado weather. She still hadn't yet gotten used to the fact that it could go from sunny and warm to ice-cold in minutes.

She entered the house just in time to see Mrs. Haggerty bundling up. "Have to get back to the ranch before the weather gets too miserable. There's stock to feed, and Lord knows what else will be coming our way. By the way Josiah's knee is paining him, it's a bad storm coming."

Not comforting words. As much as Mary would like the other woman to stay, she understood the obligations of home and family. Obligations Mary would be shirking for a while longer.

"Safe journey home." Mary hugged Mrs. Haggerty. "Thank you for everything you've done for us."

Mrs. Haggerty gave a short nod. "It was nothing.

Where would we be if we didn't offer hospitality to our fellow man?"

Her words sounded something like what Polly's ma, Gertie, would say. For the first time since they'd begun their adventure on what was supposed to be a simple trip to the Soda Springs, Mary missed home. Though her siblings' squabbles often got the best of Mary's nerves, they were nothing compared to being stuck in a barn with a bunch of cranky overindulged misses. And though she liked Emma Jane well enough, she didn't have the same jolly constitution Polly usually did. Plus, she'd gotten used to Nugget snuggled tight against her as she slept every night.

Perhaps having this time away was exactly what Mary had needed to appreciate her family. These feelings would bolster her courage when it waned due to the children's misbehavior. She'd need it for the lonely nights when she might have been tempted to question her penance.

Mary gave Mrs. Haggerty another hug. "Promise you'll call on us when you come to town?"

Mrs. Haggerty returned the embrace, smiling. "I'd be honored. I've heard Pastor Lassiter preaches the best sermons around. You're so fortunate to be living under his roof."

She'd always known that being under the Lassiters' roof was good fortune indeed, especially after the abuses she and her siblings had suffered at Aunt Ina's. But now, hearing it emphasized by a good woman such as Mrs. Haggerty, and hearing Emma Jane's tale, Mary considered herself doubly blessed.

Mary walked Mrs. Haggerty to the door, barely able to open it against the force of the wind.

"Stay inside where it's safe, dearie. I'm sure we'll meet again soon."

With a bang, the door closed behind Mrs. Haggerty. Mary turned to find Mrs. Lewis to see if there was any chance she, too, could return home today.

Instead, she was met in the hall by Will. "With the storm moving in, we're staying here. The doctor says Emma Jane shouldn't be moved yet, and even if she could, I don't think we can outrun the snow."

Glancing out the window, Mary sighed. The snow was coming down harder now. One would think they'd be safe from the danger of a blizzard in September, but Mary had heard enough stories from the old-timers that Will's worries were not unfounded.

"How is Emma Jane? Any change?"

Mary looked in the direction of the guest room where Mrs. Lewis had installed the injured woman, but the door was closed.

"She's awake, but weak."

"Why didn't anyone tell me?" She pushed past Will and darted into the room.

Emma Jane lay on the bed, her eyes open, Mrs. Lewis sitting beside her.

Mrs. Lewis rose. "Oh, good. I was hoping you'd get here soon. I need to see to my other guests, but I don't want to leave poor Emma Jane alone."

"I can take over for you. Emma Jane can fill me in on what the doctor said."

Once Mary was comfortably seated and the door closed firmly behind Mrs. Lewis, Mary took Emma Jane's hand. "So tell me really. How are you? What did the doctor say? We were so worried."

"You'd be the only ones," Emma Jane said, her voice weak and thready.

"Stop that." Mary squeezed Emma Jane's hand. "When we get back to town, I'm showing you off as my dear friend, and once the other girls get to know you, they'll say the same thing."

She didn't mention the part about how Mary herself had alienated many of the girls upon their departure. But with Polly's help, they'd figure out a way to bring acceptance to Emma Jane.

"They said some horrible things to me last night."

Was it only last night? It felt as though they'd gone through a lifetime. Years, at least.

"They're just jealous cats. All they care about is impressing Jasper Jackson, and if making fun of you or some other unfortunate girl will get a laugh out of him, then they'll do it."

Emma Jane sighed. "That's what Jasper said. He apologized for being unkind. He is rather nice to talk to. But I found that you were right. Our interests would never suit."

This time, Emma Jane squeezed *her* hand. "Thank you for being such a wise counsel. I told Jasper about our conversation, and I think he appreciated that I will only see him as a friend, not the source of my family's redemption."

"You sound much stronger."

"Physically and mentally." Emma Jane smiled. "I'm still not looking forward to facing my family, or the other girls in town, but you've shown me true friendship I'll not forget."

Mary supposed it was wrong to puff up with pride, but Emma Jane's words had that effect. She'd made a difference in this woman's life, all for the price of friendship. Another benefit of living in the Lassiter household. She'd learned that all most people needed was to have someone care about them.

"Does that mean the doctor thinks you'll have a full recovery?"

Emma Jane nodded. "He wants me to rest for several days, but he said that he sees no reason why I won't recover."

Mary leaned down and gave her friend a gentle hug. "I'm so glad my prayers were answered."

"Mine, too." A soft smile filled Emma Jane's face. "I still don't know what will happen with my family, but I'm choosing to trust what you told me and that the Lord will work it all out somehow."

Though Emma Jane's words were intended to encourage, they created a stirring in Mary's heart. She'd been keeping her secret about Ben so tight because she wasn't willing to trust that things would work out. Perhaps she needed to heed her own advice. Mary sighed. When she got back to town, she'd figure things out. There had to be a way for her to settle things with Ben without getting the authorities involved.

But for now…Mary turned her attention back to her friend. "Can I get you anything? Are you hungry? Thirsty?"

A soft smile crossed Emma Jane's face. "The doctor said I could have some broth. I don't think anyone's taken as good care of me as you, Mrs. Lewis and Mrs. Haggerty. Even Jasper's been so kind. I…"

Emma Jane looked away, toward the window, where Mary could see the snow starting to blow harder. For-

tunately the Haggerty ranch wasn't too far away. Hopefully, the Haggertys would be home safe soon.

"I don't deserve such kindness," Emma Jane finally
finished, her voice muffled.

"Of course you do," Mary said, rising. "Jesus died
for the worst of sinners, forgiving even the thief on the
cross next to him. When we get home, you should talk
to Pastor Lassiter. He'll help you understand."

Getting broth for Emma Jane was a fine excuse for
leaving the room before Mary's heart combusted and the
tears prickling the back of her eyes escaped. There was
no question that Mary had been a good friend to Emma
Jane. And she was glad to be able to share Christ's love
with the lonely girl.

But Mary Stone was the world's biggest hypocrite.
Who had she taken into her confidence about Ben? She
hadn't even taken the time to inquire of the Lord. Nor
had she talked to Frank. While she'd assured everyone
else that he'd give a sympathetic ear, she hadn't allowed
herself that same grace. Mary was so good at telling
others what was right, or what the right thing to do
might be, but she didn't have such wisdom for her own
life. She wanted to be deserving of forgiveness, but she
hadn't yet accomplished nearly enough to be worthy.

Mary pulled the door closed behind her and went
into the kitchen. "Emma Jane would like some broth."

Mrs. Lewis turned from the stove and handed her
a bowl. "You must have been reading my mind. I was
about to take her some. You're such a good girl, Mary.
You must be a treasure to your family."

"Thank you, ma'am." Mary bobbed her head slowly
as she took the bowl of broth.

The more she pondered her secrets, the more they

tightened the noose around her neck. Mary was no treasure. Yes, she took good care of her family, but the betrayal Rose felt at Mary's actions—what little she knew of them—was real. Mary had deceived her family. Worse, she'd allowed a thief access to their home so that he could rob their aunt of her most prized possession. But perhaps the worst sin of all was that she'd neglected their care while pursuing the fantasy that a handsome man such as Ben Perry could love her.

Mary could spend the rest of her life taking care of her family and helping people like Emma Jane, but she had to wonder if it would ever be enough to make up for her mistake with Ben. Frank would tell her that, like the thief on the cross, she didn't need to do anything, but she just couldn't shake the condemnation that seemed to follow wherever she went.

If she didn't find a solution soon, surely Mary would suffocate under the weight of her guilt.

Storms in Leadville were much worse than he'd seen in Denver, Will concluded after supper. The wind was howling more loudly than it had been earlier in the day, and though he knew Mary was eager to return home, he was glad they'd made the decision to stay. Sitting by the cozy fire in the parlor, Will couldn't think of a better place to be. The forced relaxation was only relaxing because he knew that in the storm, Ben couldn't do anything, either.

Jasper pulled up a chair next to him. "I've been thinking about your case. What information do you have so far?"

Will looked around. The ladies were occupied with examining some sort of cloth and paying them no mind.

In fact, Mary had done her best to avoid him since their discussion before the storm hit.

"Not much." Will blew out a breath. "All I know is that he's in Leadville. I've spotted some of his gang, so I know they're planning something. I met a woman, Mel, who confirmed that something big is going to happen, but she didn't know what. With dozens of banks, assayer's offices and mines, it could be anything."

Jasper inclined his head in Mary's direction. "How does she fit into this?"

"I don't know. They were engaged at one time, which Mary claims is off, but Ben made a spectacle of it the other night. Either way, I can't help but wonder if she knows something that can be of use. She doesn't act innocent when I bring him up."

That was the real problem. As much as he wanted to believe in Mary's innocence, her body language and demeanor told him otherwise. He'd had the same suspicions with Daisy, but she'd charmed her way around them. Though he knew Mary and Daisy were two different women, he also knew that in the area of interpreting body language, his gut was never wrong.

So, what was Mary hiding?

"And if she has nothing of value to tell you?"

Will sighed. In truth, he'd spent an awful lot of time pursuing Mary without knowing how she could be of help. What if he was wasting his time?

"I have no other leads." He went through all of his encounters with Perry since arriving in Leadville. Except…

"What do you know of The Pink Petticoat?"

"That flophouse?" Jasper shook his head. "A man's got to be desperate to go there."

"What do you think Ben Perry would be doing there?"

Jasper raised an eyebrow as if to question Will's idiocy. Everyone knew what a man did in there.

"But why The Pink Petticoat? Why not one of the, um, classier, places that seems to be more Ben's style?"

The ladies all laughed in unison. They wouldn't be laughing if they knew what Will and Jasper were discussing. Such things were not spoken of in front of ladies. But if Will didn't unravel this puzzle soon, he was going to go crazy.

Mary laughed again, the melodic notes of her voice stinging Will's heart. How could someone so innocent get caught up in Ben's game?

Jasper cleared his throat. "Could she be the target? Her family's mines are worth a pretty penny. She and her sisters are bound to be the targets of fortune hunters."

Something Jasper knew all about. Will often pitied the parade of marriage-minded mamas and their daughters chasing after Jasper's pocketbook.

"I had thoughts along that line. I warned Mary that Ben would try to get her alone to compromise her and force a marriage. She seemed terrified at the thought."

Yet she still wouldn't join forces with Will.

"Compromising a lady doesn't take a gang of men." Jasper rubbed his chin, then leaned in toward Will. "Could he be capable of something more sinister, like kidnapping?"

Kidnapping. Will hadn't even thought of that possibility. But as Mary laughed again, Will's belly turned to ice.

"I think he's capable of that, and worse."

Mary's gaze caught his. Locked, as though she knew he was talking about her. Those clear green eyes searing a warning into his conscience. Only he should be the one cautioning her.

But how? Mary had dismissed his admonition about being compromised. Kidnapping, and the sort of things that happened to young ladies who were kidnapped, was a far worse thing to be concerned about. That, at least, was something Will could do something about. He'd foiled a number of kidnappings in his day. Even though he didn't have the badge to back him up, he could protect Mary. No, not could. Would.

Will met Mary's stare. Like it or not, Will wasn't going anywhere. Not until he'd brought down Ben Perry and was assured of Mary's safety.

Mrs. Lewis seemed to pick up on their eye lock.

"It seems as though we have a young couple unable to keep their eyes off each other."

Mary's head snapped back to whatever they'd been examining. "Not at all. I was merely curious what the men were up to."

"I'm sure you were." Mrs. Lewis's voice held much doubt. "So, tell us, gentlemen, whatever could you be about that has our Mary so fascinated?"

Mary's face turned scarlet, and Will knew it wasn't from the heat of the fire. Unfortunately for Mrs. Lewis, Mary had no more interest in Will than he had in her.

Except…he wasn't *entirely* disinterested in the raven-haired beauty.

"Nothing that would be of interest to the ladies," Jasper answered for him. "Work, I'm afraid."

"Work?" Mrs. Lewis looked between the two men. "Now, this is most curious. We all know Jasper has hardly worked a day in his life. As for you, Mr. Lawson, what is it that you do?"

Will glanced over at Jasper.

"I'm between jobs," Will said quickly. "But I once worked for Jasper and his father in Denver, and I was hoping that Jasper would put a good word in with his father for me."

"Oh, mercy." Mrs. Lewis let out a long sigh. "How dreadfully dull. I suppose if there's nothing Mr. Jackson can do for you, I could ask Mr. Lewis if he has something for such a strapping man as yourself."

Emma Jane giggled, but Mary's face remained unreadable. He'd told the truth, perhaps not so much about needing a good word with Mr. Jackson, who'd told him he'd have work whenever he wanted it. But the full story, of his real intent in Leadville, wasn't to be bandied about.

Mrs. Lewis looked around the room. "I do wish he'd come out of his smoking room to join us. Such a disgraceful habit. I'm so pleased that you gentlemen don't indulge."

Though Mary appeared to be fiddling with a piece of cloth, he could feel her eyes on him. As if his answers to Mrs. Lewis's queries mattered.

Her opinion of his answers shouldn't matter, but they did. He'd like to tell himself it was only because it would bring her to trust him more, but his head was already full of things he shouldn't have put there.

"No, ma'am. My mother believes tobacco products are a scourge, and I've always respected her opinion."

"Oh my!" Mrs. Lewis clasped her bosom as though he'd given her the greatest gift. "A man who still listens to his mama. Ladies, if he's not perfect husband material, then I don't know who is."

Mary dropped the cloth she'd been holding, and

something clattered to the ground. She turned away before Will could see the expression on her face, but he had to wonder, could Miss Mary Stone have a deeper interest in him than he'd thought?

He'd just sworn to protect her from Ben Perry and his plans, especially if they leaned toward kidnapping. But now he had to wonder, how was he going to protect her, protect them, from having feelings for each other that neither had the right to?

Chapter Thirteen

"Where is my precious baby and what has that animal done to her?" Days later, after the storm had passed, the door thudded against the wall as a portly matron stormed into the room.

"Mother!" Emma Jane gasped and snapped her book shut.

Mary put a calming hand on her friend's arm. "She's perfectly safe, Mrs. Logan. Why don't you join us and I'll see if Mrs. Lewis will bring us some tea?"

Mrs. Logan continued her path toward Emma Jane, looming over them. "You poor darling. What you must have suffered."

The two girls exchanged looks. Emma Jane looked as though she was about to cry. "I'm fine."

"Oh, to hear the talk in town about my dear, sweet girl, alone all night in the wilderness with that man. And then to need a doctor's care." Mrs. Logan reached down and gathered her daughter against her in what looked to be a rather uncomfortable embrace.

Mary could almost hear what was coming. All of the Logan family's planning, despite Emma Jane's change of heart, had come true. The accusation of being alone all night with Jasper would be enough to force a marriage.

Out of the corner of her eye, Mary saw Will and Jasper walking past, having been out to check on the wagon and to be sure the roads were clear enough to travel. They'd been stuck at the Spruce Lakes Resort for a week, waiting for the storm to subside, then the snow to melt. The hope was that they could return to Leadville today.

Mary tried to signal Will to go away, only he seemed to take it as an invitation to enter. Bringing Jasper with him.

The sound of boot steps brought Mrs. Logan to attention. Mary knew the moment Mrs. Logan recognized Jasper.

"You debaucher!"

Jasper took a step back. "Ma'am?"

"You know perfectly well who I am. I'm Mrs. Percival Logan, and you, sir, are the evil man who stained the reputation of our beloved daughter. We will not allow this injustice to continue a moment longer."

More footfalls sounded in the entryway.

"Ah, there they are." Mrs. Lewis's cheery voice greeted them all, a stark contrast to the steam rising from Mrs. Logan's body.

Given the amount of contriving Mrs. Logan had gone to in order for her daughter to be compromised by Jasper, Mary had to admit that the woman's acting ability would rival anything found on any of the stages in Leadville.

"Emma Jane! My angel!" The booming voice, Mary

supposed, had to come from Mr. Percival Logan himself. "Tell me you're all right."

Mary glanced at Will. Was it her, or had she been inserted into one of those novels Polly liked to pick up in the bookshop?

Though the words were directed at Emma Jane, Mr. Logan's attention was on Jasper. "You must marry her to blot this horrible stain on my precious daughter's reputation."

Will gave Mary a look as if to tell her to stay out of it. He was right, of course, but it seemed so utterly wrong that poor Emma Jane had to suffer her parents' schemes when nothing untoward had happened.

"Sir, I can assure you—" Jasper looked as pathetic as he sounded. He knew as well as everyone else in the room that, although he had not taken advantage of Emma Jane, she would never be able to hold up her head as a respectable woman again. Unless Jasper married her.

"I've already spoken with your father," Mr. Logan said shortly. "He has agreed to make reparations."

Jasper's lips moved, as though he was swearing under his breath. Mary didn't condone such language, of course, but she didn't blame him for being upset. He hadn't done anything wrong.

"Father, no." Emma Jane tried to stand, but her mother blocked her path. "We did nothing wrong. I got lost in the woods, and Jasper saved me. If it weren't for Jasper, I'd be—"

"Your reputation would at least be intact," Mrs. Logan snapped.

Did her parents really think Emma Jane better off

dead than having spent a night in the wilderness with a man?

Emma Jane began to sob quietly. Mary had heard Emma Jane cry before, but never like this. A wailing Emma Jane was an awful sight indeed, but this defeated woman whose whole body shook with the weight of her parents' disdain was too much.

Mary stood. "Nothing improper happened. Jasper wasn't the least interested in Emma Jane, nor Emma Jane in him. They shouldn't be forced to marry when they did nothing wrong."

Mrs. Logan peered at her. "And who might you be, that you would argue with your elders?"

Mary tried not to shake. "Mary Stone. I've been with Emma Jane the entire time."

The intensity of Mrs. Logan's stare deepened. Her lips curled with greater unpleasantness. "That name does little to recommend yourself to me. Not with the scandal your family is involved in. I can hardly fathom why you'd think yourself an appropriate companion to my daughter. If anything, your influence further necessitates my daughter's marriage."

"The Stones are a well-respected family in Leadville. They own some of the most productive mines in the area." Will's voice held an edge to it that startled Mary.

Mrs. Logan's gaze didn't leave Mary's face. "Then you haven't heard."

If Mary could have described the look on Mrs. Logan's face, it would have been that of someone absolutely smug and self-righteous, worse than anything she'd ever seen on anyone before. How could someone be so positively evil?

"Heard what?" *Please, don't be Daniel again*, she

prayed, knowing that her prayers couldn't change anything that had already happened, yet she couldn't help wanting to defend her poor little brother.

A smile twisted the edges of Mrs. Logan's lips. "Why, your sister has run off with some man. And they're staying in one of those—" she mouthed the words "—houses of ill repute."

"That's not possible." Mary glared at Mrs. Logan. "I'm sure you've gotten the story wrong. My family helps with Pastor Lassiter's charitable works, and it often involves visiting those places, to give aid to the women."

If Emma Jane wanted to be rid of such a horrible family that would spread such foul words, Mary would do everything in her power to help, including giving the poor girl some of her own fortune to find a new place to settle and start over.

"It's true," Mr. Logan said, his voice just as smug as his wife's. "I saw Pastor Lassiter there myself, begging someone named Rose to please come home."

Rose. Mary's heart shattered, and she sank back into her chair. She'd hurt her sister with her selfish desire to find love for herself. They hadn't parted on the best of terms, true, but surely Rose wouldn't have preferred one of those places to their family. Rose was a good girl.

"It had to be a misunderstanding," Mary said quietly. Rose simply wouldn't do something so rash.

"I heard tell that the man Rose was with is a notorious criminal." The smile remained firmly at Mrs. Logan's lips.

Which was when Mary knew it was true. Ben. It had to be Ben. That man could talk a woman into just about anything. He'd talked Mary into violating so many principles. Except giving up her virtue, of course. But Rose… Mary had often scolded her sister for being too flirtatious. And if Ben had stopped by the house with Rose there and Mary gone, Rose's flirtations could have easily turned into something Ben took advantage of.

A tear trickled down Mary's cheek. If only she'd been honest with her sister. If only she hadn't been so afraid of getting in trouble with the law that she'd been willing to tell her family and Frank what Ben was about.

"Ah," Mrs. Logan said with some satisfaction. "See there? She knows it's true."

"Enough!" Jasper's voice echoed through the room. "Mary and her family are innocent here. Mary has been nothing but kind and a good friend. Both to Emma Jane and me. You will malign them no further. I'll marry Emma Jane."

Mary looked up at him, barely able to see through the tears that threatened to spill in earnest. "Jasper, you—"

"It's the right thing to do. Emma Jane and I know the truth. But if I don't marry her, these people and their pernicious tongues will only ruin more lives."

He stepped forward and handed Mary a handkerchief. Then he turned to the Logans. "The Stones are dear friends of mine. I'm marrying your daughter. I will not tolerate further evil talk of my friends or my future wife. You will be kind, or I will spend every last penny ruining your lives."

Mrs. Stone glared at Mary. "But her sister is a—"

Jasper held up a hand. "If you finish that sentence now, or ever, you will not see a dime of my money."

"You don't have to marry me," Emma Jane said quietly. "You've done more than anyone else has ever done for me."

Jasper's eyes misted. "Your mother's right. If I don't, your reputation will never recover. Mine won't be as bad, but I'll still never be allowed to set foot in many of the homes in Leadville. Like it or not, we must marry."

He turned toward Mr. Logan. "If you will accompany me to Mr. Lewis's study, we can go over the details of the wedding. Given the circumstances, I'm sure you'll understand why it won't be an elaborate affair."

"But it must be!" Mrs. Logan's screech burned Mary's eardrums. "My daughter's wedding should be the societal event of the season."

At least here, the Logan family's plans would be foiled. Jasper looked at her coldly. "You, madam, have no choice in the matter."

He turned and stomped out of the room, Mr. Logan trailing behind him.

Mrs. Logan turned and flopped onto a couch. "Why, I never." Then she turned her attention back to Mary. "And you—"

"I would watch your words, Mrs. Logan." Will glared at her with a deep ferocity. "I plan on remaining here, and I will report every word you speak to Jasper. Your family does not deserve his kindness."

Something in Will's defense of her made the dam holding back Mary's tears break. They ran freely down her face, and the truth crashed over her in wave after wave. Jasper's staunch support did little to change the fact that Rose had done the unimaginable, and it was all Mary's fault.

Will wished he could offer some comfort to Mary, who'd dried her tears with a handkerchief but stared at the fire as though she wished it would swallow her whole. But with the way Mrs. Logan stared at him, he knew any kindness he offered would be misconstrued.

"It'll be all right," Emma Jane said quietly, patting Mary's hand.

Mary squeezed Emma Jane's hand back. "I should be comforting you. We're in a fine mess, aren't we?"

Emma Jane looked as if she was about to say something, but Mrs. Logan swooped in. "I will not have this."

Giving Will a cold look, Mrs. Logan continued, "I may not be able to speak what I think, but that doesn't mean I will allow my daughter to be under the influence of someone who thinks that marrying the most eligible bachelor in Leadville is worthy of comfort."

At least married to Jasper, Emma Jane would have the freedom to talk to Mary again. Jasper would make sure of it, Will was certain.

Poor Jasper. Will had warned his friend that his antics would land him at the business end of a shotgun someday. But Emma Jane wasn't a bad sort. Sure, she made a lousy first impression. But she grew on a person. Jasper could do a lot worse than Emma Jane Logan for a wife.

Though he wasn't sure he could find worse in-laws than Mr. and Mrs. Percival Logan.

Jasper reentered the room, Mr. Logan at his heels. "We'll return to Leadville as soon as possible. Mrs. Lewis is having their man get the horses ready for travel. None of us have much in the way of belongings, so we will be leaving shortly."

"Surely you don't expect us to travel with—" Mrs. Logan glared at Mary.

The woman couldn't possibly be serious. The accusations were about Mary's sister, not Mary, and they hadn't even proven to be true.

Jasper met Mrs. Logan's glare with a fierce look of his own. "You and your husband will ride back in your carriage with Emma Jane. Mr. Lewis needs to go into town for some supplies, so Will, Mary and I will ride in the wagon with him."

"But you should be riding with us, so we can get to know the man who's stealing our daughter."

"I have business to attend to with Will. There will be plenty of time to get to know each other after the wedding."

The Jasper Will knew would have made a joke here, but the tightness around Jasper's jaw made it clear this was no laughing matter. Jasper had often joked about marriage being akin to facing a hangman's noose. Now on his way to the executioner, Jasper didn't have anything to laugh about.

Jasper looked at Will. "Come, help me with the horses."

Knowing Jasper, he was probably ready to explode at the inhumanity of the situation. Will didn't like it, either. Perhaps they could find a way out.

Will followed Jasper out to the blessed fresh air. Though the ground was still muddy, it was far better than being inside with all the tension.

"Are you really going to marry her?"

"I don't have much of a choice. It was bound to happen someday. Emma Jane saved my life. If saving her reputation means giving up my freedom, then I guess I owe her."

Will hadn't much considered marriage much for himself. Sure, there had been the craziness with Daisy that almost had him thinking along those lines. But he'd learned a valuable lesson in not trusting the fairer sex. Thinking you were in love only addled your brain, and if you weren't careful, you could get shot. Literally.

Truthfully, he had nothing to offer a woman. No wealth, no home, no respectability.

"Emma Jane's not too bad," Will said lamely.

"No, she's not." Jasper blew out a breath. "I don't know how I'm going to handle her family. Her father spoke of wanting to return to family back East. I'm hoping, with enough money, I can stick them on a train and be done with the lot of them."

Cold, even for Jasper.

"Won't Emma Jane miss them?"

Jasper shook his head. "Doubtful. When we were stuck in the mine, Emma Jane made it clear that she wanted nothing more than to be free of her controlling mother. That's why she pursued me so fiercely. To think I pitied her."

"Now you'll have to pity yourself."

Finally, a grin tugged at the side of Jasper's mouth. "You're telling me. I plan on staying as far away from the in-laws as possible. Which means…"

Will knew that gleam in his friend's eye. It had gotten Will into a number of scrapes when they were in Denver, and it had popped up lately when they spoke of Ben.

"I can't have a married man endanger himself by chasing down a gang that's not afraid to shoot to kill. I was fortunate to survive."

The grin faded from Jasper's face. Finally the other man saw some sense.

"Even if the man Mary's sister ran off with is Ben Perry?"

It was like being gut-shot all over again.

Of course the savvy Jasper had put two and two together as Mrs. Logan had gleefully shared Mary's family shame. Ben would do anything to get what he wanted, even if it meant taking advantage of a good woman like Mary. And if Mary wasn't available, her sister.

Will had done it again. He'd allowed his focus on a woman to get in the way of pursuing a case.

Worse, another innocent woman's life was ruined because Will hadn't found a way to put Ben behind bars.

"How bad is it?" Will finally asked, ignoring the tightness in his chest.

"Mr. Logan said that Rose ran off with Ben and they're living in sin above The Pink Petticoat. Pastor Lassiter tried to get her to come home, but Rose says she's in love, and she and Ben are going to get married."

At least they weren't married yet. The very worst thing for Rose would be marrying the scoundrel. Sure, her reputation would suffer for her mistake in allowing herself to be taken in by Ben, but it would be far better than being chained to him for the rest of her life.

Hopefully, he could convince both the good pastor and the aspiring bride of the fact. Not to mention the bride's sister.

Mary had been willing to risk her own life to marry Ben to protect her family, but would she force an innocent girl down that path?

No. Mary had seemed horrified at the idea of Emma Jane being forced to marry Jasper. And she'd seemed horrified at the idea of a future with Ben.

Maybe now, Mary would be willing to help him.

He just wouldn't allow himself to get caught up in

feelings for her. She wouldn't distract him from his primary purpose—taking down Ben Perry.

They'd save her sister, find a way to get Ben in jail, and then Will would walk away. No attachments, no hard feelings. Ben Perry had ruined the last life he was going to ruin.

Chapter Fourteen

The wagon jostled along the still-muddy ruts of the road, preventing Mary from any coherent thought.

Why had Mary been so selfish as to think that she could have some time away from home? Why had she forsaken her family for a friend? She'd been utterly useless in helping Emma Jane out of her situation, but perhaps if she'd only gone home with Polly, this crisis would have been averted.

"It's going to be okay," Will said softly as he scooted next to her. "I'm going to do my best to get your sister safely home. Jasper has promised to help."

Mary didn't look at him. "There's not much you can do if she's already ruined. I should have been there."

"And done what? If Ben's as determined to get at your family's fortune as he seems to be, you'd be ruined in her place."

This time, she stared at him. "Which would have been my due, for introducing that serpent into my family's bosom. I made poor judgment in associating with Ben, and for all of my mistakes in dealing with him. Rose is innocent."

But as she protested Rose's innocence, she couldn't help but remember the sting of Rose's hand across her cheek. Though it certainly was Mary's due, such actions were completely unbecoming of the kind of women they were brought up to be.

"Rose is capable of making her own decisions." Will's jaw set firm as he stared at her.

A thought Mary had also had. The other, more sinister, reason lurked in the shadows of her mind. "What if she's not with Ben of her own accord?"

Her question silenced Will, as though he'd also thought of that possibility. Everyone, it seemed, knew what a bad man Ben Perry was. So how was it that she could have been so easily duped by him in the first place?

"The account Jasper heard would indicate she was with him willingly. But I suppose we won't know for sure until we are there and learn the truth for ourselves."

Truth was miles away, leaving Mary too much time to consider and think the worst.

"I know you don't like me asking, but maybe it's time you told me the full details of your involvement with Ben. There might be something in your story that can help your sister."

Though Will's voice was gentle, it threatened to rip out her very soul. Yes, she'd planned on coming clean to Frank and asking for his guidance. But that was before her sister had run away with Ben. What had Ben told Rose? What was Ben using to hold her? And what could Mary say that would gain her sister's freedom?

Things she didn't know until she understood Rose's situation for herself.

"There isn't anything to tell. I met him in Ohio. We

had a secret romance. I thought he loved me. He asked me to run away with him, but I wasn't able to abandon my family obligations."

All true. The barest of facts. Scarcely scraping the surface of how deeply Mary had almost betrayed her family for love. Not almost. Had. Her family would be better off now had Mary only done the deed and run off with Ben.

"Why the scathing letter? Why the refusal to pick up where you left off when he announced your engagement?"

Those were the truths she couldn't share with Will. Only the excuse she'd given at the church. "Because I'd come to realize the importance of my faith. Despite his words at the church, I know Ben doesn't share my faith."

A lump formed in Mary's throat. How important to her was her faith, really? As much as she said that she put it at the forefront of her life, it seemed that most of the time, her faith was more of an afterthought than anything.

Even now, in the midst of this trial, Mary's faith had been lacking. Though she knew it was wrong, she still found it hard to accept that the Lord would forgive her actions. What more could she do to make things right?

Will squeezed her hand. "It's okay, Mary. I won't judge you. You can tell me what happened with you and Ben, even if you think your actions compromised your faith. We serve a forgiving God."

She yanked her hand away. "I did not compromise myself with Ben."

Of all the horrible things to insinuate. Just because her sister had deemed it wise to visit a house of ill repute with the man didn't mean that Mary had made the same mistake.

"I'm sorry, I didn't mean to imply that you did." Will sighed. "I just know how sometimes we do things that we don't mean to, thinking that we're doing the right thing. A little lie here, or hiding the truth…"

Silence filled the space between them. She'd done those things. Will knew it. Everyone knew it. Would she feel better confessing it? Perhaps. But not to Will.

He cleared his throat. "Again, I apologize. I'm just as much a sinner as you are. I have no particular knowledge of any sins you might be guilty of. I was trying to be helpful, and I had the opposite effect. So whatever it is that you feel guilty about, I hope you know that if you talk to God and confess your sins, He is quick to forgive."

Mary wished it were so simple. The trouble with confessing and even receiving the Lord's forgiveness was that none of it changed the mess you'd made of your life in the meantime. It didn't fix the lives you'd ruined and the people you'd hurt.

The compassion in Will's eyes was genuine. For a moment, she could almost make herself believe that he understood. But he wouldn't understand the depths of what she'd done. Still, he didn't deserve her acting like a petulant child when he'd been trying so hard to be a good witness to her.

"Thank you, Will. I know you were trying to help. I appreciate your kind words, and I will think on them. If you don't mind, I'm going to spend some quiet time, doing what I should have done to begin with. I'm going to pray."

Only, as she tried to form the words in her mind,

they simply wouldn't come. Why would God aid her now, when her desire for Him was one of desperation and need? The Lord deserved better from her, and she prayed that she'd be able to be the kind of woman worthy of His regard. Especially in this matter. Rose shouldn't be the one to pay for Mary's sins.

Despite the rough roads, Will was pleased to see that they'd made good time heading back to town. As the wagon rolled down Harrison Avenue, nothing seemed to indicate it was anything but an ordinary day. He stole another glance at Mary, whose red eyes spoke of grief, though he knew she hadn't yet expressed it. He'd made a muck of things, trying to get her to talk to him. He'd like to say it was just as well, since the more time he spent with her, the more he found her to be an agreeable young lady of great moral—

What was he doing, letting his thoughts go that way? It did him no good to ponder Mary's finer qualities. She was a decent woman who didn't deserve the trouble her family faced.

Had Will done his job in putting Ben behind bars in the first place, none of this would have happened.

As they passed State Street, shots rang out in the distance. Everyone in the wagon jumped, and Will couldn't help but notice the deepening lines on her forehead. Someone so pretty shouldn't have to worry so much.

Will shook his head, trying to get whatever madness was inside to fall out. No one should have to worry like that, pretty or not.

"Looks like it came from The Brass Stallion," Jasper said, looking past him to Mary.

"Is that near—" her voice dropped to a near whisper "—where my sister is?"

"The Pink Petticoat is several blocks away."

Thankfully, Jasper's confident tone didn't reveal what both men knew. Mary's sister was still in a great deal of danger.

They turned toward the church and Pastor Lassiter's house, and Will steeled himself. He needed to be sure the other man knew the truth about Ben Perry. And even if the pastor were uncomfortable, Will had to see the case through.

The wagon had barely stopped before Mary jumped out and ran toward the house.

The door opened, and Pastor Lassiter stepped out, an older matron following quickly behind. While the moment should have been reserved for a more private reunion, they didn't have any time to waste.

"Mr. Lewis, I am much obliged to you for the ride into town as well as for your hospitality at the hotel. I'm sure you'll understand that I have to—"

Mr. Lewis waved him on. "Do what you have to do, son. We'll be praying for you."

Will and Jasper climbed out of the wagon and followed Mary to the porch.

"You don't need to stay. I'll take it from here," Mary said, her voice quivering.

Will gave her a hard look. "That's where you're wrong. You're no match for a man like Ben Perry. Jasper and I will go after him."

Pastor Lassiter nodded slowly, looking at Will as if he was trying to size him up. Yes, they needed to talk.

Then the pastor turned his gaze to Jasper. "Aren't I performing your wedding ceremony this afternoon?"

The Logans sure didn't waste any time. Will glanced at his friend, who shrugged.

"I'll be there. Then I'll be back out helping Will."

If Pastor Lassiter saw anything wrong with the situation, he didn't voice his opinion. A wise move, considering. Will had tried telling Jasper to take more time before marrying Emma Jane, but apparently this shotgun wedding was almost as literal as a man could take it.

Thoughts of his friend's impending nuptials reminded Will of the nuptials they had to prevent. A woman might think that losing her reputation was the worst thing that could happen, but truth was, marrying Ben Perry was a far worse fate.

Chapter Fifteen

The rumors were true. Every last one of them. Mary had hoped that at least some of the venomous words from Mrs. Logan were exaggerated, but if anything, the stories Mrs. Logan told were missing the worst of the details.

"I don't understand how this could have happened." Mary sank into the comfortable sofa in Frank's study.

"You never told me he was a scoundrel." Polly's voice rose above the noise in Mary's head.

Her fault. That was what Polly was saying. Polly was right. This was all completely Mary's fault.

"I was ashamed." Mary looked at her lap, wishing she had a cup of tea so that she'd have something to do with her hands. This would have been so much easier had the room not been so full.

Frank, Maddie, Gertie, Polly, Will and even Jasper all stood around, discussing Rose's ruin, but only Polly had voiced the one truth they were all thinking.

Mary's shame had led to Rose's downfall.

Gertie sat beside Mary and took her hand. "He didn't—"

As the older woman's eyes searched her face, Mary

turned away and refused to meet her gaze. "No. Ben took advantage of me in other ways."

Even admitting she'd been taken advantage of was almost too much to bear.

"I can't see why Rose would..." Mary stared at the pattern on her dress. Her own dress, for the first time in days, and she couldn't enjoy it. Worse, she resented it. Because the time it had taken her to change and freshen up at Maddie's insistence was time wasted in getting her sister back.

"It's my fault," Maddie said, her voice sounding almost as dull as Mary's heart felt. "I saw them embracing in the side yard, and I told Rose that if she was going to act like a doxy, they ought to go down to State Street."

Maddie began sobbing. "I never meant for her to do it. I only thought to shock her into realizing the error of her ways."

Unfortunately, the housekeeper had not yet learned that Rose would have taken such a taunt as a dare. But even Rose should have had more sense about things.

"It's not your fault." Gertie got up and put her arm around Maddie, then looked around. "Nor is it anyone else in this room's fault. Rose has a brain, and she should have used it. There was something about Ben I didn't like from the moment he announced his engagement to our Mary."

Though Gertie's words were meant to make everyone feel better, and they seemed to have calmed Maddie's hysterics, they did nothing to ease the ache in Mary's heart.

"I should have been more open with my sister," Mary whispered, knowing that the failure to confide in Rose began a long time ago, for too many petty reasons she should have let go of years ago.

"As if Rose would ever listen to you." Polly took the seat Gertie had vacated. "If you said something was black, Rose would say it was white, just to be contrary. When I got back, she was already batting her eyelashes at him, probably just for the thrill of stealing your beau."

Which wouldn't have happened if Mary had made it clear that Ben wasn't her beau. Polly was right, though. Rose often wanted things simply for the sake of taking something from Mary.

"Assigning blame isn't going to solve anything." Will's voice broke through the melancholy threatening to swallow Mary.

"The real question is, what are we going to do to get Rose back?"

Mary looked up, noticing the grim expressions on everyone's faces, her gaze landing on Frank, who wore the grimmest expression of all.

"I'm not sure that's possible. When I went to The Pink Petticoat to try to talk some sense into her..."

The poor man looked more uncomfortable than Mary had ever seen him. Which was saying a lot, since he often went to places like that to help the women get out of that profession.

"She was dressed like the worst of them, imbibing strong spirits and sitting on Ben's lap." Frank coughed.

Mary didn't want the picture he was trying to avoid painting. But it came anyway, eating at Mary's soul. Would things be different had Mary been honest with Rose, back when Rose had a beau herself? Would they have shared confidences and been able to see the truth about the men they'd fallen for?

"All that matters," Gertie finished for him, "is that Rose refuses to come home. I'm not sure there is anything we can do if she doesn't want to be here."

A single tear trickled down Mary's cheek. After everything they'd been through as a family, now that things were finally going their way, Rose didn't want to be a part of the family. Where had Mary gone wrong?

"We can't let her stay there," Mary said.

Polly snorted. "Why not? If that's where she wants to be, then let her stay at The Pink Petticoat. They'll be tired of her whining soon enough and send her packing."

"Polly!" Gertie's tone was usually reserved for the younger children. But even Mary shrank back at the chastisement.

Mary had often wished for Rose to go somewhere far away. Had been impatient with Rose far too many times to count. Though Mary claimed to love her sister, the truth was, she hadn't treated her sister with very much love at all. Certainly Rose had always been difficult to love, but it didn't make her any less worthy of Mary's compassion.

Mary swallowed the lump in her throat. "Gertie's right. I know Rose has been difficult, but what have we given her in return? I hurt my sister with my secret romance and countless other things, I'm sure. But right now, she's hurting herself, even if she doesn't know it. We have to help her."

Polly looked doubtful, and Mary didn't blame her. Rose had done a lot of awful things to Polly, like spilling things on Polly's dress or stealing her ribbons and being downright mean to her.

Mary thought of Emma Jane, who had been one of the most hated girls in town because of her sour attitude. Once Mary had gotten to know Emma Jane, she'd realized that Emma Jane was, in fact, a sweet woman who had been crushed by her circumstances.

Could Rose be the same?

Will had handled a lot of criminals in his day, but nothing caused him more fear than Mary Stone all riled up. Her face had turned a shade of red that wouldn't even be complementary to a beet.

"I'm sorry, Mary. I can't allow you to go with them." Pastor Lassiter's voice was gentle, but it did nothing to ease the pinched look on Mary's face.

"She's my sister."

Will met her glare with a hard one of his own. "And you're a lady. Ladies don't belong in brothels."

"I visit Miss Betty's all the time." Mary puffed up her chest and stuck out her chin as if she thought it made her look tougher.

Only it made her seem all the more vulnerable.

"You visit the parlor and kitchen during daylight hours," Frank said calmly. "But The Pink Petticoat has no parlor. It's a saloon. I can't allow an impressionable young lady to go there."

"It's also not safe," Will added. "The men are all armed, and not one of them would stop someone trying to take advantage of you."

"You'll be there to protect me." Another stubborn lift of Mary's chin. Unfortunately, stubbornness got people killed. Or worse.

"I would try. But more likely than not, they'd just shoot me or knife me, and call it an accident. I'd be dead, and you'd be some man's—"

No way was he going to risk Mary like that.

He'd gladly take lead for her, but it wasn't going to be because she was too mule-headed to stay home where she belonged.

"We need to get ready for the wedding," Gertie interrupted. She sent a glance in Jasper's direction. "Especially you. Why, you haven't even washed the trail dust off you."

"Wasn't planning on it." He gave Gertie the same kind of stubborn look Mary wore. Will wanted to laugh out loud at the two petulant children in the room, but that wouldn't have done anyone any good.

"I've never heard such foolishness." Maddie reached forward and grabbed Jasper by the collar. "You're either going to go get yourself a bath and change your clothes, or Gertie and I are going to take you out back and scrub you down ourselves."

A tiny smile broke through the clouds on Mary's face. The first smile he'd seen since she'd received confirmation of her sister's fate. Her loveliness further prodded him to keep her safe. He wouldn't have her sullied by being forced to confront the ugliness at The Pink Petticoat.

Jasper's scowl deepened as Mary's smile widened. "They'll do it, you know. Go, have a bath and change into something nice. Neither you nor Emma Jane may want this wedding, but don't go into it with such an ugly attitude. I know you don't deserve being forced into a marriage, but don't make it worse for Emma Jane by further humiliating her."

The gentility in Mary's expression strengthened Will's resolve to bring Rose back safely. She'd defended Rose against Polly's attacks, just like she'd been defending Emma Jane. Neither woman likely understood what a faithful friend they had in Mary, but Will did. And even Jasper seemed to understand the implications of Mary's words.

Jasper nodded slowly. "You're right. I'm sorry. Emma Jane doesn't deserve further dishonor. I'll behave, I promise."

Then he turned and looked at Will. "But I'm still helping get Rose back. I owe Mary for her friendship and wise counsel."

Mary started to make a sound of protest, but Jasper kept her from speaking. "Don't bother. There's only so many fights you can win, and you've hit your limit."

Then Jasper sobered. "Besides, I've courted a number of the young ladies in town, and not one of them deserves to be treated the way Ben Perry has treated your sister. If we don't stop him now, who's to say that he won't move on to the next victim? Men like him who take pleasure in hurting others won't quit unless someone stops him."

Jasper was right. Ben wasn't going to stop with Rose. He hadn't stopped with Daisy, after all. Lord only knew who else Ben had hurt along the way. He thanked God that the damage to Mary had been minimal.

Gertie seemed just as determined to lighten the atmosphere in the room. "But first, we have a wedding to attend, and I expect that there will be nothing to ruin the happy occasion. Mary, I know you bathed and changed, but you could do with a prettier dress to brighten up the occasion."

"What I'm wearing is fine."

"Your brother put me in charge of this family while he and Annabelle are honeymooning, and I'm telling you that you will go change your dress. Despite everyone acting like they're about to attend a funeral, Mrs. Logan is billing this wedding as the social event of the season, and I'll not have it written up that one of our girls went dressed in rags."

If it weren't for the absolute determination on the faces of both Gertie and Mary in this showdown, Will would have laughed at the absurdity of it all. Gertie was worried about a mention in the newspaper's social column over Mary's dress when they all should be worried about mention of Rose's new residence.

Or maybe that was Gertie's way of distracting Mary from the foolishness of thinking she could help with Rose's rescue.

Women. He'd never understand them, but at least in the battle of wills with Mary, he had a few allies he could count on.

Pastor Lassiter coughed, and Will turned his gaze to the other man long enough to catch his wink. He'd remain to talk to the older man alone.

As soon as the others left the room, Will turned to the pastor. "I'll find a way to leave them behind."

"I'm counting on it." Pastor Lassiter nodded slowly. "Jasper's father says that there's no better man for the job than you. You'll be in my prayers."

Clearly the news of Will's downfall had not been passed on. "Sir, I appreciate your faith in me, but you've got to know—"

"Henry Jackson believes you were set up."

Will let out a long breath. Of course Jasper's father would have good things to say.

"I've made my share of mistakes."

"Of course you have." The pastor gave a slow nod. "We all have. Which is why I'm grateful for a forgiving Lord." Then his expression hardened. "What do you know of this Perry fellow?"

"There's no greater evil walking this town than Ben Perry. He was the mastermind behind the Century City bank robbery and, as far as I can tell, behind a lot of other crimes."

Will neglected to mention Ben's propensity for harming women. The pastor didn't need to have more to worry about with Rose being in Ben's clutches.

"Sounds personal."

The sympathy in the other man's voice was a balm to Will's soul. "My life was ruined because of that robbery. But many others have been harmed as well, and I won't rest until Ben is brought to justice."

His words seemed to change the expression on the pastor's face. "Justice? Or vengeance?"

Will wasn't sure how to respond, but then the pastor continued.

"Don't fool yourself into taking a vengeful path. Vengeance turns a good man into the kind of man who needs taking down himself. We serve a good God, and even when our human plans fail, God will always prevail. Don't make the mistake of taking what is God's into your own hands."

Easy enough for the pastor to say. Will had been asking for the Lord's assistance in the matter, and the Lord had not seen fit to step in and stop Ben. An evildoer like Ben Perry had to be stopped. If the Lord wasn't going to do it, well, Will was up for the challenge. He'd take care of Ben. No matter what the cost.

Chapter Sixteen

Mary had never witnessed anything as opulent as the Jackson mansion. Everything seemed to be plated in gold, or perhaps even encased in solid gold—from the wall fixtures, to the furnishings, to the scrollwork in the floors they walked upon. Despite her family's new-found wealth, she'd never dreamed of being in a place so fine. Joseph had begun construction on a family home for them all to live in, but he'd said from the outset that they would not be spoiled by their wealth. As Mary ran her hand along the balustrade, she was grateful for her brother's sensibilities.

She entered the ballroom, where Jasper and Emma Jane sat upon a raised dais, like two overstuffed, unhappy dolls. People mingled but mostly ignored the newlyweds.

They were only here for the prestige of attending a party at the Jackson mansion, a traitorous voice inside her said. Not one of them approved of the goings-on, and had Jasper been worth less money, they all would have snubbed Jasper and his new bride. At least the girls would no longer be unkind to Emma Jane's face.

Still, as she passed by a group of giggling, whispering girls, Mary couldn't help wonder if this was the worst fate. She marched right up to where Emma Jane and Jasper sat.

Mindful of Mrs. Logan's eyes on her, Mary said simply, "I pray for God's abundant blessings on your marriage."

Emma Jane nodded slowly, her eyes filled with tears. Had anyone wished her friend well?

"Thank you," Jasper responded. "You've been a good friend to us, and you'll always be welcome in my home."

He sent a glare in the direction of Mrs. Logan, almost as if he defied her to disagree. The best thing to come of this mockery was that at least Emma Jane would finally be out from under her mother's thumb.

"Thank you." Mary tried not to let her eyes fill with tears, but Emma Jane noticed her struggle. She leaned forward and hugged her.

"You are a true friend, and I am grateful for you."

The room around them stilled, and Mary knew that others had taken notice.

"Pay them no mind," Emma Jane whispered. "I'm Mrs. Jasper Jackson now. They can say all they want, but when the dust settles, they'll be begging for invitations to our home. If they're not kind to my friends, they won't be welcome."

There was no meanness in Emma Jane's voice, only strength. Some of the weight fell off Mary's shoulders. Emma Jane was going to be all right. Mary gave Emma Jane another hug. Funny how just a few days before, Mary was assuring Emma Jane that she would be using her influence to make sure none of the girls snubbed her. The tables had turned.

"Thank you for being my friend."

Mary stepped away, making room for other well-wishers to have a chance to greet the bride and groom. None came forward but instead stood gawking. Mary had no doubt that they would come around eventually. At first because they longed for the prestige of being associated with one of the wealthiest families in town, but then they'd see what a good heart Emma Jane had.

She walked toward the refreshments, intent on finding something to drink. As she walked, she looked around the room for Will. He wasn't in the ballroom, but a crush of people were still arriving. Apparently, none were willing to miss the chance to attend a reception at the Jackson mansion.

Mr. Jackson stood by the door, and Mary couldn't help but go to him to thank him for his hospitality. He was most likely doing his best to make the most of a bad situation.

"Hello, Mr. Jackson. I'm Mary Stone, and I—"

Suddenly, the impropriety of her actions struck her. She was used to reaching out to others in church, but this was high society, and things were done differently.

"Miss Stone, of course." He smiled at her. "Thank you for being such a good friend to my son."

She stared at him. Emma Jane had just thanked her for her friendship, but weren't all of the parents thinking her the enemy?

"You're welcome?" She raised an eyebrow, not sure how else she was supposed to respond.

"Jasper told me of your role in helping save his life. Our family is indebted to you. If there is ever anything you need, I am your servant."

"Well, sir, I didn't do it alone."

Mr. Jackson's smiled broadened. "Of course not. I've known and respected Will for years. There's no finer man on this earth than Will Lawson. I can't tell you how grateful I am to have him in my son's life. Still, Jasper spoke highly of you, and I respect my son's good opinion."

The open honesty of Mr. Jackson filled Mary with hope. Not all of Leadville society had the same prejudices and intolerance. Emma Jane would do well in this family. Once again, Mary was genuinely happy that there was good in her friends' unfortunate circumstances.

Flora and a group of girls started in the direction of the refreshments but spotted Mary and stopped. They turned directly around and went the other way.

"Pay them no mind. Flora Montgomery has been chasing my son for years. She's merely taking out her frustration at being thwarted."

Mary swallowed. "I'm afraid it's more complicated than that."

The sympathy on the man's face was almost too much to bear. "Ah, yes, your sister's regrettable situation. Her actions have no bearing on your character, and those who would believe otherwise are not worthy of your regard."

If only others had similar convictions. Besides, Mr. Jackson didn't know the full story. Still, his support meant that her family would be able to move past the scandal of her sister's actions.

He looked at her intently. "I meant what I said about there being anything I could do. I know Jasper intends to help in the matter, and while I would prefer my son act in the interest of his safety, I can't argue. If any of my resources can aid in your sister's recovery, please, come to me."

How could her prayers have been answered more perfectly? True, she did not have her sister returned safely, but she did have the backing of the most important person in town. And she knew, beyond a shadow of a doubt, that if there was assistance Mr. Jackson could give, he would. The situation, while still dismal, didn't look as hopeless.

"Thank you." She smiled at him, then looked around. "I'm sorry to be rude, but have you seen Will? I'd like to find out what he has planned for Rose's recovery."

Mr. Jackson didn't look at all offended. Rather, an affectionate look filled his face. "Of course you're anxious for her. I shouldn't have kept you. But I am glad you stopped to talk to me so I could offer my support."

He stopped, looking past her, then back at her. "That's odd. Jasper seems to have disappeared, as well."

A groan slipped from Mr. Jackson's lips. "He's handling this the best he can, poor fellow. Emma Jane's just as good as any of the others chasing him, so he might as well settle for her. Still, I need to find him before his mother gets upset. If I see Will, I'll tell him you're looking for him."

As Mr. Jackson departed, Mary knew exactly where both Will and Jasper had gotten themselves off to. They'd gone to find Rose without her. She straightened her back. They weren't going to lose her that easily.

She'd leave this sorry excuse for a party, find her sister and then make her life right.

For a man who thought he was above the law, Ben Perry wasn't taking any chances. Two members of

The Perry Gang stood in front of The Pink Petticoat, their hands so casually upon their holstered guns, only a trained eye would notice that they were on high alert. Even with his hat pulled low over his eyes, Will wouldn't get past them. He recognized the one on the left as Colt—nicknamed as such because he knew how to use one. More important, Colt was the kind of guy to shoot first and ask questions later. Actually, Colt probably never asked questions. The man was deadlier than a kicked-over rattlesnake nest, and there wasn't a lawman in the state who'd go after him.

Will hung back in the shadows, watching as the two men examined every man who walked into the saloon. When they stopped to frisk a well-heeled gentleman, another armed man stepped out of the shadows of the door. They weren't just guarding the door; they had enough backup to signal they expected trouble.

At least he'd managed to give Mary and Jasper the slip. Mary would have been too hotheaded to understand the danger. Jasper didn't need the trouble, either.

He turned back, looking for an alleyway that would give him access to the back of the notorious house. Back in '76, when he'd taken down the Mahoney brothers, he'd slipped in through a coal chute.

The alley reeked of vomit, human excrement and something else so unpleasant Will wasn't sure he wanted to put a name to it even if he could. He tripped over a passed-out figure that moaned softly as his body made contact.

As Will bent to make sure the person wasn't too badly injured, he caught the flash of a knife.

"Begging your pardon, sir," Will said with a tip of

his hat. "Just wanted to be sure I didn't hurt you with my careless misstep."

The figure grunted, and Will moved on.

No, this was no place for a lady.

Will turned into the back alley, where he noticed a couple of Ben's thugs standing by the back door smoking. So much for thinking he'd be able to sneak in the easy way. He sighed. Was there a way in on the other side of the building? The front and back were covered too well for him to get past.

He turned back the way he came, wondering how he could get around to the other side of the building. Surely this place had a fire escape or something. The man he'd encountered remained in a heap, but this time, Will gave him a wide berth. No sense in disturbing an already disturbed man.

When he reached the main street, he sucked in large, deep breaths, though the air here wasn't much better than in the alley. His timing couldn't have been better, for as he looked up, he spied the face of a familiar groom.

"Jasper! What are you doing here?"

Jasper stopped and looked at him. "Backing you up, of course. I can't believe you left without telling me. I thought we were in this together."

The betrayal in his friend's eyes almost made Will feel bad for leaving Jasper behind. But as gunshots rang out from the direction of the front door of the saloon, Will's conscience cleared.

"Ben's got all of the entrances covered." Will gestured toward Colt. "With some of the best guns in the West. There's no way we're getting in."

"So, we're just giving up?" A female voice piped up from behind Jasper.

Mary.

"At the risk of repeating myself, what are you doing here?"

Mary squared her shoulders. "Same thing as you are. My sister is in there, and I've got to save her."

As much as Will admired her courage and loyalty, Mary had no idea the kind of people they were dealing with. Whatever her history with Ben, she'd clearly not witnessed the level of violence the man was capable of.

Will grabbed her by the shoulders and pointed her in the direction of the saloon. "Do you see that tall man by the door?"

Mary nodded slowly.

"His name is Colt. Do you know what his hobby is?"

This time, Mary shook her head.

"He collects the badges of lawmen he's killed. He's never lost a gunfight. Never."

Despite the noise from the street around them, Will heard Mary swallow.

Will continued with his dose of reality. "Every door is covered by at least two of Ben's men, and from what I've seen, they have backup waiting in the wings. Ben is just waiting for someone to come rescue your sister, and he's got enough firepower to make sure that who- ever comes doesn't come out alive."

"That must mean she's there against her will." Mary's plea made it sound almost simple. "Besides, they let Frank visit the other day."

More sweet simplicity that failed to comprehend the duplicity Ben operated under.

"They let the pastor in to talk to Rose in broad daylight. I'm sure Ben knows I'm back, and he knows that I won't let his actions stand. It's me he's prepared against."

Mary looked at him, so intently that even in the growing darkness, he could tell that she wasn't going to let him off as easily as she had in the past.

"Who are you that he would need so many guards to keep you out?"

She would never trust him again. Not if he told the truth. But of all the things his association with Ben Perry had turned him into, he wasn't about to add liar to the list.

The weight of Mary's stare increased.

"He's the best lawman this side of the Mississippi," Jasper answered with the kind of puppy-dog pride that served only to shame Will.

"Keep your voice down," Will hissed. "That's not a fact a man goes bragging about in this part of town."

He swallowed the shame welling in his throat and looked at Mary. "Besides, I'm not anymore. That bank robbery Ben's responsible for? It cost me my badge."

And a whole host of other things, but the gist would have to do. Especially since they were starting to attract attention.

"Come on. Let's head back toward a more respectable part of town. People don't stand around here jawing for as long as we've been."

At least now Mary seemed willing to listen to him. Maybe he should have told her to begin with.

"I had no idea," Mary said quietly. "I wish…"

Poor thing already blamed herself for her sister's troubles. Now she was probably feeling worse, given her refusal to talk to Will when he'd first come to town.

Will took her by the arm and quickened his pace toward the more civilized part of town.

"It's not your fault. Even if you'd been open with me, and I'd told you about Ben, he still would have found a way to target your family's fortune. If not marrying your sister, then he'd have tried something else—robbery, kidnapping, extortion…"

Mary sniffled a little, as though she was trying to hold back tears. She'd had no idea what sort of man she'd been up against. It made him realize that as much as he'd thought he'd been helping Daisy, the other woman had never been as genuinely horrified by Ben's actions.

Will should have never put Mary in the same category as Daisy. Mary was too sweet and innocent to have realized what a dangerous game Ben played. He only regretted that some of that innocence had to be lost in seeing Ben's game play out.

Chapter Seventeen

Mary tried shutting her ears to Will's words. If she'd told her side of the story to the sheriff, maybe he'd have believed her. Maybe Ben would have been arrested and be in jail. Then he wouldn't have robbed the bank, and Will would still have his badge.

Yes, Mary was right in keeping her misdeeds from the former lawman.

She stole a glance at the handsome man. She'd guessed correctly that he'd had some affiliation with the law. He was too strong, too smart, too…

Her face warmed. What was she doing, mulling over the man's finer qualities like that? Surely if he knew the truth about her, he'd see her as being very much the kind of woman to avoid. Respectable lawmen didn't involve themselves with women who'd allowed themselves to be so thoroughly taken. Besides, she could hardly prove her innocence.

She'd thought the worst of her crime of silence was how it had hurt her family. But now she could see that so many others were hurt, too. Sure, she'd paid secret restitution, but how had that given them a feeling of safety?

Had she given any thought to Ben's other victims? The good people in town he'd stolen from? The bank that'd lost its money? Will, who had lost his badge? Who else had Ben hurt in the course of his crimes?

No more.

Mary wasn't going to stand around anymore, waiting for Ben's next move. That was fine if everyone else wanted to wait until it was safe. But who else would Ben hurt?

She stared hard at Will. "I am not running away from this. It's time to stand up to Ben and put an end to his hurting others, once and for all."

Will took her by the arm, pulling her into an alley. "Keep your voice down. No one said anything about running away. But going in there, tempers blazing, is only going to get you killed. If you die, your sister's share of your family's wealth gets bigger. Ben has no reason to not harm you."

The talk of armed guards had frightened Mary to be sure, but to have her death so callously discussed sent a darkness into her heart. Ben had done a lot of things, but to kill her? Over money?

Her throat ached from unshed tears. Though she heeded Will's caution to not attract attention, she wanted to shout from the rooftops and let everyone know of the grave injustice being done.

"What if he hurts my sister?"

Mary hardly dared speak the words, but if Ben wouldn't be above killing Mary, what was to keep Rose safe?

Jasper came around the other side of her and gently patted her arm. "They're not married. She's worthless to him dead. Until he has his money, your sister is safe."

His words weren't as calming as she'd have liked them to be. "Has he asked for money?"

The two men exchanged glances. When would they realize she wasn't a delicate flower they needed to protect?

"You can't hide the truth from me for long. I'll find out eventually, so just tell me."

"Yes," Will said, his voice taking a more somber tone. "Ben asked Pastor Lassiter to give them her share of your father's claim. He told them that only Joseph has that authority and that they'll have to wait until Joseph returns. Ben wasn't happy. I don't know what he'll do if Joseph isn't back from his honeymoon soon. He's not a patient man."

It would be several more weeks, at least. Not only were Joseph and Annabelle going on their honeymoon, but Joseph had also wanted to take care of some business that would help modernize their mining operations. Plus, Annabelle had mentioned wanting to spend time with her East Coast relatives. When they'd left, both Mary and Frank had assured them that they could take all the time they wanted. Gertie had moved into the Lassiter house with her family to help Mary take care of the children and get everyone settled. Between Gertie, Polly, Mary and Maddie, the housekeeper, no one had foreseen the need for Joseph and Annabelle to hurry home.

A tear rolled down Mary's cheek before she could stop it. She didn't want to spoil Joseph's happiness. Of course, that was what had caused so many of her problems in the first place. Though she'd let Joseph know that things with Aunt Ina weren't good while he was gone, she'd kept the worst of Aunt Ina's abuses from him. If Joseph had known that Aunt Ina was forcing the little ones to go without food so that she could have a new dress with the money Joseph sent, he'd have come straight home. And if Joseph had been home, she'd have told him about Ben, and Joseph would have set her straight.

One more thing Mary should have done and didn't.

She swallowed against the coming tears and focused her attention back on Will. "Does Joseph know about any of this?"

Will shook his head. "Pastor Lassiter said that he was waiting for us to return with news. Joseph and Annabelle are traveling right now, so the soonest he would be able to reach them is Monday."

Three days. And then the agony of deciding whether they would return. Well, of course they would return. But the journey home would take some time, even if they took the train.

"We can't wait until Monday to try to rescue Rose."

"Agreed." Will glanced at Jasper, then back at Mary. "But we also can't go charging in. Now that we know what we're up against, we need a plan."

Despite being partially shielded by the alley, a spray of water from a too-fast buggy in the street hit Mary, soiling her dress.

"We need to get you to a safer part of town," Will said, taking her by the arm again.

Mary tugged away. "It's just muddy water. After all we've been through, I can take a little mud."

She brushed away the worst of it, only then realizing that she should have taken off her gloves to complete the task. She could feel Will's eyes on her, knowing exactly what he was thinking.

"It'll wash." The gloves, anyway. Her new dress was probably ruined. She should have changed out of her wedding clothes and into something more practical, but that would have kept her from following Jasper out the back door and finding Will.

As much as Mary had been prepared to go it alone in recovering her sister, and as much as she'd prefer Will not knowing the truth of her background, it was clear that she needed him.

Unbidden, a verse from the last meal they'd had as a family, before Will and Ben came to town, came to mind. "Trust in the Lord with all your heart. Lean not on your own understanding. In all your ways acknowledge Him, and He will make your path straight."

Mary had made a lot of mistakes leading up to this moment—from the day she'd allowed Ben Perry to walk her home from the mercantile, to the day she'd lied to her sister about running an errand so she could meet Ben and every single moment in between.

She closed her eyes and took a deep breath. The real reason they were all in so much trouble was because of Mary's poor judgment. At the core was her failure to rely on God. In all of this, she'd trusted her own judgment. She'd thought her ways the best way, and not once had she considered that the Lord would have a better way.

With every bit of strength Mary had in her, she prayed. *Help me. Help us. Show us how to bring back my sister safely. Lord, I'm willing to do this Your way. Please, show me.*

Will watched as Mary closed her eyes and murmured softly to herself. Probably praying. Such a virtuous girl should not be caught up in this. He glanced at Jasper, who nodded over his shoulder.

Someone was watching them.

Will turned and glanced behind him. Mad Mel.

"I know her," Will told his friend. "I'm going to talk to her and see what I can find out."

He left him with Mary, who'd apparently ceased praying and now watched him with wide eyes. Hopefully, Jasper could get her to understand that this was not the time for her to be involved.

"Mel," he said as he approached. "Are you looking for me?"

Mel glanced around, as though to make sure she wasn't being watched. "I saw you from the window. They're expecting you. Ben figured you'd try coming after Rose, and he's got men waiting for you. He left orders that he wants you alive, but the men are joking about how alive is alive. They have something big planned, but I don't know what."

"What do you know of the situation with Rose?"

"He keeps her locked in a room upstairs. She acts like it's some kind of game and plays the princess role to the hilt. The other girls are getting tired of her antics."

Will didn't know Rose, but from the conversations he'd heard, he could see where this would happen.

"So, is she there as a prisoner or is she free to go?"

Mel shrugged. "If there weren't a lock on the door, one of the girls would probably sneak in and slit her throat. But when she throws one of her hissy fits because Ben isn't giving her enough attention, Ben doesn't let her leave."

He squeezed his eyes shut for a moment, trying to focus on saving Rose, when really, he wanted to throttle her for being such a spoiled brat. Her family was worried about her, and she was holed up in a brothel throwing fits because she didn't get her own way.

"Any chance we're going to get her out?"

"Not without a fight."

Will figured. He'd handled his share of fights. Then he glanced over at where Mary stood waiting with Jasper. He'd just never had so much at stake before. "Any idea how we can make the fight go our way? I have a young woman standing over there who would do just about anything to rescue her sister—including walking right into The Pink Petticoat."

Mel made a noise in the back of her throat. "That'll just get her killed."

She looked around him, studying Mary before bringing her attention back to Will. "Maybe not right away. She's a pretty young thing. Ben would like her."

"She used to be engaged to Ben."

The noise around them seemed to stop as Mel stiffened. "She's the one?" A dark look crossed Mel's face. "There's no way Ben will let her out alive."

Not the best news, but Will could have figured that out for himself. "Mary is determined to rescue her sister."

As annoying as it was to have her follow him, endangering herself, he couldn't help but give her respect for being willing to do what others weren't.

"You like her."

The intense look Mel gave him made him want to deny it, but he couldn't. "Yes."

"They say she helps with the pastor's ministry."

"She does."

Mel's lips pressed together, hard, as if she was trying to keep from saying more. Instead, she turned her gaze back to Mary.

"Think she can climb a rope?"

If Mary were any other woman, Will would have given an emphatic no. No respectable woman, certainly not one as fine as Mary, would be willing to so scandalize herself. Not to mention not having the kind of strength to accomplish such a feat. But something in Will told him that Mary would do it. If not of her own strength, but of the sheer determination to see her sister safe.

Will nodded.

"Go around the block so you aren't passing The Pink Petticoat. I'll lower a rope from one of the upstairs windows of the boardinghouse on the far side. Ben's men won't see you from that direction. I'm not supposed to have guests, but if Alma catches us, she'll be delighted to know I'm associating with one of the pastor's girls."

"I'm assuming you'll get us into The Pink Petticoat via the passageway you took me?"

Mel nodded. "They don't know you know about it, and as far as I know, it's not being guarded. I'll watch and be sure it's safe, though."

Will looked up at the building, noting that even with a rope, getting to the second floor of the boardinghouse wasn't going to be easy. "There's no way we can go in one of the doors?"

"Not without Ben's men seeing you."

He supposed, as far as a plan went, it was the best they were going to do.

After glancing again down the street at Ben's men, Will turned his attention back to Mel. "You need to get back before they notice you're gone."

"I'm not working tonight. Far as they know, I'm at the boardinghouse where I'm supposed to be."

"Still, I don't want them seeing us talking here on the street."

Mel pulled the cloak tighter around her. "I'll be fine."

She turned to leave, then grabbed him by the sleeve. "You know I'm risking my own neck here. When this is over, I expect you to find my sister."

Looking her square in the eye, Will gave a nod. "You have my word."

Understanding passed between them, and Mel let go of his sleeve, disappearing into the night.

Will returned to where Jasper and Mary waited. Even as he crossed the street, he could see the tension and anxiety in Mary's pose. Mel's assistance was the break they needed. Still, as he relayed the plan, he couldn't help the feeling of dread that came with bringing them all into danger.

Chapter Eighteen

In all her days, Mary never imagined she'd find herself ensconced in the room of a notorious lady. She'd been scandalized enough delivering food to Miss Betty's kitchen, but this…

Mary shook her head. It didn't matter. She'd known this was what rescuing Rose would come to; only now that she was sitting in Mel's bedroom, Mary wondered if perhaps this was more of her foolishness. Still, she'd prayed, and what had happened next was that Mel had approached them and told them that the only way in was through her window at the boardinghouse.

If God wouldn't open a door, well, didn't they say you were supposed to go in the window? She'd asked the Lord for guidance, and this had been the answer to her prayers.

"I'm afraid I don't have any tea," Mel said, her voice like sandpaper. "Don't want to get Alma involved unless we have to."

Mary swallowed. "I'm fine, thank you."

A loud banging sounded at the wall. If the person on the other side hit the wall any harder, surely it would break. Mel motioned for them to get behind a changing screen in the corner of the room. Will went first, pulling Mary with him. Then Jasper followed, sandwiching her between the two men.

"There's a secret door leading to the brothel," Will whispered in Mary's ear. "It could be one of Ben's men."

Mary shivered, despite being pressed between Will and Jasper.

"It'll be all right," Will whispered. "Just be still. If something goes wrong, Jasper will take us out the other door to safety."

"Now, Colt, you know I can't see customers here." Mel's voice cut through the worries going through Mary's head.

Mary tried to turn to Will, but he held her still. Surely Mel wouldn't do…that…while they were trapped in her room?

"I ain't no ordinary customer, and you know it. I set you up here real good, and you'd best not forget it."

The bed creaked as someone, presumably Colt, sat upon it. "I gots me one of them headaches, and you're the only one who knows how to make it better with the stuff you rub on my neck. Help me so's I can get back out there and stand watch. Ben's sure that dunderheaded Lawson's gonna show up tonight. He may have lost his badge, but I'd still like that trophy."

Mary fought the urge to gasp. Fought the desire to turn to Will and…and what? A man wanted to kill Will. Such a thing was hardly news to any of them. But hearing it from a would-be murderer made the situation all the more dire.

"All right." Mel let out a long sigh. "Take off your boots and lie down. I'll get my special cream."

"And whiskey," Colt croaked.

The sound of bottles clinked in the background as Colt shifted and took off his boots. One of the boots landed close to the screen. If Mary thought the smell was bad before, it was nothing compared to the odor coming from the empty boots.

"You know Alma doesn't allow whiskey in here," Mel said. "Drink this instead."

Whatever she gave him made him cough.

"Now lie back. I'm sure it's just your neck all tensed up from being on watch. You must really want to get this Lawson the way you're all worked up."

"He messed things up good for us in Century City. We were going to own that town, but he had to step in with his refusal to look the other way. We even had a pretty plum to tempt him, but not even she was enough to distract him."

Mel made a soothing noise. "Pretty plum? I don't recall you gentlemen having a lady with you when you arrived in town."

"She's at the ranch." Colt let out a groan. "Oh, not there. That spot hurts real bad."

Will tensed next to Mary. She wished she could do something to ease whatever was causing him discomfort, but with the man who wanted Will dead so close, she couldn't risk giving away their position.

"It's all the tension," Mel said softly. "Just relax. Tell me about this plum of yours. Should I be worried?"

"Nah. She's in the family way. Don't know why Ben doesn't just get rid of her and the brat, but I think he thinks it might be his. I s'pose a man needs someone to carry on the family name."

"I don't believe I've ever been to the ranch," Mel said, her voice gentle.

"I'll take you there, baby. Just help me get rid of this headache."

"Is that where he's taking the new girl he's got locked up? He doesn't seem to be sending customers her way."

Colt gave a soft snore, then snorted, as though he'd been falling asleep but jerked awake. "Her? No. Once he gets her money, we've got an accident planned."

Mary drew in a breath, and Will's hand immediately came over her mouth.

"What was that?" The bed creaked.

"Shh…lie down." Mel's voice came again, as sweet as honey. So different from the gruff woman who'd grudgingly welcomed them into her room. "I had a bit of a tickle. Didn't mean to distract you. Now close your eyes. Let's think nice thoughts. That ranch sounds real nice. I always wanted to live on a ranch."

"You?" Colt's voice sounded far away. "I never took you down for the domestic type."

"Oh, yes. I was raised on a ranch, don't you know? I always thought that, someday, I'd like to be around animals again."

"Mmm…" Colt sounded almost asleep. "You'd like this ranch. Down near the river, with a right pretty view of the lake. I'd like…"

It seemed as if Mel was putting the man to sleep. Mary didn't blame him. Despite her own discomfort, the melodic sound of Mel's voice was almost hypnotic. Relaxing. The warmth of Will's body next to hers, comforting.

And, as she burrowed closer to Will, Mary couldn't help but notice that he smelled far better than whatever she'd been smelling. He smelled of clean, of good soap and something a little tangy.

Colt let out a long, loud snore, jerking Mary out of her reverie.

What had she been thinking?

She tried moving away, but wedged between Will and Jasper, Mary had no place to go. Why had she been thinking these things about Will? After all, Jasper was right on the other side of her. True, he'd just married her friend. But why couldn't she have moved closer to Jasper instead?

It was as if she had some kind of invisible connection to Will, always drawing her closer to him. And if she had any room for fancy in her life, she might have allowed herself to entertain thoughts about him. But fancy, and thinking that she could find happiness for herself with a man and a family of her own, was exactly what had landed her in this predicament to begin with.

Mary squeezed her eyes shut. She was not going to think about Will. Not in that way. Not in any way that brought her comfort or made her think that she could have anything more than what she had.

Mel was good; Will had to give her credit for that. But did she realize exactly what Colt had given away? The pretty plum was Daisy, Mel's sister. He wished he could get Mel to ask more about the ranch's location, but as Colt's voice trailed off into a snore, Will knew it was probably hopeless.

At least they knew something. Daisy was alive and well. Living on a nearby ranch. True, she was with child, but at least she was all right. Will waited for the expected pang at the thought of Daisy carrying another man's child. But as Mary's head rested gently at his back, he found he couldn't resurrect any of those old feelings.

If anything confirmed that Will didn't love Daisy, it was the woman next to him.

Will's reality prevented him from being the kind of husband a respectable lady deserved. He'd seen the pained look on her face as the other ladies at the wedding had snubbed her. Once her sister was safe and time had passed, people would forget the scandal, and Mary would be one of society's darlings. The man on the other side of her would make sure of that. Jasper might have married in scandal, but the Jacksons were too wealthy and powerful for people to remember long.

Mary would be all right.

As for Will, well, he would get his man. Ben Perry had ruined too many lives. And now, knowing that poor Daisy was carrying the miscreant's baby, it was just one more reason the man didn't deserve to live. She'd been a good girl, too. But now, like Rose, her life was ruined because of one man's greed.

Will supposed he should pray, but what good would that do? He'd prayed for so many things, and the Lord hadn't provided. Not selfish prayers, but things about bringing Ben to justice, keeping people safe, and none of them had done any good. Yet the pastor's earlier words rang in his head. No one was beyond the Lord's aid. Not an exact quote, but enough to make Will sigh. *All right, Lord. I'm asking. Help us.*

Mel's face appeared at the edge of the screen. "Come on. Colt's asleep."

Will scooted out from behind the screen, then offered Mary his hand to help her out.

"What if he wakes up?" Mary's voice trembled. As Will felt her hand in his, he realized that it was colder than the mountain air in the dead of winter.

Mel chuckled. "I gave him enough laudanum to knock out an elephant for a week. Colt's not going anywhere."

Will looked over at the sleeping man. For a hired gun, he looked almost childlike and innocent.

Mel seemed to know the direction of Will's thoughts. "Colt's been a friend to me for a while now. If a customer gives me any trouble, Colt takes care of it. He just…" Mel turned her gaze on Mary, and for once it didn't look as hostile as it usually did.

"Folks don't understand that we don't choose this life. It chooses us. You do what you have to do to survive, and sometimes, you become something you never thought."

Would Mary understand Mel's words? Probably not. But if she sat and talked with Mel as a friend, she'd realize that the two women had far more in common than she would have guessed. Will looked around the simple room. Mel had done all this for Daisy. Though he suspected the idea turned Mary's stomach, if living this life was what she'd need to do to save Rose, she wouldn't hesitate.

The thought of Rose and Daisy brought Will back to the task at hand. He forced his attention back on Mel.

"Do you know the pretty plum Colt was talking about?"

Mel shook her head. "I'm surprised Ben is taking care of her. He just threw a girl out for finding herself in the family way."

"Be glad." Will swallowed the lump in his throat. "I'm pretty sure he was talking about Daisy."

"No." Mel took a step back. "I don't understand how… I did everything to protect her." She sank onto the bed, looking at Will as though her world had ended.

"Who's Daisy?" Mary leaned in to Jasper to ask the question, presumably not to interrupt Will, but Jasper wouldn't know.

Will cleared his throat. "Daisy is Mel's sister. Mel took up this life so Daisy wouldn't have to. Daisy went missing a while back, and Mel's been working to get in with Ben's gang so she could get information on her sister's whereabouts."

The compassionate Mary Will knew and loved made a small noise. She was finally putting all the pieces together about things not being what they seemed. And, knowing Mary, probably feeling guilty for judging.

Mary sat on the bed beside Mel. "I'm so sorry about your sister. I guess we have more in common than we thought."

Will's chest tightened. She was such a good woman. Oh, to be able to deserve her.

"This doesn't mean I'm coming to any tea parties or those suppers you folks have for the poor at the pastor's house." Mel shot Mary a harsh look but then took her hand. "But I thank you for your kind thoughts."

Mel brought her attention back to Will. Eyes narrowing, she once again resembled the tough-as-nails woman who'd threatened him with a gun when he'd first met her.

"If she was the plum used to tempt you…"

"No." Will took a step back. "I absolutely am not the

father of her child. Yes, I was involved with your sister, but I courted her properly, taking no liberties."

If only his words didn't break Mel's heart. Her face filled with the kind of lines that made her look older than her years. All the hard living she'd done caught up to her in that moment.

"She was in a convent school," Mel whispered. "I'd worked so hard to be able to afford that school for her. Where she'd learn how to be a lady and have the kind of religious upbringing that would teach her right from wrong. Why would she…"

Mel looked around the room. "And with Ben?"

One more question Will wished he had the answers to. Now that they were in the middle of trying to rescue another young lady from Ben's clutches, it was even clearer that they had to stop Ben—before anyone else was hurt.

Chapter Nineteen

The heartbreak coming from Mel made Mary wish she hadn't been so quick to judge. She thought back to all of Frank's sermons and how, even when she questioned why they were giving charity to one of the most notorious brothels in town, he often told her that the road to sin was often paved with desperation.

Had Mary spoken up about Ben to begin with, he might never have had the chance to ruin Daisy.

Mary swallowed the lump in her throat. So many ways Mary's mistake had hurt others. She'd barely begun to atone for what she'd done to hurt her family, but how could she fix the way in which she'd wronged Daisy and the child she carried?

Glancing over at Will, she realized that perhaps she'd also wronged Will in another way. Had Will loved Daisy? His words about their courtship seemed to indicate such. It was just as well that the secret feelings Mary harbored for him were never to be expressed or acted upon. Though Mary might have a fondness for him, his heart was already spoken for.

"Ben is a con man," Will said as he crossed the room.

"I'm sure your sister isn't the first woman he's tricked out of her virtue, and if we don't do something, I'm sure she won't be the last."

Will was right. They had to do something. But after realizing just how badly following her own heart kept ending, Mary wasn't going to make any rash decisions. She took a deep breath, then sent a prayer heavenward.

"What do you suggest we do?" she asked, looking from Will to Jasper, then at Mel. "If Rose is kept in a locked room next door, how do we rescue her?" Mary took Mel's hand. "And Daisy. How do we help her?"

Someday Mary would have the courage to tell everyone that this whole mess was all her fault. She'd been so intent on protecting herself from harm and from Ben's false accusations. How would any of them ever forgive her?

She'd ruined the lives of every single person in this room. Well, all excepting Jasper. But if she hadn't caused this damage, Jasper would be at home with his bride.

Mary looked over at Jasper. "You really should go home now. It's your wedding night. Emma Jane will be worried."

"I saved her reputation," Jasper said, scowling. "I've done my duty. We both agreed that this is the extent of our marriage. Emma Jane expects nothing."

The matter-of-fact tone Jasper used put an additional heaviness on Mary's spirit. It hardly seemed fair that Emma Jane had to resign herself to this. But at least Emma Jane had a husband. Jasper might be angry about the marriage now, but he'd come around. They'd find their way and someday might even have children.

For Mary, such a thing was impossible now.

Colt let out a long snore, as if to remind everyone that he was in the room.

"You're sure he'll stay asleep?" Will looked at Colt as though he'd just as soon put a bullet in the other man. Mary didn't blame him. He had, after all, made it clear that he'd do the same to Will.

But surely, all this killing wasn't the answer.

"All night, and probably all day tomorrow," Mel said with a grin. "I've used it on a few of my customers. They all leave, happy as can be about the entertainment, never knowing that all they did was sleep. Best nights' sleep I get sometimes, that's for sure."

Now that Mary had stopped judging Mel for her profession, she had to admit that Mel reminded her a lot of Polly and Gertie. The two women always told it like it was, and Mary always appreciated never having to decipher what they meant.

That had been the trouble in her relationship with Rose. Rose never spoke plainly and always left Mary guessing as to what was going on in her head. She'd never enjoyed talking with Rose because it was always such an exhausting endeavor. From now on, Mary resolved, she'd do a better job of communicating with her sister.

"All right, then." Will began pacing the room. "How do we get to Rose?"

"She's in Ben's private quarters. We'll have to wait until folks have cleared out for the night and the other girls are busy with their customers."

A loud crash sounded from the other side of the wall.

"Judging from the sounds next door, I'd say we have a while yet." Mel sighed. "Ben's gang hit one of the mines today, so they're celebrating."

"But if the ore can be traced back to the mine, why would they do such a stupid thing?" Jasper looked at Mel with the kind of amazement that showed he had no idea just how brash Ben could be. After all, he'd stolen from the houses she cleaned in broad daylight.

"Not the ore. The payroll."

"Do we have evidence we can use to pin it on Ben?"

Will's wisdom gave Mary hope that they could resolve this situation without bloodshed. With Ben finally in jail, this madness would stop. Despite Mary's initial fear of Will's connection to the law, she was grateful that he had the knowledge to get them all out of this situation alive.

Mel laughed. "Ben? He doesn't dirty his hands anymore. He plans the jobs and tells everyone what to do, and in the meantime, he sits in the saloon at the Rafferty, where enough respectable men can vouch for his whereabouts."

Just like no one could prove that Ben was at the houses Mary cleaned. It would be her word against his, exactly why she'd never risked defending herself.

"Think anyone would turn on him?" Will didn't sound hopeful, but Mary had to believe that someone in this organization harbored ill will toward Ben.

"Not likely. The whole reason Ben's in charge is because he shot Iron Mike, former leader of the gang. Everyone who crosses Ben ends up at the better end of a bullet."

Which meant it all truly was hopeless. Mary closed her eyes, drowning out the sounds of Mel, Will and Jasper debating the ways they could get Ben arrested. If Ben didn't go to jail, he'd be free to roam the streets, inflicting more harm on the good people of this and any other town he visited.

Lord, it's just not right. Don't let anyone else pay for my mistake. The evil has gone on long enough. Help us find a way to stop Ben.

Will knew what he had to do. Not a day went by when he didn't fantasize about putting a bullet in Ben's head. The man deserved death. Death was actually doing the man a kindness compared to what he deserved. He'd heard Pastor Lassiter's cautions against vengeance, but in truth, vengeance would be subjecting Ben to the level of torture he'd put so many through. Justice was killing the man.

That didn't mean he had to like it, though.

He glanced over at Mary, who appeared to be praying.

Dragging his gaze away, he refused to let himself feel guilty for what had to be done. It wasn't as if Will had never killed before. He had. Every shot he'd taken had been in defense of himself or another life. With Ben, it wouldn't be an immediate danger he was saving someone from, but he was still saving lives.

Mary could pray all she wanted. But it didn't change what had to be done.

He brought his full attention to Mel. "Can I use your gun?"

Mel snorted. "Sadie? She's mine." Then she pointed at the still-sleeping Colt. "He won't be needing his, though."

Will walked over to the bed and reached for Colt's side. But as the other man's coat fell away, Will jumped back.

Colt had Will's father's gun.

Will's father had been awarded the gun as a sign of his bravery in saving a mining baron's wife. It reminded Will of his legacy to protect others. A legacy Will had failed.

The same gun that had been used in the bank robbery. Sheriff Horton had said Will had to have been involved because the mother-of-pearl inlay was so unique, so distinctive. No one but Will would have been carrying that gun.

And now Will had the proof that he'd been set up.

"Did a rattler jump up and bite you?" Mel's laugh shook him to the core. But it wasn't a laughing matter.

Would the gun be enough to get anyone else to believe he'd been set up?

Resisting the urge to pick up the gun, he looked over at Mel. "Do you know where he got that gun?"

Mel shrugged. "We don't talk about things like that."

Then Mary turned to him. "Why is the gun so important?"

"The gun used to belong to my father. He gave it to me when I became a deputy. Said he wanted me to have it so my mother wouldn't worry. It went missing right around the time I was investigating Den's gang in Century City. A witness saw someone shooting the gun at that bank robbery. Everyone thought it had to have been me. But seeing Colt here with it…"

Will sighed. It didn't exactly prove that he wasn't involved. He couldn't prove that the gun had been stolen. He couldn't prove that Colt had stolen it.

"You know how Colt is about taking trophies." Mel's words confirmed his suspicions but did nothing to prove the truth.

"I don't suppose we could get Colt to confess that he

stole the gun." The thought sounded even more stupid now that he'd uttered it.

"No," Jasper said, crossing the room. "But you do have us as witnesses that you found it in Colt's possession."

"Go ahead and take it," Mel said.

Even Mary looked as though she thought it was the right thing to do. But as Will grasped the slick mother-of-pearl handle, he wasn't sure he'd ever be able to use it again. How many people had Colt killed in cold blood with his father's weapon?

His hands warmed to the feel of the weight of the metal. Oh, he could still use it all right. At least in the dispatching of Ben and his gang.

They couldn't be allowed to continue their evil. And with Will all but rendered useless, this gun was the only thing standing between them and more crime. He'd tried justice the legal way, so maybe it was time to become everything he'd said he wouldn't be.

An outlaw.

A heaviness settled on Will's heart, and he wished he didn't see Mary's bright green eyes shining over Jasper's shoulder. In them, he saw the face of Pastor Lassiter, bringing to mind the words of the Bible and not repaying evil for evil.

He thought of David being pursued by Saul and how David pleaded with the Lord for rescue.

"Lord," Will said to himself as he closed his eyes. "I'm no David. But I know what I have to do. And I sure hope that what Pastor Lassiter said was right and that you'll forgive me when this is all over."

Will's eyes flew open. Did the Lord forgive premeditated sin? And was it a sin when he was only trying to keep more people from being hurt? If the Lord had only stopped Ben from succeeding in the past, Will wouldn't be facing these seemingly impossible questions.

If he asked Mary, she'd probably pray for him. Might even be able to give him some of the pastor's wisdom on how to proceed. But Mary was too good, too pure to know the ugliness lurking in Will's heart. If she knew the truth about him, she'd never understand.

No, he'd do the best he could do, what he had to do, and in the end, he'd simply hope that God would forgive the depth of his sin.

Chapter Twenty

They waited for what seemed to be ages. No one spoke much, and Mary figured it must be so that no one would overhear. Occasionally, she peeked out Mel's window and watched the drunken men passing the alley as they walked down the street.

She'd hated this lifestyle for so long. But something in her had softened when she realized that Mel was merely doing the only thing she could do to protect her sister.

Mary glanced at the man snoring on the bed. Colt's facial hair was scruffy and scraggly, so unlike the neat appearance of a decent man. His boots had smelled like something died in them, and she was certain the rest of the man was just as foul.

Mel entertained men like him for the sake of her sister.

Would Mary do any less?

Once again, Mary stole a glance at Mel. Now that evening was fading, and so too Mel's meticulously applied paint, Mary saw a girl who couldn't be all that different than she.

It made her think about her father, and the woman he'd taken up with after arriving in town. Was she like Mel, merely doing the best she could with what she had? She'd kept and cared for her child. Mary could never bear to hear Nugget go on and on about her mama, but now...

Her heart ached as she realized that she'd been denying her half sister the chance to mourn a dearly loved parent. A woman who, aside from her profession, seemed like a decent woman. Like Mel.

Lord, forgive me for judging Nugget's mama. I don't know why my father betrayed my mother with her. I don't know why she took up her profession. But she loved Nugget and was a good mama to her. Help me help her deal with her grief.

Perhaps Mary was the wrong sibling to do right by her sister. After all, she'd failed Rose miserably. Mary took a deep breath. No. She'd rescue Rose, and then she would do better by her sisters. She would be a better example and would devote her life to their loving care. She would make up for her mistakes. Just like she'd always planned.

Mel scooted back in her chair and got up. "Sounds like things have quieted down."

Mary glanced over at Will, who shrugged. Jasper grinned. She hadn't been able to talk him into going home to Emma Jane, and Will had finally told her to stop interfering in their business. When this was all over, Mary would go to Emma Jane and do what she could to soothe the poor girl's feelings.

Mel opened the door and peered out. Then she turned back to the others. "It looks like we're safe. But I'm going to do some scouting to be sure."

She hadn't even closed the door behind her when the men sprang into action. Will removed the gun belt from the still-sleeping Colt. Whatever Mel had given the man, it had definitely worked.

Suddenly, it felt cold in the room, and Mary rubbed her arms. This was really happening. They were going to rescue her sister, and it would take guns to do it.

How could Mary have been so deceived?

How could Rose?

Rose wouldn't have suspected Ben of anything nefarious, considering he'd already wormed his way into the family's good graces by claiming engagement to Mary.

But how could Rose have believed he'd fall in love with her so quickly after declaring himself to Mary?

None of this made sense, particularly when Mel returned, carrying two large guns. She held one in Mary's direction.

"You ever use one of these?"

Mary shook her head. Mel rolled her eyes. "Figures. What about you, pretty boy? Does the son of the richest man in town know how to shoot a gun, or do you get people like Will to do it for you?"

Jasper snatched the gun out of her hand. "Thanks to Will, I'm probably almost as good of a shot as he is."

"Good." Mel tossed a look at Mary. "Your job is to keep her from getting killed. I'd just as soon have her gone, but I'm not keeping a woman from saving her sister, even if she is completely unprepared."

Mary supposed her words were meant to be an insult, but they felt like a compliment. At least Mel saw that she was trying to be a good sister.

"Things have slowed down for the night. Mitch says Ben stepped out, and it looks like most of the guards have found companions for the rest of the evening. They probably figure you saw they were ready and gave up."

Mel directed them through a passageway, which Mary realized brought them straight into the notorious house. When they reached the room at the end of the hall, she pulled a set of keys out of her pocket. "Swiped it off Colt. Being Ben's second, he's got copies of all the keys."

Mary never would have guessed that she'd end up admiring a fallen woman, but Mel's resourcefulness was a quality Mary wished she possessed. Actually, Mel had a lot of qualities Mary wished she possessed, like bravery and the willingness to do the hard things, even when it didn't sound right. Mary wasn't stupid enough to believe that Mel would walk away from this without getting in trouble herself. Once they got out of here, Mary would make certain that Frank helped the other woman find a better situation.

The third key did the trick. But rather than entering a room to find Mary's sister asleep on a bed, they came face-to-face with the barrel of Ben's gun.

"So you're the traitor," Ben said calmly, staring down the barrel at Mel.

Will stepped in front of Mel. This wasn't her fight. "She just wanted to keep another innocent young woman from being kidnapped."

"Kidnapped. Such a vile word." Ben kept the gun trained on Mel. "Rose is here because she wants to be. Isn't that right, Rosie?"

Mary's gasp at the sight of her sister coming out of the shadows in a revealing dress brought Will's attention to Mary, not Rose. Everything on her face told him that her sister's appearance shattered something in Mary's heart.

Will turned his attention back to Rose. She bore the look of every working girl in this place, and the haughty way she held her head told him that she didn't mind a bit.

"Of course." Rose sauntered over to Ben and kissed him.

"Please, spare us." Mel stepped forward and approached Ben. "He doesn't love you. It's just a game with him."

Will let out a breath. Thank goodness for Mel bringing some reality to the situation. The gun at his side called to him, but he knew that while he could shoot Ben now, doing so would only turn Rose into the grieving widow, or at least whatever she would be, considering they didn't have the benefit of marriage. A fallen woman. With no chance at redemption.

"Ben loves me. He told me so," Rose said in a honey-sweet voice.

"He was with me this morning, you twit."

"Mel!" Ben pointed the gun at her again. "Don't make this harder on yourself."

Mel smiled at Rose. "Surely you aren't so feeble-minded as to think that he'd meet you and be so overcome with love for you that he'd forsake all of his wild ways?"

From the crestfallen look on Rose's face, it seemed that she had, in fact, believed just that.

At least Mary had managed to remain silent. Will was certain that she'd start in on Ben, but she seemed to be going along with Mel's tactic of making Rose see what kind of man she'd settled for.

Ben cocked his pistol, but Mel laughed. "Really,

Ben? I'm standing on your favorite Oriental rug. You won't shoot me here. You'll never get the blood out."

Then she brought her attention back to Rose. "Go home with your sister, little girl. You don't belong here."

Ben let out a long belly laugh. "So that's what this is about. Mad Mel's jealous."

As he laughed, he set the gun down. Unarmed, he was the perfect target. But with Rose so close to him, Ben's grip tightening around her, Will didn't dare risk putting her in harm's way.

"I forgive you, baby. Why don't you go pick something nice out of the jewelry box I keep on the dresser and go back to your room? I'll deal with you in the morning. I do thank you for bringing me these unfortunate souls who just don't know how to mind their own business."

Mel turned and walked toward the dresser, and Ben brought his attention back to them.

"It's a shame, Will Lost-his-badge. You're going to die here today, and word's going to get out that you died trying to rob me." Ben let out a long, dramatic sigh.

"We're witnesses." Mary stepped forward and then turned to her sister. "Rose, surely you don't want to be with a man like this. A murderer?"

Rose kissed Ben again, and Will could feel Mary's shudder even though she wasn't touching him. The spoiled brat deserved Ben. Did Rose have any idea what her sister had gone through to rescue her? Did she even care?

Of course not.

When Rose finished kissing Ben, she tossed her head and looked back at Mary. "You're just jealous. You had your chance with Ben, but you spoiled it. Instead of meeting with him to discuss your wedding, you went on that church picnic, leaving him alone with me. Ben confessed how cold you were and how terrible he felt that he loved you so deeply, but you, you thought you were too good for him, just like you think you're better than everyone else."

"That's not true!" Tears ran down Mary's face, and Will wished he could do something to make it better for her.

"Mary is a devoted friend and sister," Will said. He glared at Rose, who still looked more smug than any person had a right to. He'd give Ben credit; at least he'd found someone just like him.

"You have no idea how much she worried about you. How much she risked to save you."

"I don't need saving."

"Yes, you do." Will glanced over at Mel, who was still digging through the jewelry box. Clearly, she was looking for something. He only wished she'd informed him of her plan.

"Has Ben told you about Daisy? She loved him, too. And you know where she is? Stashed on a nearby ranch because she's carrying his child."

Mel dropped whatever she'd been rooting for. Ben looked in her direction. "Haven't you found something yet? You're a hard one to please. Grab something and get out."

Mel walked back into their line of sight carrying what looked to be a brooch. She held it up to him. "What about this? It's ugly as sin, but I think Celeste would like it. Tomorrow's her birthday, and I didn't get her a gift."

"That's Aunt Ina's!" Rose jumped up and snatched

it out of Mel's hand, then turned to Ben. "Where did you get this?"

Ben leaned back in his seat. "Why, I got it from your sister, of course. She gave it to me to pawn so we could pay for our train tickets out of town. Only she didn't show up when we were supposed to meet, and then I had family troubles. I couldn't bear to part with the symbol of our love."

The man looked positively wretched as he stared at Mary. "I know we had some larks together and you stole some things from your employers from time to time, but I can't believe you'd steal from your own family."

Will wanted to think Ben was playing some kind of game, but as he watched the devastation cross Mary's face, he had to wonder if he'd made another mistake in trusting the wrong woman. Especially as Rose's words seemed to confirm it.

"That's how you were able to afford those spectacles for Bess? By stealing? Aunt Ina whipped *me* because I was the last one to dust her dresser before the brooch went missing. But it was you all along."

Rose began to sob. "What other punishment did I take for you? Everything I've ever lost has been because of you."

As the guilt washed over Mary's face, Will's gut turned over. He'd believed Mary to be everything good and honorable in a woman. Finally someone he could trust.

Apparently his instincts had failed him again.

Chapter Twenty-One

Rose's theatrics were something Mary was quite used to. And yet, nothing tore at Mary's heart worse than knowing Rose had been beaten for the loss of Aunt Ina's brooch. They'd had an unspoken agreement about the beatings, her and Rose. When one of the little ones was at the end of Aunt Ina's switch, either she or Rose would take their place.

She should have known someone would have been beaten for the missing brooch. She should have put two and two together and realized that because of the promise she and Rose had made, Rose had taken the punishment.

But Mary had been too busy being blindly in love to realize it.

"I didn't steal," Mary said as calmly as she could. "The money for Bess's spectacles came from her Sunday school teacher, but she didn't want anyone to know, so I said I took on extra work and bought them."

Aunt Ina had taken a switch to her for that. She'd been irate to think that money that could have been used for one of her fripperies had been wasted on spectacles for a child.

Rose stared at her. "How do I know that's not another one of your lies? You admit that you lied to me about Ben. You admit that you lied to me about your whereabouts when you were sneaking off to see him. How can I ever trust you again?"

If Ben hadn't been smirking, Mary might have been tempted to tell her sister that she didn't blame her. That she'd do whatever she had to do to earn her trust again. She'd admit how duped she'd been by the smooth-talking charlatan. And she'd promise to spend the rest of her life making up for her mistakes.

Instead, she looked to Will for guidance. Only, he looked at her as if he believed her to be the miscreant she was accused of being.

Even Will believed the lies.

Mary had been right to keep everything a secret. No one believed her now, just like they wouldn't have believed her then. Ben had been right.

"Please, forgive me, Rose." Mary had no other words, no other excuse she could offer.

It was just as well that the slowly developing feelings Mary had for Will would never be returned. She'd never allow herself to be blinded by her love for another person again.

"Never." Rose glowered at her, then smiled, running her hand up and down Ben's chest. "When Ben came looking for you, I knew what I had to do. You ruined my chances of happiness with the only man I will ever love, and now I have stolen yours."

Rose's eyes glittered in the gaslight. Her sister was a vain, spoiled girl, but the tears were real. Despite Rose's bravado, she felt no joy in her victory.

Swallowing her own tears, Mary took a step toward Rose. "I think, then, you should reconsider your actions.

I don't love Ben. I broke it off with him before we moved here."

She turned and looked to Will. "You wouldn't happen to have that letter you confronted me with, would you?"

"No. It's in my room at the boardinghouse." He still wore the look of accuser, but as he continued, Mary's heart hoped. "But I can verify the veracity of Mary's statement. Her letter condemned what she called Ben's scandalous behavior and stated in no uncertain terms that she no longer loved him and could not marry him."

Will seemed to consider each word slowly, as though having to repeat them finally made him understand what she'd been trying to tell him all along.

But did it mean he believed her about not stealing?

His good opinion shouldn't matter so much to Mary, but as she tossed that question in her mind, she realized that his coldness hurt far more than Rose's.

"Rose, please, don't marry him. Not to get even with me. I wronged you, and I am sorrier than I can ever express. Yes, I lied to you. But I promise, I didn't steal. And I promise, it wasn't my fault that Silas married Annie. It's not too late to come home."

Her promises, she knew, meant nothing, given that she'd already admitted to being a liar. But surely she could appeal to the goodness in her sister's heart. The love of their family that made her step in when Bess got the switch for spilling the milk because she couldn't see the steps.

Mel stepped forward, carrying the box from which she'd taken the brooch. "Listen to your sister, girl. If Mary was a thief, then why does Ben have all the jewelry? If Ben is penniless, then why does he have such a fancy room? Why does everyone bow down to him?"

Mary watched her sister for any sign that logic was swaying her emotion, but then turned her gaze to Will. Did Will see that Mary couldn't have stolen all these things? That if Ben had been telling the truth, he wouldn't have a box full of jewels?

"Enough!" Ben stood, adjusting his fine clothes. Finer clothes than what he'd worn when Mary had known him back in Ohio.

"So I had a spell of luck after I met Mary. I was hoping to surprise my bride-to-be with my good fortune after we married. I don't need your brother's money. I fell in love with my beautiful Rose, who comforted me after my heart was broken by Mary."

Ben turned to Mel, his eyes glittering with malice. "As for those trinkets, they were all gifts from lady friends. No need for me to steal. Mary gave what she had freely."

"Liar!" The word burst out of Mary's mouth as she forgot all decorum. "I saw the contents of your satchel the day we were supposed to have run off together. Jewelry and money, all things you shouldn't have had, if your claims of poverty were true."

"It was a friend's." Ben's answer was so smooth, Mary again doubted how anyone would believe her over him.

But then Mel stepped in again. "Even if you were given the jewelry as gifts, as you say, how does a respectable man come into your line of work?"

She turned her attention back on Rose. "Think about it. Do you truly believe that he intends to make you his wife? I can introduce you to at least a dozen girls in this place who were tricked into thinking that Ben loved them."

Mel didn't sound bitter. In fact, she sounded more factual than anything else. As if she was reading from one of the newspapers.

"You're just jealous," Rose cried. "Just like Ben said. You've been replaced."

Mel laughed. "I made my choice, and it wasn't for the love of a man. I chose the life I did to give my sister a better life. If not Ben, there's a dozen other places I could go. Miss Betty's been trying to get me to move to her establishment ever since I got here."

Mel chose her life for the love of her sister. Perhaps it wasn't the life Mary would have chosen for herself, but in the end, both women were doing the same thing. Mary nodded at the other woman. A look of respect, or what seemed to be such, passed between them. And there, in Mel's eyes, Mary saw something else. Sadness. Mel had sacrificed for her sister, only to have it all be for nothing. Daisy was shut away on a ranch somewhere, carrying Ben's child.

Mary's own sister would not suffer the same fate.

All this bickering was getting them nowhere. Will examined Ben's face. Why was he tolerating this going on for so long? True, he seemed to enjoy watching the women arguing over him, but he bore the look of a man expecting something more.

Will glanced over Ben's shoulder toward the window. The lace curtains were sheer enough that he could see out the window and into the alley. The two guards had been joined by several other men, likely members of Ben's gang. They appeared to be waiting for some kind of signal.

Stepping between the women and facing Ben, Will pushed the other man's gun aside. "What's your game here? You haven't shot anyone, and you act like you're at the theater for the evening. This isn't a show. Let Rose go, and we'll be on our way."

Ben chuckled. "Rose is free to go anytime she wants. But you don't want to, do you, Rosie?" He twirled his fingers in her hair, but Rose looked slightly uncomfortable.

"Why haven't you found someone to marry us yet?" Rose pulled from his grasp and stared at him. "You said we'd be here only for one night, and then we'd stay in respectable lodgings."

"Now, Rosie…" Ben reached for her, but she stepped away.

"Don't 'Rosie' me." When Rose put her hands on her hips, Will knew exactly why the two sisters never got along. They were too much alike. Sure, Rose was the flightier of the two, and definitely pettier, but they were as their last names suggested—stones.

He stole a glance at Mary. Perhaps he was too quick to leap to conclusions in his comparison to Daisy. Daisy was like the flower, weak and easily wilted. Not so with Mary. Mary might have admitted to a few lies, but she was no liar.

Rose strode toward her sister, pulling up the bodice of the revealing dress as best as she could. "If you truly want to marry me, then you will do it right now, or you will take the time to court me properly. I'm not going to let you take advantage of me."

For a moment, Will almost thought that Ben was

going to give in. He looked at Rose with such a calculated expression that it was almost easy to believe that Ben had genuine feelings for her. But then his lips curled into a sneer, and Ben threw back his head and laughed.

"Do you think it will be so easy for Rose to walk away? Even if she hadn't given up her virtue, her reputation is in tatters. No honorable man would be willing to have anything to do with her."

And then with a look that was typical Ben, he grinned. "Except buy her for a night."

Jasper glared at him. "Not all men are bothered by such trivialities."

"Says the man forced to marry a shrew."

"Emma Jane is a decent and kind woman. I'm proud to call her my wife."

"So proud that you're spending your wedding night in this establishment."

"To save another good woman from ruin."

"She's already ruined." Ben's tone couldn't be mistaken. Especially as he grabbed Rose and pulled her back into his lap. "You've got nowhere else to go."

Will knew this was how a lot of women got trapped into this life. Until today, he couldn't say that he understood ministries like Pastor Lassiter's. But seeing an innocent girl like Rose being given no options, he knew.

How many people fought for girls like Rose? How many simply turned their backs the second they left home?

He looked over at Jasper, who held his hand out to Rose. "For now. But it won't be forever. Don't let his lies get to you. Yes, people will talk for a time. But then some other scandal will hit town and yours will be forgotten."

Will was glad his friend could be here to help Rose see reason.

Tears streamed down Rose's face. "You don't understand. I am truly ruined. No man will take me for a wife."

But she slid off Ben's lap and took a step in Jasper's direction.

Jasper reached forward and wiped at the tears on Rose's face. "A man worth having would."

"It's true, Rose," Will added. "I've met many respectable women who once had unsavory pasts."

As the single man in the bunch, the right thing to do would be to say that he'd be honored to have a woman like Rose for a wife. But he couldn't hint at a promise he'd never be able to make. Marrying Will meant taking dishonor for a name, and he wouldn't do that to anyone, not even to salvage the kind of damage Ben wrought.

He glanced over at Mary. How could he consider offering to marry someone else when he knew that she was the only one who could make him happy?

"My family will never take me back." Despite her words, Rose took another step toward them.

Mary took her sister by the hand and led her to the rest of the group. "Why do you think we're here? Of course we want you back. Frank is beside himself, wondering what he could have done wrong."

As Will watched Mary put her arm around her sister, Jasper indicated the direction of the window. Will realized that several more gunmen were approaching the building.

"If we're free to go, then why do you have so many hired guns surrounding the place?"

"I said Rose was free to go." Ben's eyes glittered in the moonlight. "As for you, well, I have other plans."

"Me?" Will could easily guess what they were. Fine by him. He could take Ben before Ben's men entered the room. As long as he could ensure the safety of Jasper, Mary and Mel. "What about the others?"

Will looked over at Jasper, who nodded slowly in the direction of the window. Sharpshooters were getting into place as though they were waiting to take a shot. Ben had no intention of letting any of them leave the place alive.

"I haven't decided yet—I have a score to settle with Miss Mary Quite Contrary."

Mary didn't flinch. Instead she stared directly at him. "I'm not afraid of you."

"No, you aren't, are you?" Ben looked at her intently. "That's all right. You will be."

Will turned his attention to Rose. "This is the sort of man you fall in love with and want to marry?"

Rose blanched. "I didn't mean what I said about hurting Mary, Ben. I was angry. She's my sister. The fact that she came here for me and said that the family is willing to take me back... Don't hurt her."

"We all know Mary is a liar," Ben said, so smoothly it would have been easy for anyone to believe him if they didn't know any better.

And it seemed Rose did. Was she really such a fool to believe in Ben even after all the evidence to the contrary had been presented?

"We're supposed to forgive one another's sins, and Mary is my sister." Rose's voice wavered.

"I thought you said you weren't sure you believed all that Pastor Lassiter taught you."

Couldn't Rose see what Ben was doing? Twisting her words to turn them into what he wanted? Was it any wonder no one believed Will when he said he was innocent? Will glanced at Mary. Now more than ever, he was convinced that there had to be a reasonable explanation behind Ben's accusations—one that had been twisted into something that made Mary look bad.

"What are you going to do to her?" Rose looked at Mary as if she finally believed her sister might be in real danger.

"Nothing she doesn't deserve."

Will tried to determine Mary's reaction, but she remained expressionless. Mel, on the other hand, looked as though the end of her fuse had been lit, and she was about to blow.

"What do you know of what Mary deserves? Despite the risk to her reputation and safety, she climbed to my window to rescue a spiteful sister who wanted to steal her beau. Rose should be grateful for such a sister."

"Stop." Mary glared at Mel. "I appreciate you taking up for me—but this is between my sister and me. Rose, I hope that we can work this out between us. If you truly love Ben, despite what everyone here has told you, then I'll support your marriage. I only want you to be happy. But I hope that you'll decide to come home with us tonight."

What was Mary up to? Will could hardly imagine that Mary would actually leave Rose here. Not after everything they've been through. So, why was she acting as if she would countenance the match?

Rose looked at Mary. "You would support me? Truly?"

"I would."

"So touching." Ben snickered. "But where was this sisterly devotion when Mary left poor Rose to tend Daniel even though she'd promised Rose the afternoon off? When Rose didn't show up to meet Silas, he went over to Annie Garrett's for a piece of pie. Then he married Annie instead."

"How do you know about that?" Rose said, her voice barely above a whisper. "I never gave details. And the pie? How do you know he went for pie? I didn't even know that."

Rose slowly began to back toward the door, toward where her sister stood. Will could only hope that Rose was finally beginning to realize that this situation had nothing to do with her, and everything to do with Ben's evil plans.

The door flew open, and three armed men entered, led by Rusty Horton, Century City's sheriff. He'd always suspected Rusty was dirty, and now he knew for sure.

"Will Lawson," the spindly man said, not masking his unpleasantness. "I've come to arrest you for the robbery of the Colorado Citizens Bank and the murder of Eldon Wormer. I do hope you resist, because putting a bullet in your head would be a pleasure."

Rusty grinned, showing a few more missing teeth than when Will had seen the man last. "Now that I see you with the murder weapon you said had been stolen, getting a conviction will be easy. That is, if the lynch mob doesn't get you first."

As Rusty's men barked their laughter in unison, Will met Ben's eyes. This whole thing, from the moment they'd walked into The Pink Petticoat, had been a setup.

He should have killed Ben when he'd had a chance.

Chapter Twenty-Two

A murderer? Mary looked over at Will in hopes that he would deny the charges. He was too good of a man to be involved in such things. Besides, Mary already knew that the gun had been taken from that other man, Colt.

"Then you have the wrong man," Mary said, looking at the sheriff. "Will borrowed that gun from a man named Colt."

"Ah, yes, Colt." Ben got up from his seat and walked over to them. "And where is my dear friend?"

Ben's gaze landed directly on Mel. From the intensity of it, Mary was glad it wasn't her.

"He had one of his headaches. I gave him something to sleep it off."

But of course, Mel wasn't her, and she had so much strength that Mary admired. Why, she didn't look frightened at all.

"Idiot." Ben turned and walked over to the sheriff.

"You said he'd do the job for me," the sheriff whined.

"And he will. As soon as he wakes up. That Mel creates havoc with all of her potions she gives out. Can we hang her for that?" Ben smiled in such a way that made Mary's stomach turn.

"I'm the sheriff. I can hang whoever I want."

Mary should have known not to trust any lawman af-filiated with Ben. But she'd have liked to have believed that they weren't so easily persuaded. She looked over at Mel, who didn't appear worried.

"You won't hang me, and you know it." Mel stood straight and proud. Mary wished she had the kind of courage the other woman had. She glanced over at her sister, who seemed to finally be realizing the full ex-tent of the evil they were dealing with.

Mary didn't need to know anything about criminals to know that these were bad men. This sheriff might have a badge, but she didn't feel safe knowing a man like him was the law. And, from the looks of everyone else in the room, they all felt the same way.

Mel continued staring the sheriff in the eye. "Will took the gun off Colt. If you're looking for the man who had the gun, then you need to look in my room. Will is no murderer."

"Isn't he?" The sheriff looked at Mel with stone-cold eyes that made even Mary shudder. "You've just named him a thief. Is it so hard to imagine he might also be a murderer?"

This time, when the sheriff asked his question, he looked at Mary, as though he was trying to convince her of Will's guilt.

Only Mary knew better.

"He didn't steal the gun. It was his to begin with."

"So he says."

Reasoning with the sheriff was as futile as reasoning with Ben. The two men were cut out of the same rancid cloth.

Mary glanced over at Will, whose hand rested on his gun.

"Go for it," the sheriff urged. "Though I've been looking forward to a hanging, no one will fault me for killing a man who drew on me."

"Do you know who my father is?" Jasper stepped forward, his hands out. Anyone who shot him would be labeled a coward, if they lived long enough to tell their side of the tale.

"Accidents happen." Ben spoke smoothly, easily. He pointed his gun in Mel's direction. "It wouldn't be unheard of for a disgruntled soiled dove to shoot a man. Everyone knows that you married the town shrew. No one would be surprised you spent the night here."

"That's a dirty lie!" Jasper's face reddened.

Ben shrugged. "The victor is the one who gets to write the history."

"You're not shooting him," Mel said quietly. "He has no part of this."

Jasper glared at Ben. "Despite what you think of my marriage, I aim to be a good husband to Emma Jane."

Mary should have found comfort in his words, but Emma Jane was still at home alone on her wedding night.

Ben laughed. "Don't make no never mind to me. You couldn't pay me enough to tolerate that shrew."

Such a harsh description of her friend made Mary cringe. Though she was certain Ben had no such opinion of a woman he couldn't possibly know, she knew his words had nothing to do with Emma Jane, and everything to do with riling up Jasper. The redness to Jasper's cheeks told her it was working.

"Stop calling Emma Jane a shrew." Jasper pulled out his gun. "Emma Jane is a decent woman."

Though it didn't look as if Jasper had any intention of shooting, Ben drew his gun and fired. Mel seemed to catch the motion of Ben drawing because Mary heard her shout something just before jumping in front of Jasper.

Next thing Mary knew, Will had shoved her to the ground. His body trapped her against the soft carpet. She couldn't see what was happening, but the sound of rapid gunfire echoed through her ears. *Don't let Will die for my sake*, Mary prayed. She thought to Jasper, and Mel and Rose. She tried to lift her head, but as soon as she moved, Will pushed it down with his hand. "Don't be stupid."

"But—"

"Stay still and be quiet or we'll both be dead."

A bullet grazed the floor beside them. Mary clamped her mouth shut. Then the shooting stopped. As suddenly as it began, all was quiet. Still. Like death. Though it must have only lasted a few seconds, the exchange seemed to have gone on for hours, Will's body pressing her against the ground the entire time. He'd been so close. Making her feel so safe.

Yet as the air stilled around them, Mary was more terrified than ever. She'd come to rely on Will.

"You idiots," Ben said, his voice growing louder as he crossed the room toward them. "I was only trying to nick the boy and teach him a lesson. What were you thinking, opening fire like that?"

"Sorry, boss," one of the men mumbled. "We thought—"

"I don't pay you to think."

Will stirred, allowing Mary to shift her head to watch as Ben hit one of the men with the barrel of his gun.

How had she fallen in love with a man like Ben? No, that wasn't love, Mary realized as Will's solid mass remained firmly covering her. Love was a man who would shove a woman to the ground and cover her with his own body to keep her from getting hurt.

Not a man who would use a woman as a cover to steal.

Ben's boots crunched the floor around him, probably from the broken glass of lamps being shot out, and stopped in front of them. "You can get up now. These numbskulls aren't going to shoot."

Will rolled off Mary and got to his feet before helping her up. Once they were standing, she saw her sister, huddled in a corner, but obviously alive.

Mary looked over to where Mel had covered Jasper. Mel lay motionless.

"Get a doctor!" Jasper's voice was muffled by Mel's body.

None of this was supposed to have happened. Will dashed over to Mel and Jasper, quickly rolling Mel off his friend.

So much blood.

"I'm fine," Jasper said before Will could ask. "It's Mel. She's been shot good."

"No doctor," Mel rasped. "No time."

The gurgle coming with her voice agreed with her. Her lungs were filling with blood, and she'd be dead before the doctor arrived. Even if a doctor arrived before Mel died, there was no saving her. Will had watched too many others pass this way.

"I…" Jasper looked worse than Mel as he seemed to comprehend what she was saying. "You saved me. Why?"

"Can't let an innocent…" Mel gasped, choking on her blood. Will tried to prop her up better to make it easier. Not that there was anything easy about dying this way.

Mel's sacrifice humbled Will. Sure, Jasper was the son of one of the wealthiest men in the state, but Mel's sacrifice wasn't about money. It was about doing the right thing and protecting an innocent man.

"I can never repay…" Jasper's voice wavered as he shifted to better accommodate Mel and make her last moments more comfortable.

"Yes," she said, her voice thready and garbled. She wouldn't last much longer. "Help."

Mel tried to cough, but the effort took more color out of her skin. "Daisy."

The word was but a whisper of a breath and barely discernible. But Will heard. And from the look on Jasper's face as Mel closed her eyes for the final time, so did he.

Ben gave them no time to reflect or mourn. As Mel slipped from the earth, Ben let out such a cackle that Will had to wonder if such evil could exist in a mere mortal.

"Touching, but let's not waste our breath on a harlot. We still have the matter of Will's arrest and—" Ben blew on his nails in such an affected gesture that Will wanted to punch him "—a wedding to arrange."

Ben turned his gaze toward where Mary had crawled over to Rose. "Personally, I've had the younger sister, so I'd much rather the elder. But, my dear, you've turned into quite the shrew yourself. I suppose the question is, which one of you can I most tolerate as my bride?"

"You don't honestly think you're going to get away with this? Pastor Lassiter won't allow it."

Will took a step toward Ben, but Rusty pushed aside his coat, showing his guns. "The noose or my revolver. Don't tempt me."

He was serious. Just as serious as the look on Ben's face.

"Here's how I see it. We have a dead woman of no consequence. A man about to go to jail. A sheriff and his deputies who will testify to the truth of whatever I say. Which leaves me with two potential brides and a dandy who skipped out on his wedding night. Having made myself a reputation in gambling circles, I can safely say that marriage to one of these young ladies is a good bet."

Another cackle twisted Ben's face into an expression that bordered on demonic. "I have enough ladies here who can make sure that their tales of Jasper Jackson's wedding night make anything he has to say sound like the ravings of a madman desperate to keep his wife from knowing the truth."

Lies. All of them. And as the memory of Will's persecution in Century City flowed through his brain, he knew that Ben would ruin Jasper's good name. He'd marry either Mary or Rose, and do away with the other, enabling himself to lay claim to a hefty fortune.

Why did God allow such evil to exist? And why couldn't Will have found the courage to have shot Ben when he'd had a chance? Fair fight or no, this man deserved to die.

Unbidden, a verse about trusting the Lord with all

your heart ran through Will's brain. Could he trust in the Lord enough to let the chips, as they were, fall? Would letting the Lord have control of the situation impact the outcome?

Will took a deep breath. *Lord, I know we haven't exactly been on the best of terms. I've blamed You and denied You, and tried taking matters into my own hands. But in all my chasing of Ben, none of it has done a lick of good. No one's believed me. There's a dirty sheriff on Ben's side. The room is full of gunslingers who shoot for the fun of making a kill.*

I can't do this on my own.

The heaviness pressing on Will's chest lifted. Yet no angels burst through the ceiling, or even through the door. No, Ben still stood before him, eying Rose and Mary as if they were as scrumptious as the wedding cake that was supposed to be served at Jasper's reception.

"So what's it going to be, ladies? Which of you lovely creatures will love, honor and, most importantly, obey me?"

"Neither!"

In a movement that could have only been planned, Mary grabbed a kerosene lamp from a nearby table as Rose did the same. Mary tossed hers at Ben, and Rose aimed straight for Rusty.

The result was chaos. Giving Jasper and Will enough time to reach the girls, then run through the door.

Ben let out a howl, and Will didn't need to look back to know he was hot on their tail.

Hot being the operative word as they ran down the hallway and flames followed. The room shouldn't have caught fire from those two lamps, but as a loud boom sounded behind them, Will realized there must have been some other explosives in the room, ignited by the smaller fire.

Whatever it was, they weren't safe in this building. Nor was anyone else.

Will grabbed Mary's hand, pulling her behind him as they headed for the stairs leading to the exit.

"Fire," he yelled, hoping that the inhabitants of the other rooms would hear him in time.

As they reached the stairs, Will noticed US marshal Dean Whitaker standing on the landing, looking ready for a fight. It figured he would show up at some point or another. The marshal had been trailing Ben almost as long as Will had…but now was not the time to think about such things. Another boom sounded from the room they'd just escaped.

"Arrest them," Ben shouted. "All of them. Those crazy women are trying to burn the place down."

"No time!" Will kept moving forward. "We have to get all these people out of here!"

The air was so thick with smoke that it was a wonder any of them were able to yell at all. Doors flew open, and people, mostly half-dressed, poured out of the rooms.

In the melee, they were able to get past the marshal and even slow up Ben. Too many people wanted to escape the impending disaster.

"Don't give up!"

Will turned to see Jasper tugging at Rose. Mary turned as well, moving in their direction.

"We have to keep going. You have to keep going." He stared at Mary for a brief moment, long enough to hopefully instill the sense of danger they faced, but not so long as to lose himself in those eyes. Face streaked with sweat and soot, Mary Stone was still the loveliest woman he'd ever beheld.

And the smartest.

"We'll never make it through the door," Mary said instead. "The crowd is already too thick."

She was right. Mary pointed to a window.

He didn't need further encouragement to head in that direction. Jasper followed, pulling Rose, who seemed to find the strength to carry on at the sight of the freedom so close.

Will picked up a chair and hurled it through the window. He started to help Mary out, but she looked in her sister's direction. "Get Rose first. She's coughing a lot."

Rose had grown pale and, just as Mary said, was coughing, struggling to breathe in all of the smoke. "I didn't mean for it to cause such a terrible fire," she said between gasps.

"No time for that." Will picked her up and lifted her through the window. "Be careful of the glass."

After making sure Rose made it to the ground safely, Will turned to Mary. "Your turn."

Over Mary's shoulder, Will noticed that the marshal had gotten trapped underneath a fallen beam. Though the marshal cried for help, no one stopped, as they were all too busy trying to save their own lives.

"Jasper," he said, turning to his friend. "The marshal's stuck. Let's get Mary out and then try to help him."

Jasper gave a quick nod of his head, as though he'd been thinking the same thing. Will lifted Mary.

"Let me stay and help."

"No. Tend to your sister."

He didn't let Mary argue further as he guided her through the window. There'd be time enough for that later.

"Go to my house," Jasper said, leaning out the window. "Father has men he can send, and the doctor is next door. Besides, it's closer than the parsonage."

Mary nodded. She looked as if she wasn't going to obey, but as her sister started coughing again, Mary took her sister's arm and tugged her down the street.

At least Mary was safe, and Will wouldn't have to worry about her. But as another beam crashed down in front of them, Will had to wonder if his nobility had been nothing but suicide.

Chapter Twenty-Three

What had Mary been thinking, letting Will and Jasper remain behind like that? She passed a group of firemen, but she knew they weren't going to save the building or its occupants. Their only concern would be to keep the nearby buildings from catching fire.

"I'm sorry," Rose gasped as they turned the corner by Jasper's house.

"Don't talk nonsense. That fire's not your fault."

Technically, they had started the fire. But neither of them had realized that it would so quickly get out of hand. Or spread to the entire building.

Please, Lord, Mary prayed. *Let everyone get out safely.*

She should have stayed behind to help. But then Rose coughed again, and Mary knew that Will had been right to send her home with her sister.

"It's not much farther," Mary said, putting her arm around Rose and helping her the last few feet to the stairs leading to the imposing Jackson mansion.

They'd barely set foot on the first step when the front door flew open, and Emma Jane came rushing out. "What happened?"

"There's a fire at The Pink Petticoat. Jasper and Will are helping get people out. Rose needs a doctor."

One of Mr. Jackson's men came and grabbed Rose, carrying her into the house, while another rushed past Mary, presumably to get the doctor.

"Are you all right?" Emma Jane examined Mary as she arrived at the top of the porch.

"I'm fine."

Emma Jane led Mary to a sitting room that looked too elegant and immaculate to hint that it had been full of people only hours before.

"I'll ring for some tea."

The absurdity of such a statement made Mary want to laugh, given that the clock in the hall said that it was two o'clock in the morning. Who would want tea at such an hour? But as Mary examined the lines on her friend's face, she knew it was best to keep Emma Jane occupied and not focused on the fact that her new husband was in a burning building.

"We should send word to Frank, as well. I'm sure he'll want to know Rose is safe."

Mary forced herself to sit on one of the rather stiff-looking chairs. This perfect room was a far cry from the comfortable sitting room at the Lassiters'. Emma Jane looked equally uncomfortable in this space, taking a seat across from Mary with her old sour expression firmly planted on her face.

"Mr. Jackson has already seen to it."

Stiff, formal. Like the old Emma Jane who was too prickly to approach.

"You call your father-in-law Mr. Jackson?"

Emma Jane sighed. "Mrs. Jackson requested I do so. I'm not yet family, it seems."

Poor Emma Jane. "You married their son."

"Who didn't even stay until the reception was over."

"I'm sorry." Mary wasn't sure what else to say, and her words hardly seemed sufficient to cover her guilt in allowing Jasper to be a part of Rose's rescue.

Mary moved to the edge of her seat. "I should see to Rose."

A maid bustled into the room with the requisite tea tray. Having spent some time working as a maid in Ohio to help support her family, Mary pitied the poor girl, who'd likely still have to be up at dawn to tend to her regular duties.

"That's not necessary, miss," the maid said, as she arranged the tray on a nearby table. "The doctor's just arrived, and he's asked for privacy. I'm to come get you when she's able to have visitors."

The Jacksons, it seemed, had everything in hand. And from the expression on Emma Jane's face, this was going to be the rest of Emma Jane's life. Emma Jane poured the tea and handed Mary a cup. She wanted to say that she didn't want it, nor the sandwiches so nicely displayed upon the tray. But she found, as she took her first sip, that she was parched. She hadn't had anything to drink since she'd gone in search of lemonade at the reception.

The reception seemed as if it had happened decades ago, not the mere hours that had passed. Emma Jane, too, had aged, turning back into her former self, filled with a resignation devoid of light.

Emma Jane asked about the events of the evening, and Mary recounted them as best as she could. "Mary!" Frank burst into the room. "I came as quickly as I could. Polly and Maddie remained at the house in case one of the children wakes, but Gertie has gone to the sick-room to see if she may be of assistance to Rose. You're uninjured?"

Mary nodded slowly, realizing that if she had been injured, she wouldn't have noticed. Upon reflection, her body felt tired, sore, but nothing that needed treatment. Except a deeply wounded heart.

Unfortunately, no salve for such things existed.

"How bad is the fire at The Pink Petticoat?"

Mary glanced at Emma Jane, not wishing to alarm her friend, but also knowing she couldn't keep the truth from Frank, particularly when he might be of assistance.

"I don't think there will be anything left. The smoke was terrible, and Will and Jasper went to rescue a man trapped under fallen beams."

The horrible images flooded her mind again, especially as she recalled the people scrambling for the exits. "Those poor women," Mary said, tears filling her eyes. "It's our fault the place burned down. Rose and I only meant to start a small fire, enough to distract that terrible Ben, but something happened, and there was a loud noise, and suddenly the whole place was engulfed."

Frank wrapped his arms around her. "It's all right. The kerosene in one of the lamps must have ignited something flammable. I know you wouldn't have intended to cause anyone harm."

Though his comfort was reassuring, it wasn't enough. Mel's lifeless body clung to the inside of her memory like sticky goo. "Part of your ministry is helping those women. They're going to need a place to stay. Can you help them?"

Helping them wasn't the pastor's responsibility. "That is to say, I would like to help you help them. I don't approve of their lifestyle, but a wise woman taught me that many of those women are not in that profession by choice. Surely there is something we can do for them, especially now that their home and livelihood is gone. I'm responsible for what happened to them, and I need to make it right."

He nodded slowly, looking at Mary as though he understood what she needed to do. "Mary, I appreciate your heart in wanting to help. And we will do something for those women. But I need you to understand something about grace."

Grace? What did grace have to do with any of this? They weren't talking about God or salvation, but about women who'd been hurt because of her.

"Grace doesn't have to be earned. When you sin, you don't have to do something to make up for it. God's love is boundless."

The man made absolutely no sense. Mary stared at him, trying to understand why she was getting a lecture on something she'd known her whole life.

"I've seen how you react to things going wrong. You hold yourself far too responsible for everything bad that happens. Polly said that you even blame yourself for Rose's predicament. She said that you promised to never leave your siblings alone and that you'd spend the rest of your life making up for this mistake."

Mary's eyes filled with tears. She had told Polly those things. But her friend shouldn't have repeated it to Frank.

"You can't make up for it. God doesn't place such a large burden on our shoulders. We can't control everything. Don't you think that I felt guilty for allowing that man into our house? Of course I did. But I don't need to spend the rest of my life serving some penance as a result."

"You don't understand!" The words burst out of Mary as a new flood of tears flowed down her cheeks. "This is all my fault. I knew Ben was a bad man. But I was afraid that the lies he threatened to tell about me would be believed and that I would get in trouble, so I said nothing. I refused to expose him because I feared my own exposure. Had I been open with my sister, with my family, with my friends, none of this would have happened."

Her heart thudded in her chest, the weight of the enormity of her mistake nearly crushing her. So strong, the pain pinned her to her chair.

"So what?" Frank stared at her calmly. Too calm. "It did happen. Nothing you can do will change it. Nothing you do will make up for it, because you've put too much guilt upon yourself. Jesus has already forgiven you, so forgive yourself."

Forgive herself? Did the pastor not understand how selfish she'd been?

"But I owe them."

He knelt in front of her and spoke softly. "Mary. Look at me."

She had no choice but to obey. Not because he was forceful, but because something tugged at her heart.

"When Christ died on the cross for your sins, He paid a debt that you can never repay. Grace is about not trying to pay Him back. If you accept Christ's love, then you have to accept that you cannot spend the rest of your life atoning for your sins."

The insides of Mary's heart tore wide-open. If she

couldn't atone for her sins, how was she going to live with the guilt?

"He's right, Mary," Emma Jane said. "You have to let go if you're going to be free. You taught me that by loving and accepting me even when I was completely unlovable. The expectations you have of yourself— they're not what God wants of you."

Mary closed her eyes and tried to shut out all of the voices accusing her of the many things she'd done so wrong. She understood what Emma Jane and Frank said, but it seemed so inconceivable against the weight of the lives that had been damaged because of her reticence. And yet...

Just a few weeks ago, Frank had spoken on the parable of the debtors. Mary had marveled at what it must have been like to have the enormity of forgiveness these men experienced. Could it be that as much as Mary said she believed, she'd never fully experienced the full freedom of the forgiveness of God?

Lord, forgive me for I have sinned. I've been trying so hard to turn my faith into a checklist of the right and wrong things to do that I've forgotten Your love.

Mary turned to Frank and Emma Jane, and as she wiped the tears from her eyes, she realized that for the first time, she was truly free.

Chapter Twenty-Four

The air was getting thicker with smoke by the second. Will pulled the lapel of his coat over his mouth and nose, crouching low to the ground, where the smoke wasn't as thick. It occurred to him again that the fire couldn't have started by the small lamps Rose and Mary had tossed. The explosion had sounded a lot like dynamite.

Will and Jasper reached the marshal, lifting the beam off him.

"Come on, we've got to get out of here," Will said, tugging at the other man's arm. "I have no idea what other explosives are in this place. It's only a matter of time before the whole place goes up."

The marshal coughed and put a handkerchief up to his face. "Then we'd better get the rest of these people out of here."

Will nodded, looking around. Though most people had reached either the door or one of the windows, he could spot pockets of people trapped in the thick smoke. No one was going to die, not if he could help it.

Jasper pointed to a place where a group of women

appeared huddled together. "I'm going to help them. There's a window not too far away."

Another beam crashed to the ground, trapping a group of people that had been trying for the back door.

Will didn't wait to see what the marshal would do. He started for them, looking for something he could use as a tool to move the burning rubble. A discarded buffalo robe lay at his feet. Though the heat was stifling, Will wrapped it around himself to offer some protection from the falling debris. As he got closer to the site, he spotted a pick leaning against one of the tables. Probably belonged to a miner with no place to stay, so he kept his gear with him.

Offering a silent prayer of thanks for the miner leaving it behind, Will grabbed the pick. He swung it through the stack of burning beams to clear a path. Above, more timbers burned, clinging precariously to the beams that held them up. He had only minutes, maybe less, to get these people out of here.

"Come on!" Will set the pick down and held out his hand. "We've got to get out of here, now!"

A scantily dressed woman took hold of him, and he pulled her toward the mercifully clear space that would soon be engulfed in flames.

"Head to the window, there!" Will pointed to an open window where it looked as if the marshal was helping people exit.

Will ushered four more women toward the escape, then noticed a man lying in a crumpled heap beside the bar. Hopefully, he wasn't dead. Will checked the burning timbers. Helping the man was a risk, but he had to believe he still had a chance.

Holding the buffalo robe high above his head, Will

made his way toward the bar. As he got closer, he realized that he'd risked his life for Ben.

The man he wanted to kill. Could have killed. Should have killed.

For an instant, it occurred to Will to just leave Ben there, but as the man moaned, Will realized that he had to have been led to find Ben for a purpose. All along, thoughts of vengeance had consumed him, combined with Pastor Lassiter's words cautioning him that it was a dangerous path to follow.

Could Will let a man die when he'd been clearly led to save him?

Will knelt beside Ben. "Are you hurt?"

Ben coughed. "Got to get to my safe."

The man was knocking on death's door, and he was worried about the contents of his safe?

"The ceiling is about to cave in and kill us both. We've got to get out of here. Can you stand?"

Ben struggled to get up but quickly fell to his knees. Will put his arm around him and helped Ben stand just as the ceiling collapsed across the path Will was going to take to get them both to safety. Will looked around for an alternative exit. The back door was only a few yards away, but the path was blocked by several burning timbers. Still, if they were quick, they could dodge the timbers and get to the exit.

"Come on!"

Will tugged at the other man, looking around to be sure there weren't any others in the building. He couldn't see beyond the wall of fire blocking them in. *Please, Lord,* he prayed, *get everyone out safely.*

They arrived at the back door, which was blocked by a burning beam. Ben slumped to the floor as Will looked around for a tool he could use to move the beam safely. Thick smoke clogged his lungs, and Will coughed, pulling the coat more tightly around his mouth and nose. He knew enough about fires to know that if he didn't get fresh air soon, he wouldn't be much use to anyone, especially himself.

He spied a rifle lying haphazardly on the floor, probably abandoned by one of Ben's men in the melee. Hoping the heat wouldn't ignite any of the powder within, Will grabbed the rifle and used it to poke at the burning beam. The beam practically crumbled underneath the effort.

The fire was hot, too hot to have been caused by two kerosene lamps.

Will glanced up to see more flames rushing toward them. He gave another good swipe at the burning beam, then kicked at the door to open it. Air, fresh, blessed air greeted him. He tugged at Ben. "Come on!"

Will pulled Ben out of the building just as the fiery mass came crashing down. They'd both have a few singed hairs, but at least they were alive.

As Will gulped in the fresh air, he had to wonder why God would put him in a position to save the very man he'd sworn to kill. The man who deserved to die and not be allowed to victimize another human being.

"Don't think this changes things, Lawson," Ben gasped. The man could barely breathe, barely talk, and he was still fighting their old battle. "I own the law in all these mining towns. You should've let me die, because tomorrow, you'll be facing a noose. Especially when folks realize you're responsible for the fire. You're only a hero if you didn't start the thing."

Yup, he should've left Ben to die.

"You and I both know that the fire couldn't have been started by those lamps."

Ben coughed. "New powder to use in the mines. A spark from one of the lamps must've hit the crate holding it."

He grinned, the flames behind him giving him an eerie, more wicked glow. "But everyone will know you did it. And those girls…they'll be so desperate for me to keep their names out of it that they'll do whatever I ask."

Another cough wracked Ben's body. "At least I got the contents of one of my safes. Now I really need to marry one of them."

It took everything Will had in him not to shove the other man back into the burning building.

"Will!"

Will turned to see Jasper running toward him.

"Thank God you got out of there all right. When I saw that ceiling fall in, I was sure you were done for."

The other man clasped him in a bear hug. "You all right? The doctor's around front, treating some of the people who were badly burned."

"I'm fine." Will patted his friend on the back, then stepped away. "Did everyone get out?"

"As far as we know. We were fortunate. The marshal said that your quick thinking saved a lot of lives."

"In a fire you caused," Ben said, his voice raspy and strained with smoke damage.

"That's a dirty lie!" Jasper started for him, but Will held an arm out.

"Don't. It's not worth it."

Suddenly weary, Will looked for a place to sit. He was tired of fighting. Tired of running. If he met his end at the end of a rope thanks to Ben's lies, so be it. Will's conscience was clear. He'd meet his Maker knowing he was innocent and knowing that instead of taking a life, he'd saved it. He trusted the instinct that said his actions honored God, and he'd like to think that, just as it said in Hebrews about faith being a man's credit to righteousness, God would credit this to Will's.

If there was anything to regret, it was that he couldn't tell Mary how he felt about her. In the flames, all he could see was that he loved her. He'd tried to tell himself it was admiration and respect. Sure, those two things played a part in his feelings, because after all, a man couldn't love a woman he didn't admire and respect.

Jasper seemed to sense his need and led him to a crate. "Here. You can sit here. The marshal asked us to stick around. I figure we ought to oblige him, given that maybe saving his life might account for something in keeping us out of trouble."

"That's not why I saved him."

"I know," Jasper said solemnly, nodding in the direction of Ben, who remained lying on the ground. "You're a good man, Will Lawson. And even if people want to believe the dirty lies about you, there are people who know the truth, people who are honored to call you friend."

Will thought back to Mary and how he refused to express his feelings for her because he couldn't give her a respectable life. If he hanged, it wouldn't matter, because there'd be no life at all. Earlier, Jasper had chided him for not letting his friends help him. For not letting his friends make their own decisions about his character.

If Will had one more chance to see Mary, he'd give her the same opportunity. A woman deserved to know when a man admired, respected and, yes, loved her. Mayhap it would all be for naught, but Mary needed to have the choice.

Will closed his eyes. The heat from the burning building was almost scalding. Would it feel this way to hang? Or would it be worse?

The crunch of gravel interrupted Will's thoughts. He opened them to see the marshal standing before him.

"Marshal."

"Lawson."

"Ben's over there. He needs a doctor." Will barely had the energy to move his head.

The marshal made a motion with his arm, and Will realized a number of men were already tending to Ben.

"Ben says he has evidence that proves your involvement in the Century City robbery."

"He thinks he does," Will said slowly. "But a man's got to wonder how Ben seems to know so much about a crime he didn't commit."

The marshal seemed to think for a moment as he gazed at the burning building. "A man does have to wonder. I've been following the activities of Ben's gang for a while now."

"When I asked for the marshal's office to look into Ben's activities, I was told their hands were tied."

Marshal Whitaker shrugged. "You know we can't talk about an ongoing investigation. And you were a suspect."

Were. As though there might be a chance Will was in the clear.

"And now?"

"Seems to me a guilty man would have run. But I've been dogging your tail long enough as you've tracked

Ben to realize that you've been doing your best to help us catch him."

Will watched as a group of men carried Ben off on a makeshift stretcher. By the time the other man told his tale, most people would look at Will with more askance glances than he'd been receiving since the accusations first began. Even if he went to trial and was exonerated, there'd always be some people who thought him guilty. Either way, Will would never be able to walk around without a stain on his honor.

Especially since the marshal hadn't said Will was off the hook.

"I've got Rusty Horton around front demanding your arrest. He claims he's got definitive proof that you were involved in the bank robbery."

Will didn't have the heart to fight it. He pulled aside his jacket to reveal his father's gun. "This is the gun used in the Century City Robbery. I found it on Colt this evening, and I took it. I reckon it's my word against his, but until tonight, I haven't seen the gun since before it was used in the bank robbery."

The marshal paused in thought again. "I suppose, though, if the evidence burned up in that fire, I wouldn't have anything to hold you on."

Will thought about the gun he'd slipped into his holster. He had Jasper to back up his story, even if the law wouldn't listen to what Mary and Rose had to say. But would it be enough?

"I have too much respect for the law to destroy evidence," Will said.

With a loud rush, the rest of the building caved in with a burst of flame and smoke.

"It's not too late," the marshal said. "I believe you, but I can't guarantee you'll get a fair trial."

The trouble with being convicted by the Holy Spirit to do the right thing was that it didn't hold any guarantees of not facing human consequences. He had to do the right thing, no matter what the cost.

"I know. But I can't live with the thought of having to look over my shoulder for the rest of my life."

At least this way, Will knew he'd done everything he could to keep his integrity intact.

"I'm gonna have to take you in." The man said the words slowly, sounding as if he regretted them deeply. But Dean Whitaker was the kind of lawman who followed the law, and as much as he believed in Will's innocence, he had to follow the evidence.

"Would you be willing to let me turn myself in, in the morning? I'd like the chance to get my affairs in order."

Will watched the shadows cross the marshal's face. To let a man accused of bank robbery walk when the safest bet was to take him in was unheard of. But the marshal believed in his innocence. Plus, the first time Will had faced accusations, he'd turned himself in. At the time, he'd stupidly believed that he'd be released after he explained things. That hadn't happened. He'd only obtained his release after they'd determined they didn't have enough evidence to hold him. His possession of the gun changed things.

"I'll give you the gun," Will said slowly. "If I don't show up tomorrow morning, my face will be on every wanted poster either side of the Divide."

The marshal held out his hand. "You're a good man, Will Lawson. I'll do what I can to put in a good word for you."

Will shook the other man's hand, then pulled out his gun, holding it out so the marshal could take it. "Take good care of this, will you? If I come through this, I'd like to have it back as a reminder of my father."

"He was a good man, too. Raised you right. Shame about what happened to him."

The marshal's words gave Will hope he hadn't dared hope before. Since his father's death, not one person had expressed kindness toward the situation. Perhaps others felt the same way but were too afraid, given the high sentiment running against him.

"Thank you, sir."

"Now I'm going to turn my back, real slow, so's I can examine the progression of the fire. When I turn around, I'll expect you to be on your way. I've got some deputies due soon, and if they spot you, I'm going to have to bring you in. Understand what I'm saying?"

Will would be leaving the place a wanted man. With just enough time to say his goodbyes before he'd be put in jail to await a trial.

"Thank you."

The marshal didn't say anything but turned around very slowly. Jasper grabbed Will's arm, helping him up.

"Let's get out of here."

The men ran, sometimes with Jasper dragging Will's fatigued body down the street. Fortunately, they weren't far from the Jackson mansion. Rather than going in through the front, Jasper took him around back through the servants' entrance.

The entire place was lit up, and Will wondered if coming here was a mistake. It was likely the first place anyone would look. But he didn't protest as Jasper guided him through the house and into a quiet room.

"You'll be safe here," Jasper said, pointing to a bed before exiting the room and closing the door behind him.

Will couldn't help but collapse onto the bed. Yes, he was safe. For now. But in the morning, he'd be on his way to jail and an uncertain future.

Chapter Twenty-Five

Rustling noises around Mary made her wake with a start. She looked around the elegantly appointed sitting room and realized she'd fallen asleep on the couch. Daylight streaked the room, and she saw that the tea tray had been taken away. Emma Jane and Frank had disappeared.

How had she fallen asleep at a time like this?

Mary rose and exited the room, looking for signs of life. The maid who'd attended them last night stepped into the hallway.

"You're awake," she said, smiling. "Mr. Jasper would like you to join him in his sitting room. Follow me."

Mary looked around for signs of life. The entire house remained still. Quiet. Like a tomb. "What about Will? Is he here? Is he all right?"

The maid looked startled. "I can't say, miss. Mr. Jasper returned alone last night."

Alone. Tension knotted Mary's stomach. He wouldn't have left Will behind. Not unless—

No. She wouldn't countenance such a thing. Will had to be all right, he just had to be. Now that Mary had finally realized she couldn't continue punishing herself by denying her own happiness, she had to let Will know her true feelings. She had to tell him that she'd intentionally pushed him away and refused his kindness because she feared falling in love with him.

Of course it was too late to worry about such fears. She'd already fallen in love. And hard. What she'd had with Ben was a girlish infatuation. Now that she knew real love and the sacrifice of an honorable man, she couldn't settle for anyone less than Will Lawson.

The doctor exited a room, closing the door behind him. Mary stopped. "How is my sister?"

"Sleeping." He smiled at her gently. "She'll be fine. I gave her something to help her sleep, to allow her body to heal. You've all been through quite the ordeal. I hope you'll heed my words and get some rest."

"Of course."

Mary continued following the maid down the hall, grateful that her sister was going to be fine but even more eager to hear Jasper's news. Surely Will was all right.

The maid opened a door at the end of the hall. "In here, miss."

"Thank you." Mary smiled at the girl, who'd probably had a rough time with all the excitement. "What is your name?"

"Alice, miss." The maid curtsied and started to turn away, but Mary stopped her.

"Thank you, Alice. Your help has been much appreciated."

The maid colored slightly before bobbing another curtsy and walking away. Mary entered the room.

Jasper lay on a sofa, clad in pajamas and a dressing

gown. He smiled as she approached. "I apologize for my improper appearance, but mother insists I be treated like an invalid. I'm perfectly fine, I can assure you."

"Were you badly injured?"

"Nothing a few days' rest won't cure." The impish Jasper grin filled his face, only now it held an air of maturity Mary hadn't seen in him before.

Their experience had changed him. Changed them all. Which was why talking to Will was imperative.

"Where is Will?"

The grin slipped from Jasper's face. "He's safe. For now."

Jasper gestured to a nearby chair. "Please, sit. I can't think with you hovering above me."

Being told that Will was safe didn't make sense with the way Jasper was acting. If Will was truly safe, he'd be in the room with them.

"Thanks to the sheriff's words against him, and the discovery of the gun, Will is now wanted by the law. Father has arranged for him to be transferred into custody later today." Jasper's voice cracked slightly.

"He's going to jail, Mary. He'll stand trial for the robbery in Century City as well as for starting the fire at The Pink Petticoat."

Mary stared at him. "But he didn't start that fire! Rose and I did."

"Yes, and you'll keep quiet about your involvement. Will and I have agreed to take the blame." Jasper coughed. "Actually, Will insists on taking the entire blame himself. Father is working on getting the top lawyers in the country to take Will's case, but in the meantime, we're to keep quiet about what happened. Once we've consulted with the lawyers, then we can tell our side of the story to the authorities."

"But that's lying." Mary looked at him, incredulous. "I can't countenance such a thing. We didn't mean to burn the place down. Surely they know it was an accident."

A door creaked open, and Will stepped through. "Please, let me do this, Mary."

"Will!" She couldn't help herself. She ran to him and threw her arms around him. "I was so worried."

As if it were a herculean effort, Will returned the gesture, holding her close to him. "You and your sister won't survive in a jail cell. Especially not with the power Ben's gang holds. I've talked with Mr. Jackson, and he believes we can find enough evidence to exonerate me, both of the fire and the robbery. But you have to be patient and do as I ask."

His breath fanned her hair, and Mary didn't want him to let her go. The safest Mary had felt in a long time was right here, in Will's arms, and the thought of him going to jail for her, even temporarily, was unbearable.

"But what of Ben's threats of a lynch mob?"

Will let her go and looked into her eyes. This man had never let her down, and as she looked at the light shining in his dark orbs, she knew she could trust him.

"The marshal is on our side. Between his men and the men Mr. Jackson hired, I'll be perfectly safe. There's still a chance that the jury will convict me, but we've already got people working to ensure I have a fair trial."

Though she supposed Will meant to comfort her, it all seemed such an impossibility. Not with the kind of weight Ben carried in this region. He was the slickest of criminals, and he'd managed to evade being caught so many times.

"What about Ben?"

Will smiled. "He was found with a number of stolen gems in his possession when he escaped the fire. He's got some explaining of his own to do."

At least Ben was finally getting what was coming to him—as long as he didn't wiggle his way out of it.

Still, at the hope shining in Will's eyes, Mary had to trust that things would work out. After all, they'd come this far.

"Will, I have to tell you—"

"No." His eyes took on an unfamiliar look. "I have some things I need to say first. The marshal's men will be here any time now, and I have to go with them as soon as they arrive. I need to leave with a clean conscience."

Go. Perhaps never to return. Those thoughts burned in Mary's chest, even as she fought to cling to hope.

"I care for you, Mary. I've fought my feelings because I didn't think it was right declaring myself to a woman when I had no honor to give her. But I've come to realize that honor isn't about what others think of you, but of being right in the eyes of God. I had the chance to let Ben die, and I didn't."

Mary couldn't imagine a more honorable man standing before her, even if he had allowed Ben to die. But she continued listening, giving him the chance to say what he needed to say.

"So I am declaring my love for you, Miss Mary Stone. I love you, and I hope someday to be able to give you my name. It may not be a name most people think of as being a good name, but I hope it will be good enough for you."

Unbidden, tears streamed down her face.

"Of course it's good enough for me. I'd be proud to carry your name and give you sons to carry on what is the noblest name I have ever known. I hadn't dared hope to find a man I loved. I thought I owed it to my family to make up for what I've done by devoting my life to them. But I don't need to serve any penance for sins the Lord has forgiven. I love you, too, Will."

Will kissed her then, and as she melted into his arms, the sounds of the deputies coming to arrest him clanged in her ears. But Mary didn't care. As her heart swelled with love for the man kissing her, and the peace of God settled around them, she knew that in the end, it would all work out according to God's plan.

Several hours later, as Will sat in a Leadville jail cell, he wasn't so sure that turning himself in had been the best idea. Colt had been locked in the cell next to him, and he was looking for a fight.

"You know we'll both hang, Law-lost-his-badge."

"I'm counting on the evidence to say otherwise." Will turned his back and laid on the uncomfortable cot.

"I heard you saved Ben from the fire."

Will grunted, then closed his eyes. Saving Ben wasn't something he wanted to talk about. He'd made his peace on that issue with Mary and God, the only two people whose good opinions of him mattered.

"That was pretty stupid, considering Ben's just going to testify against you."

He'd figured, but at least with all of Ben's other crimes, that testimony wouldn't matter as much. Will had put his trust in the Lord, and while he didn't understand why events had happened the way they had, he had to trust in the Lord's good purpose.

"Is it true Ben killed Mel?"

This question made Will sit up and look at Colt. "What's it to you?"

"I know what she did for a living, but she was still my girl. Mel was a good woman, and as soon as I had the money, I was gonna set her up real nice."

"By stealing from other people?"

Colt grunted. "You wouldn't understand."

Will jumped up and approached the other man. "You're right. I don't understand. Tell me why I'm sitting here in this jail when you know as well as I do that I had nothing to do with that robbery. Tell me how you ended up in possession of my father's gun, a gun someone who wasn't me used to kill an innocent man. And then tell me how all that adds up to giving a decent woman like Mel a better life."

Despite knowing it was wrong to engage Colt, Will couldn't help it. Mel shouldn't have had to die.

"You tell me it was Ben, and I'll give them everything they need to hang him."

Those words should have brought Will the comfort he needed. One word, and Colt would give the authorities the testimony they needed to end Ben's reign of terror once and for all. The trouble was, Will wasn't sure that word was the truth.

Yes, Ben had fired, but he'd claimed it was only to scare Jasper. Ben's men had also fired their weapons. So, whose bullet had hit Mel? Will couldn't definitively say. He'd been too busy trying to keep Mary safe.

It hadn't been right to let Ben die in the fire, just as it wasn't right to give Colt the answer he sought.

All Will had to say was yes, and everything Will had come to Leadville for would be accomplished. Ben would face justice. Will's name would be cleared. He could give Mary the honorable life he'd hoped to be able to give a woman someday. But there'd forever be a stain on his soul.

Will looked at the other man, whose face looked more worn than Will had ever remembered seeing it. His grief was real.

"She betrayed you, you know. By helping us."

Colt nodded slowly, as if he still couldn't believe Mel would do such a thing. "What'd you have on her?"

"Nothing. She was trying to find out what Ben had done with her sister." If anything good could come of this conversation, maybe it would be that they'd finally find where Ben's gang was keeping Daisy.

"I didn't know she had a sister." Darkness flitted across Colt's eyes. "Why wouldn't she have told me?"

"Because her sister's the pretty plum Ben used to tempt me in Century City. Mel didn't know if she could trust you."

Colt's face crumbled. Not in the way a pretty girl started to cry, because there were no tears. Just the utter devastation of a man who had nothing more to lose—or gain.

"I wish she'd told me."

The calmly spoken words were unlike anything Will had ever heard from the other man. He sounded almost…human. Even the cold-blooded killer who'd struck fear into the hearts of many a lawless town had loved another, and loved her deeply.

Could Will play on that love to get the information they needed to find Daisy?

"All Mel wanted was for Daisy to be taken care of. It's why she took up the life she did. Why she came to Leadville."

"She'll be taken care of just fine. Ben's seen to that." Colt eyed Will as though he dared him to say otherwise.

"An outlaw's life is no life for a woman. Mel wanted better for Daisy. If you loved her, you'd grant her dying wish."

The disgust on Colt's face was unmistakable. "I ain't no rat."

"You'd put your loyalty to Ben over Mel's dying wish?"

"It's not Ben I'm protecting. But if he killed her..." Colt turned his head, and Will caught a glimpse of him wiping at his eyes.

Once again, Will wished he could tell Colt what he wanted to hear. Especially when Colt turned to him with red-rimmed eyes. "You're not going to tell me who killed her, are you?"

Answers. Funny how regardless of which side of the law a person was on, all anyone ever wanted was answers. Not even Will had the ones Colt sought.

"I honestly don't know. Ben and his men were all shooting, and I was too busy trying to get Mary to safety to see who shot who. All I know is that when the dust settled, Mel was dead."

He left out the part about her saving Jasper. The last thing Jasper needed was for Colt to decide to hold him responsible. There seemed to be too many vendettas going around these days.

"He deserves to hang, you know."

Will swallowed. All he'd been able to think about for

months was Ben's body swinging from the gallows. And now... "I suppose that's for a judge and jury to decide."

"You know he won't live long enough for a trial. Folks are already outside clamoring to see Ben's neck in a noose. I heard tell that he stole from some mighty important people."

How could Colt discuss the case as though they were sitting in a parlor discussing town gossip over tea? Especially when Colt had been part of it all?

"I guess you'd know more about that than I would."

Colt snorted. "I suppose you want me to be sorry for what I did. Look, I never stole from no one who couldn't spare the loss, and I never killed a man who didn't deserve killing."

In some ways, Will could relate to Colt. Not so much in the stealing part, but hadn't Will himself thought Ben worthy of killing? The good Lord had seen fit to remind Will of what was right, before Will had the chance to take the man's life; but as Will looked upon the other man's remorseless face, Will prayed that Colt would understand the love of God for all of His people.

"God loves you, you know."

Colt stared at him as if he'd gone daft.

"I rightfully earned my spot in the hereafter. I'm not going to get all religious and pretend otherwise. The Lord ain't never had a place for me in His life, and I reckon I ain't never had room for Him in mine. It's nothing personal."

"I used to think the same thing," Will said quietly. "But I learned that God loves all kinds. If He could love Paul, who persecuted the early church before becoming a follower himself, then why can't He love sinners like us?"

Colt walked over to his bed and sat down. "I s'pose if you consider yourself a sinner, then that's all good and well. But I didn't choose the life I led. It chose me."

He stared at Will as though he expected a fight. But this wasn't Will's battle. Given that Colt uttered the same words Mel once had, Will knew the battle was bigger than that. It was waging in Colt's soul, and Will could only pray that, somehow, the truth of Will's words, of God's word, would get into Colt.

Before today, Will would have never believed Colt wasn't a bad person. But seeing Colt's love for Mel, combined with the self-righteousness of feeling as if he'd been acting in some warped form of justice, made Will realize that Colt was just as lost as the rest of them.

"Just remember it's never too late. To let God in, or to tell me where I can find Daisy. She'll have a good, honest life with us. The pastor has promised to help with that."

"Maybe she likes the life she has."

With that last defiant statement, Colt lay down and rolled on to his side so his back was to Will.

Will had done his best. Tried talking sense into Colt, but Colt felt too much justification in his actions. All Will could do was leave it in the Lord's hands, and that was enough.

Turning to sit onto his own bunk, he watched as the door to the cell area opened, and Marshal Whitaker entered.

"Lawson. You're free to go."

He opened the cell, but Will didn't come forward. "Am I going to be back in here in a few days when there's more evidence against me?"

"Is there evidence against you?" The marshal cocked an eyebrow at him.

Colt's bed rustled, and Will turned to see the other man coming to where their cells met. "None that wasn't manufactured."

"That's what I thought." Marshal Whitaker nodded and held his arm out toward the door. "A diamond necklace from the Century City bank robbery was sewn into the lining of Ben's coat. Sheriff Rusty Horton has a few stolen items of his own to explain. Between that and some other evidence we've found, I think I can safely say you won't be back in here anytime soon."

Marshal Whitaker looked over at Colt. "As for you, well, I'm not sure I'll be able to say the same."

Colt shrugged and went back to his cot. Before Will could say anything, Mary burst into the room.

"I know they said I should wait out there, but I am not waiting another minute to see my fiancé."

Will held out his arms, and though it was hardly the proper thing to do, he held Mary close. "I am so glad God gave me this chance."

She smelled of lilacs and summer, even though fall was upon them and they'd soon be knee-deep in snow. Will wasn't a man for fancy notions, but if he had to say what blessings smelled like, this was the scent he'd choose.

Marshal Whitaker cleared his throat. "Speaking of chances, I got word from Mayor Harris that they're looking for a new sheriff in Century City. He feels real bad about siding with Rusty against you, considering it was Rusty all along."

After giving Mary a final squeeze, he turned to look at the marshal. Just a few weeks ago, this would have been the very opportunity Will would have desired, even though he'd have never believed it possible.

"I appreciate the offer. But I need to stay in Leadville to help my fiancée and her family."

He held out his hand to the marshal and was given a firm shake in return.

"You ever need a job, you let me know, and I'll put in a good word for you."

"Thanks."

He turned his gaze back on Mary, whose eyes were shining more brightly than any silver pulled out of the hills. "I mean that, Mary. I'm here for you. And your family. Especially that rascal Daniel I keep hearing stories of."

The loving but exasperated smile Mary rewarded him with confirmed to Will that he was making the right decision. As much as the events leading up to this point had made him question his life and his faith, they'd brought him to this place of complete and utter peace.

There was no place he'd rather be than here, now, with Mary.

Sounds of the jail around him reminded him that perhaps here wasn't exactly right.

"Shall we?" Will held his arm out to his bride-to-be.

Arm in arm, they walked out of the jail. Will, a free man, without the stain of his past or the accusations that had once followed him. And Mary, a woman of such strong faith and willingness to face her past that Will could hardly believe himself worthy of such a blessing.

Epilogue

It was a fine day for a hanging. Or at least that was what the good people of Leadville kept saying. For Mary Stone, however, there was no joy to be found in this day. As Will put his arm around her, they silently walked away from where the crowd had gathered to watch the vigilantes hang Ben. The warmth of his arm reminded Mary that she did, indeed, have something to be joyful about.

Becoming Mrs. Will Lawson, which she would be in just a few short months. The weather was getting colder, and with his mother's health, they'd agreed to wait until spring so she could attend the wedding.

"This wasn't justice," Will said as he led her away from the scene. "There should have been a trial, and Ben should have been convicted by a jury of his peers."

As if to confirm Will's words, an icy wind hurled down the mountains, causing Mary to shiver.

"We should get you home. There'll be snow by morning." His gentle smile reminded her of the last snow they'd gotten and how, despite everything, it had brought them closer together.

Daniel and Nugget ran past them, but just as Mary started after them, Will pulled her closer.

"They'll be fine. Joseph and Annabelle are up ahead, so they won't let those two get far. Best to let them get all their running out now, before the snow hits."

Having a man around had helped Mary's younger brother. Though Daniel was still often far too energetic, Will was giving him a fine example of how a gentleman should act. Joseph, too, now that he and Annabelle were back from their honeymoon.

When Mary had confessed all to Joseph, he'd been angry at first, but mostly hurt that she'd tried to do so much on her own. Even her relationship with Rose was improving, now that all of Mary's sins were in the open. Despite everything, they were still sisters, and they still needed each other.

Not perfect, of course, Mary thought wryly as she adjusted her cloak against another gust of wind. Rose had been cross with her for leaving her to tend Bess, who was home sick with a cold. But Will had been asked to come to the sheriff's office today, and he'd wanted Mary to accompany him.

"Are you going to accept the deputy position he offered you?"

Mary looked up at him, and he smiled down at her. "I'd like to, but that's a decision we need to discuss as a family."

A family. One that Will had gladly accepted as his own when he'd asked Mary to be his wife. He understood about Mary's need to help take care of her siblings; but where she'd once thought she'd have to do it all on her own, now she knew what real family meant. No more carrying their own burdens on their own shoulders. Now, sharing and discussing with one another, it seemed almost inconceivable how they'd managed before.

His eyes twinkled, and again, Mary's heart filled with gratitude that this fine man was going to be her husband.

"I think you'd make a fine deputy." She gave his arm a squeeze.

The look Will gave her in response made her heart want to burst. How could she have ever believed anything less than this deep love was the real thing?

"I want to be sure it won't be an imposition on Joseph and Frank."

"But you already have your first case."

Will stopped, released her arm and turned to look at her. "What do you know about that?"

"If you and the sheriff didn't want me to overhear your conversation in his office, you should have closed the door." She grinned at him and took his arm again.

"Finding Daisy and keeping your promise to Mel is important. She died helping us save my sister. How could we do less for her?"

He shook his head slowly. "We are not going to do anything. Jasper has already left with a party to follow up on the latest lead."

After a quick glance at his pocket watch, Will turned his attention back to her. "They should be about halfway there."

Then he gave her the kind of stern look he usually reserved for Daniel. "And no, we are not following them. You can go help Emma Jane work in the women's home if you need something to do. But you are not putting your safety at risk. Not again."

The intense expression softened, and he pulled her a little more closely than was proper, especially in public. "You're too dear to me. I love you, Mary, and I aim to keep you safe for the rest of our days."

A lump clogged Mary's throat as she recalled that horrible night. Her worry hadn't been so much for her own safety as it had been for Will's. The level of anxiety she'd felt for him was far too much to bear again. No, she wouldn't have him have to endure that again, either.

"And I love you. Which means I won't give you cause to worry." She gave him a reassuring squeeze, then pulled away into a more respectable posture. "I'll go help Emma Jane so she has someone to keep her company instead of worrying about Jasper."

"I'd kiss you right about now, but we wouldn't want to get the town's gossips wagging." Will nodded in the direction of a group of women in front of the mercantile.

"I'll take you up on that later." Mary winked at him as she gave a small wave to the women.

They waved back and tittered among themselves. She could almost hear their words. "That's her. She's the one who burned down that horrible place."

The citizens of Leadville had agreed that burning The Pink Petticoat down had done the community a great service. Everyone had gotten out safely, and the only harm done was the destruction of the building. While some of the ladies had found work in other houses of ill repute, Frank had opened a women's home that helped the women find other positions that didn't involve compromising their morals. In the end, the true story of what happened did come out, and Mary enjoyed a little notoriety of her own.

No one had cared that it was an accident. Nor that

the real culprit was a box of explosive powder Ben had been storing in the room. No, all they saw was Mary Stone, the woman who brought down one of the most notorious houses in the West. She'd been invited to tea with all of the town's most prominent women. But unless those invitations were extended also to Rose and Emma Jane, Mary politely declined.

After all, what was the sense in being notorious if you couldn't use that power for good?

And then, partially out of the confidence of her notoriety and partially because she recognized the impatient look on Will's face, Mary stopped. She stood up on tiptoe and gave the man she loved the kiss he deserved.

Let people talk. Mary's real confidence wasn't in her reputation, but in a man who loved her, and a God who loved them both.

* * * * *

Dear Reader,

When I began thinking about which Leadville character I should write about next, I couldn't let go of the idea of writing about Mary Stone. I kept wondering what was so interesting about a seemingly perfect sister who'd sacrificed so much for her family. After all, perfection doesn't make for a very interesting story. As I dug deeper, I thought about the things a young lady would have had to have given up, like love, and that's when the rest of Mary's story came to me.

So many times, we look at the perfect exterior of another person, not realizing the secrets they carry or the past they may have overcome. Fortunately, the Lord knows all these things, even the darkest places in our hearts, and He loves us anyway. That was a lesson Mary needed to learn—that God loved her, and she didn't have to do anything to make up for her past sins.

I hope you find encouragement in Mary's story. If there's something in your past that you're struggling with, take it to God. He already knows, and He loves you just the same. You're precious to God, and He doesn't want you to have to carry that load.

I love connecting with my readers, so please, stop by danicafavorite.com and say hello.

Blessings to you and yours,
Danica

REQUEST YOUR FREE BOOKS!

2 FREE INSPIRATIONAL NOVELS
PLUS 2 *FREE* MYSTERY GIFTS

Love Inspired® HISTORICAL

YES! Please send me 2 FREE Love Inspired® Historical novels and my 2 FREE mystery gifts (gifts are worth about $10). After receiving them, if I don't wish to receive any more books, I can return the shipping statement marked "cancel." If I don't cancel, I will receive 4 brand-new novels every month and be billed just $4.99 per book in the U.S. or $5.49 per book in Canada. That's a saving of at least 17% off the cover price. It's quite a bargain! Shipping and handling is just 50¢ per book in the U.S. and 75¢ per book in Canada.* I understand that accepting the 2 free books and gifts places me under no obligation to buy anything. I can always return a shipment and cancel at any time. Even if I never buy another book, the two free books and gifts are mine to keep forever.

102/302 IDN GH6Z

Name	(PLEASE PRINT)	
Address		Apt. #
City	State/Prov.	Zip/Postal Code

Signature (if under 18, a parent or guardian must sign)

Mail to the **Reader Service:**
IN U.S.A.: P.O. Box 1867, Buffalo, NY 14240-1867
IN CANADA: P.O. Box 609, Fort Erie, Ontario L2A 5X3

Want to try two free books from another series?
Call 1-800-873-8635 or visit www.ReaderService.com.

* Terms and prices subject to change without notice. Prices do not include applicable taxes. Sales tax applicable in N.Y. Canadian residents will be charged applicable taxes. Offer not valid in Quebec. This offer is limited to one order per household. Not valid for current subscribers to Love Inspired Historical books. All orders subject to credit approval. Credit or debit balances in a customer's account(s) may be offset by any other outstanding balance owed by or to the customer. Please allow 4 to 6 weeks for delivery. Offer available while quantities last.

Your Privacy—The Reader Service is committed to protecting your privacy. Our Privacy Policy is available online at www.ReaderService.com or upon request from the Reader Service.

We make a portion of our mailing list available to reputable third parties that offer products we believe may interest you. If you prefer that we not exchange your name with third parties, or if you wish to clarify or modify your communication preferences, please visit us at www.ReaderService.com/consumerchoice or write to us at Reader Service Preference Service, P.O. Box 9062, Buffalo, NY 14240-9062. Include your complete name and address.

LIH15

Love Inspired

Love the Love Inspired book you just read?

Your opinion matters.

Review this book on your favorite book site, review site, blog or your own social media properties and share your opinion with other readers!